Alexa's head whirled. "Are you vexed because I am enjoying myself by dancing tonight? This is a ball, is it not?"

"I need no reminder of that," he replied arctically. "But perhaps you need a reminder that you are supposedly engaged to me."

"Your insinuations are rude! Furthermore, you have no right to chastise me for my behavior in any arena. Our engagement is one of form only."

"Our engagement may be of form to you and me," Winslow said with a tight smile, "but while my sister and your brother consider us all but betrothed you shall have to appear more the thing!"

Not a moment too soon as far as Alexa was concerned, the music ended and she departed in high dudgeon. He was without doubt the most insufferable man she had ever known!

Another Fawcett Crest Book
by Clarice Peters:

SAMANTHA

THE FALSE BETROTHAL

CLARICE PETERS

FAWCETT CREST • NEW YORK

for my mother and father

One

In its one-hundred-year existence, the proud Palladian mansion on the hillock overlooking Winslow Park had withstood fire, two floods and a score of childhood complaints. But it was now, in this July of 1816, undergoing its severest test.

"And I," the fourth earl of Winslow acidly informed his valet as he stood in the middle of the dressing room preparing to knot his cravat, "am being driven mad with distraction! What, pray, do I know of betrothal parties?"

As befitted a faithful servant, James knew whenever a question demanded an answer, and he confined himself in this instance to a sympathetic murmur. Later, however, in the back rooms of the country estate, the valet unbent long enough to confide with crushing pretension to the country staff that his lordship was holding up tolerably well for someone going through all the fuss and botheration of a betrothal party that weren't even his own!

That the betrothal plans under way did not herald his own impending march toward St. George's Hanover Square was the only thing remotely of merit that Winslow could discern about the current situation. The party and all its attendant honors belonged to his eldest nephew, Mr. Leigh Denning, whose mama—the earl's sister—had managed to wrangle Winslow's consent to the hare-brained scheme of holding a modest gathering at his country seat on the grounds that a dazzling match would soon be forthcoming between Lady Rowena's firstborn son and one Miss Fornhurst.

While the earl bowed to his sister's greater knowledge of matrimonial matters, he did not totally agree with this assessment. Not that he had any grave complaint to lodge against Miss Fornhurst, whom he recalled vaguely from chance encounters in London as a comely enough chit if one's taste ran to blondes, which Leigh's evidently did. No, the issue wasn't Miss Fornhurst but Leigh, who at twenty was much too green—in his uncle's opinion—to contemplate taking on a leg shackle. Winslow had ventured to offer this opinion to his sister, who had airily dismissed the remark out of hand as being all one could expect from such a confirmed bachelor as himself.

At the moment, Leigh, his prospective bride and both sets of parents had failed to put in an appearance at Winslow Park; however, a full contingent of servants had arrived bearing provisions for the party including, at last count, three baskets of fresh asparagus, a dozen strawberry plants, a turtle and the pièce de résistance, a milking cow. Such largess was courtesy of Lady Rowena, who was by no means assured that someone as inured to the single state as her brother knew what to lay in front of his guests. During the past forty-eight hours the flow of provisions had been fortuitously stemmed, a circumstance that had more to do with a rainstorm pelting the region than with any change in Lady Rowena's opinion about her brother's household.

With his cravat now tied flawlessly *à la Mathematique*, Winslow dealt a last oblique look into the mirror James held out. A vainer man might have lingered for considerable time at the glass, since the image reflected was the very epitome of masculine good looks: high, noble forehead, squarish jaw, generous mouth and two vivid blue eyes. The hair, cut in the Corinthian mode, shone to a burnished gold and in sunlight had been known to dazzle the more susceptible females of his acquaintance.

Happily, no such females were present now as Winslow, finishing his toilette, nodded his satisfaction to James and then strolled over to the window for his first glimpse of the day. The clear view of the poplars lining the great driveway cheered him. The rain had lifted. With any luck at all, Leigh might yet arrive and, after that, his parents and the Fornhursts, and this dratted party would be over and done with, leaving the earl free to follow his normal pattern of summer activities. In July, this usually meant the pursuit of salmon in Scotland.

Suppressing a wistful sigh at the memory of the capital sport he had enjoyed there only a summer ago, he went down the stairs, checking his progress at the sight of the morning mail laid out on the gold ormolu table at the foot of the staircase. There was no need for him to resort to his quizzing glass, for he had unerringly recognized the four hastily scribbled missives in the middle of the silver plate as being from his beloved sister, constituting in his jaundiced opinion a gross abuse of his franking privilege!

Letters in hand, Winslow headed for the morning room, wondering how he had agreed to any of this. The answer, of course, was simple. Rowena had forced him into it. True, she hadn't called it force at the time, merely the return of a favor due her.

"A favor due you?" he had drawled some two weeks ago as she flitted about his London drawing room straightening and rearranging his prized Chinese dragons on the mantel. "My dear Rowena, I fully agree that I owe you numerous favors over the years. You saved me from Nanny's paddle more times than I care to recall, but why do you choose to remind me of the debt now?"

"Because it's important," Rowena replied testily, her attention drawn away from the dragons and back to her brother. "And I am speaking of much bigger favors than poor Nanny, God rest her soul." She fixed her brother with an eye almost as imperious as his own. "You shan't deny that 'twas I who single-handedly saved you from the clutches of that harridan last year who had all but bewitched you and who would as soon have married you as look at you until I providentially dropped word in her ear that you had dissipated your entire fortune during a night of tempestuous play at Watier's?''

Winslow accurately recalled the harridan in question as a particularly ravishing and strong-willed creature and shuddered slightly.

"If you bring her up, I know the matter must be serious, Ro. Pray tell me just who it is you wish me to murder?''

His sister recoiled. "I wish you would not talk fustian, Sebby. Murder, indeed. The very idea! It's the merest trifle, and I wouldn't ask it of you if it weren't *geography*!''

Despite the somewhat flighty exterior Lady Rowena displayed, notably in a head of guinea-colored curls and blue eyes dancing perennially with mischief, Winslow had always considered her to have a tolerable head on her shoulders—for a female! But her words now tempted him to alter that opinion.

"I didn't know you were so interested in geography, Rowena," he said mildly, settling himself more comfortably on his crocodile-legged couch. "I daresay you are getting to be a veritable bluestocking!''

"I am no such thing," Lady Rowena denied, flouncing back toward him. "It's merely that Winslow Park is within a day's journey of Wiltshire and that, you must know, is only a stone's throw from Bath.''

The earl received this news with unabated affability. "Did you venture here to give me directions to Bath, my dear sister? It is very good of you, but I am well versed with the location and how to get hither and thither . . .''

"Don't be idiotish, Sebby!" Lady Rowena cut him off briskly.

"Rowena, why don't you cut line and let me have it, whatever it may be.''

Instead of replying at once, Lady Rowena twisted an intransigent curl about her finger and eyed his handsome figure garbed in a coat of Bath blue superfine and matching kerseymere trousers. "Oh, very well, if you must know, it's the Fornhursts."

Whatever the earl had expected in the way of an announcement it was not this. "The Fornhursts? Pray, what does that dismal family have to do with you or me?"

"Everything!" his sister shot back, running her kid gloves over the folds of her lilac morning dress. "Their cousin has his seat not five miles from Wiltshire, and they are quite in the habit of visiting him each summer."

"No doubt that is of considerable interest to you, Rowena," Winslow said faintly, "but I fail to see—"

"And," Lady Rowena swept on, paying no heed to her brother, "it could not be more convenient, for while Mrs. Fornhurst detests travel as a rule, even she shall consent to undertake a journey of a few miles, and before you say anything else, Sebby, do think of Leigh!"

The earl, who had been lifting a pinch of Mr. Berry's finest snuff to one nostril, paused to demand just what part of his nephew played in his sister's twaddle.

"He has everything to do with it. I wish you will attend to what I am saying. Leigh is thinking of offering for that Fornhurst chit and has been growing quite particular in his attentions. I wonder that even you did not notice, but I daresay you don't move in the same circles, which," she acknowledged, "is all to the good, for I couldn't bear it if he wound up in some sluicery!"

The earl's eyes were bright with laughter. "Sluicery? My dear Rowena, you shock me. And what type of disrepute do you think I am?"

"Oh, I don't think you a disrepute at all," his sister said hastily, "which is why I hope you shall consent to sponsor a small party at Winslow Park for Leigh and Miss Fornhurst. Nothing so very grand," she added as a frown descended briefly on his brow. "Oswald and I mean to pay every penny of the expense. We shan't hang on your sleeve! At Winslow Park, we'll have the opportunity to become better acquainted with the Fornhursts."

Winslow shook his head sadly. "You'll be sorry," he predicted. "For I am already acquainted with them, and I wish to heaven I weren't. Mr. Fornhurst, by my recollection, is a bobbing block, and that wife of his is an invalidish ninnyhammer!''

To his surprise, Rowena accepted this scorching indictment with surprising equanimity. ''Yes, I daresay you are right. But their daughter is an acclaimed beauty and her dowry is ample, and Leigh is quite besotted with her!''

The earl snorted in disgust. ''Bah! He's much too green to even think of marriage. Nine years my junior!''

His sister leaned forward, her index finger prodding him lightly on the chest. ''Don't be a gudgeon, Sebby,'' she commanded. ''Just because you are addicted to bachelorhood there is no need to condemn Leigh to share a similar fate. I daresay many gentlemen wed at an even earlier age than Leigh!''

The earl grimaced. ''Then they all have my complete pity.''

Lady Rowena inhaled a majestic breath but thought better than to waste it on arguing the merits of connubial bliss with such a hardened bachelor as her brother.

''About the use of your estate, Sebby,'' she said, returning to the matter which had prompted her call.

The earl hesitated not a jot. He was genuinely fond of his sister and saw no reason to deny her request, particularly since he meant to spend his summer in Scotland.

''You may have full run of Winslow Park,'' he told her, ''and invite whomever you want to, including those dismal Fornhursts. I just hope you shan't be bored to tears. I'll have no need of the seat for the month, since I've already made plans to go to Scotland.''

''To Scotland! But you can't!'' Lady Rowena sprang up from the couch. ''You must be at Winslow Park with us. How very odd it shall look otherwise. Mr. Fornhurst is a high stickler for the proprieties, and I'm certain he'll think it dashed peculiar of me just to usurp your household!''

''But Ro, I know next to nothing about betrothal parties!'' he objected.

''Then it shall be very good practice for you,'' his sister had replied, easily nipping in the bud this argument and the others her brother put forward during the rest of her visit. "For surely," she had quizzed as she took her leave of him at the door, "even you must contemplate matrimony sometime in your future."

"But if I ever did," Winslow murmured now as he fed the last of Rowena's letters into the fire, "I should have given over that notion by now!"

A leisurely breakfast of ham, buttered eggs and an assortment of country muffins restored Winslow's normal good spirits, and an hour later he was speculating about possibly reviewing the ledgers of the estate with his bailiff. Happily, for the task always proved to be more tedious than at first anticipated, he was interrupted before he could put it into action by the clatter of riding boots in the entrance hall and a voice calling, "Uncle Sebby!" at the top of its lungs.

Leigh! Winslow opened the door to the breakfast room, crossed the black-and-white lozenges toward the entrance hall and arrived in time to discover his nephew involved simultaneously in the tasks of interrogating Jenkins, the butler, and raking his fingers through his hair, the latter an activity that encouraged the earl to hope that Leigh might submit to a trimming before the arrival of Miss Fornhurst.

Aside from the deplorable length of his hair, Mr. Leigh Denning more than fulfilled his uncle's expectation of what a lovesick Romeo ought to look like: petrified! His countenance was pale, his manner agitated and, to cap it off, he was swathed in a great-caped driving coat that seemed rather too familiar to suit Winslow.

"How now, Leigh," he said, effecting a prompt rescue of his butler. "You look as though you've had the devil's old time getting here. I suppose the rain delayed you. Where are Rowena and Oswald, and where the deuce did you get that coat? I swear I have a twin to it somewhere in my wardrobe."

"I wouldn't be at all surprised," Leigh answered the last in his uncle's barrage of questions. "Mama commissioned it for me, and she always claims you are the last word in fashion, so it's no surprise if it's very like yours. But Uncle

Sebby, I have more pressing matters on my mind than driving coats. You must help me. I'm in a fix."

"Yes, I know," Winslow murmured calmly, one arm flung about his nephew's shoulders. "Thinking of getting hitched, are you not?"

Leigh frowned. "Yes, but that's not the fix, sir."

Winslow had been leading the way into the privacy of his library and was startled by the emotion in Leigh's voice. His eyes narrowed slightly.

Despite the obvious trappings of his youth, attested to by the length of his golden locks and his evident struggle with a neckcloth, there was nothing about Leigh to give anyone a fright. Tall and slender, he stood a mere fraction of an inch shorter than the six feet the earl himself measured. Always an appealing child with easy-going manners, Leigh had grown into an engaging young man who at the moment reminded his uncle of a skittish colt fighting the rein.

"It's just such a mull, Uncle Sebby." Leigh moaned as he dropped into the nearest chair.

"Come now," the earl said bracingly, handing him a glass of sherry from a tray of restoratives kept at hand. "Marriage is always alleged to be something of a mull. I thought you knew that. But luckily it's not too late to turn cat in the pan since, as I understand it from Rowena, you haven't formally offered for the Fornhurst chit."

"I'm not turning cat in the pan over that!" Leigh exclaimed impatiently.

Winslow paused, his sherry glass halfway to his lips. "Oh, no? Then what is this coil you've been prattling about?"

Leigh hung his head. "Devil take it. Just please, Uncle Sebby, don't rip up at me when I tell you."

"When did I ever make it a habit to rip up at you?" Winslow asked quietly.

Leigh flushed. "You're right. You've always been a complete hand."

"So then tell me what's amiss. In some scrape?"

"The very worst imaginable! I've gone and compromised a lady."

"You've gone and done what?" Winslow choked.

"Compromised a lady," Leigh repeated as he held his head between his two hands. "It was that curst rain. I was soaked through, and she would come along and offer me shelter for the night. I couldn't stay out in the storm like a nodcock, now could I?"

The earl, shaken to the core, took advantage of a moment's pause to replenish his wits and his glass of sherry. He had a notion he would be needing several glasses of sherry before Leigh's recitation was complete. He had heard of young men sowing wild oats before but never during a rainstorm.

"I trust the forces of nature were very strong, and the pair of you lost your, er, heads during the thunder and lightning?"

Leigh stiffened. "Do you take me for a flat, sir? We didn't lose our heads, either one of us. We were caught in the storm right enough. That's all. She was in her carriage having a devilish time what with the mud. Had been intending to set out for her brother's when the storm broke and forced her back. Since I was nearby she graciously offered me shelter until the storm cleared."

"Civil of her," the earl commented, feeling his way carefully.

"Well, she is a lady," Leigh insisted stoutly. "Only, of course, the rain didn't clear but came down even harder. And she wouldn't think of letting me go out in it."

"A woman of considerable persuasion," Winslow drawled, taking a minute to admire the polish on his high-glossed Hessians. "Am I to deduce from all this that you stayed the night under your benefactress's roof?"

Leigh nodded. "But I slept in the library!"

Winslow pressed his twitching lips tight. "If such is the case I fail to perceive the fix, unless you believe it to be a trap to be sprung later by this pernicious female."

Leigh's face registered alarm. "Heavens, no! And she's not pernicious, sir. She treated me more than civilly, much the way an aunt might, bidding me to go and dry off by the fire. And while she's not married, I'm certain she must have had offers even though she is an older female.''

''And how old would that be?'' the earl asked, curious to know what might constitute an older woman in his nephew's eyes.

''At least five-and-twenty, sir,'' Leigh answered, speaking in a hushed voice appropriate to communicating such a secret.

His uncle shouted with laughter. ''Impudent puppy. Five-and-twenty, indeed! Well, never mind that. I still do not see your problem. The lady harbored you for the night but is not the type to demand marriage from you as payment for her hospitality. What, pray, is the fix?''

Leigh drained his sherry. ''There wasn't a fix until this morning,'' he reported glumly. ''I was taking my leave at dawn, thanking her for all her kindnesses, when one of her neighbors drove up in a carriage and saw us together. I knew then what she was thinking.''

''Are you a mind reader in addition to your other accomplishments, lad?''

He flushed. ''Anyone could see what an evil mind she had, Uncle Sebby. And just for a minute I wished I were you, for I would have given her one of your setdowns. Odious wretch, looking at us in such a speaking way before driving off. I realized then how it must look with the two of us under the same roof and no servants about.''

All trace of amusement faded from the earl's face. He put down his sherry carefully. ''No servants about? That is the first time you've mentioned that fact to me, my boy. I'd assumed your benefactress kept a slew of servants or at least had an abigail underfoot.''

Leigh shook his head. ''She was on her way to her brother's and is quite in the habit of driving herself. She had dispatched her servants to Bath to open up the family home there, intending to go on to Bath after visiting her brother. And her abigail was called home on the death of her father. Now you see what I mean by a fix. Her neighbors knew about the absent servants. And that old biddy, Mrs. Nettles is her name, would have to appear today!''

''More to the point, lad, does this Mrs. Nettles know your name?''

''It was hardly the type of scene that warranted introductions, Uncle Sebby,'' Leigh said dryly.

The earl winced. ''And what did your hostess make of her neighbor's sudden, untimely appearance?''

''That's the odd thing, sir,'' Leigh replied in a bewildered voice. ''All she *would* do was laugh. In fact, she treated the whole episode as a lark and paid no heed to what I said. She even scolded me for making such a Cheltenham tragedy of things.''

''Obviously a woman of superior sense.''

''Oh, she has that,'' Leigh assured him, ''but I needn't scruple to tell you that that Nettles creature shan't hold her tongue. And I'll be dashed if I ruin any *honorable* female's good name.''

The earl's eyes crinkled in amusement. ''Most commendable,'' he agreed. ''But you, young Galahad, haven't really *seduced* her as far as I've determined, and since she is content to treat the matter as a lark, my advice is to follow suit.''

''You sound just like Miss Eiseley,'' Leigh accused.

The intrusion of this name for the first time into their conversation caused a frown to sprout on Winslow's forehead. ''Miss Eiseley?'' he asked. ''Pray, what does Miss Eiseley have to do with things? Did you perchance encounter her on your way here? I'd heard she was staying at Pembroke this summer.''

Leigh stared at him. ''Uncle Sebby, haven't you been attending to a word I've said? Miss Eiseley is the lady I compromised!''

For a moment, the earl was frozen in his chair, then he rose with an awful languor to tower over his nephew. ''You and Alexa Eiseley? *Impossible!*''

The younger man bristled. ''Of course it's impossible. I just finished explaining about things—''

''About things, *yes*! But not about Miss Eiseley,'' Winslow said thickly. "Why didn't you tell me it was her from the start?"

"I thought I had," Leigh answered, startled by the lightning-swift change in his uncle's benign expression. "That's why I went with her to Pembroke, for I knew she was a firm friend of yours and Mama's and Grandmother's. But now you see what an untenable position I've placed her in. I shall have to offer my protection."

Winslow, who had gone to the tray of restoratives again, halted and turned to fix his nephew with a baleful eye.

"Are you speaking of matrimony, halfling?" he demanded, boggling at the image of his green nephew with one of the ton's leading ladies. "Don't tell me you have forgotten Miss Fornhurst!"

"I haven't forgotten Miss Fornhurst," Leigh insisted. "Once I've explained everything carefully to her, she will see the necessity of my marrying Miss Eiseley. And it shall only be a marriage of convenience. I'll obtain a bill of divorcement as soon as possible and then marry Miss Fornhurst."

Lady Rowena, known to be a prodigious reader of lending library romances, might have been proud of her son's cleverness in concocting such a scheme, but her brother was far less impressed. A more bird-witted idea he had never heard in his entire life, and he took it as further proof that the lad was still wet behind the ears.

"For the moment you shall do nothing," Winslow ordered. "Through no fault of yours you have made mincemeat of your own plans as well as of Miss Eiseley's unblemished reputation. I just hope Alexa is right in thinking this affair shall die down. In a day or so I'll ride over to Pembroke, and perhaps together she and I can deduce a way out of the coil if it hasn't died down."

"But she's not at Pembroke, sir," Leigh informed him. "As soon as the weather cleared she set out for her brother's estate at Ferring."

This news came as a blow to the earl. Alone together he and Alexa might have thrashed out a suitable solution to the problem, but that brother of hers would undoubtedly complicate matters. The earl's acquaintance with Mr. George Eiseley was slight, but he had heard him described at length as the soul of propriety, and he saw no reason to doubt the veracity of his informant—Alexa herself!

Two

Several miles away, at the estate known as Ferring, a young woman still habited in her traveling dress could be seen stifling a yawn behind one slender hand. Her arrival twenty minutes earlier had sparked an impassioned lecture from the gentleman in the chair opposite her, the bulk of which concerned his unexpurgated opinion of his unmarried sister being so hen-witted as to drive herself alone up to his front door.

Despite such evident signs of brotherly displeasure, Miss Alexa Eiseley, sitting in a gilded curricle chair in the Ivory Saloon, was not gravely alarmed. Indeed she would have thought poor George in queer stirrups if he hadn't found something to pinch and scold her about within minutes of laying eyes on her.

George, she had realized long ago, was a dreadful bore, and as he stormed and ranted at her now she wondered again at the improbability of their being brother and sister, doubtless a thought that had often plagued him as well.

Their physical resemblance was slight and lessened even

14

more so by their differences in sex and age. At forty-three, George's blond hair was beginning to silver and the slenderness of his salad days had given way to stout middle age.

Temperamentally he was a moralist and never more so than when the issue concerned his only sister, whom, in private, he was prone to call a rather ramshackle chit.

To the members of the ton, Alexa Eiseley would never be characterized in such an unflattering way. In London, she was feted as an acclaimed beauty with a full score of admirers languishing after her. While her face and figure might not be perfect, they were judged to be as close to perfection as possible in a mere mortal, accentuated by two hazel eyes usually brimming with laughter, an exquisite crop of copper-colored curls and a mouth deemed soft but mischievous. Her chin bespoke character, and her voice was alleged to be just what a lady's should be: serene and yet somehow compelling, without a hint of shrewishness.

The sum effect of these female virtues was usually sufficient to dazzle most gentlemen of her acquaintance. A few, however, were immune, and into this latter category fell her brother.

"Such a sad want of conduct," he repeated now for what had to be the fourth time since her arrival, "as though you were naught but a gypsy!"

Alexa repressed the urge to laugh. Poor George! Her real if tepid affection for him was continually strained to the breaking point at every meeting. She thought him deplorably starched up while he considered her a flitty gadabout. And she could not help wondering now why she had decided to visit Ferring.

Actually it was on account of Penny, her sixteen-year-old niece, George's daughter by his first wife, Constance, who had died nearly fifteen years ago, that Alexa consented to the visit. Not a week ago, hard on the heels of Maria's invitation—which Alexa was certain to decline, for nothing, she told herself, would be more boring than to visit George and Maria in July—had been a second message. This time it was from Penny, with the lines crossed and recrossed, betraying the young writer's agitation.

In the letter Penny had begged Alexa to remember the promise she had made to take her to Bath later in the summer. Alexa's first thought had been to fob the child off, but as she reread the letter she found a growing sympathy for the girl, and after some deliberation she penned a letter of acceptance to George and Maria.

"I had thought you wanted me here, George," Alexa said, realizing with a start that a lull had fallen in the room as he paused to mop his brow with a handkerchief. "If my conduct is so wanting, I shall quit your establishment immediately lest I reflect so badly on your position."

"It's not your presence I object to," her brother replied, relenting a little, "but your curious mode of arrival!"

Alexa threw up her hands. "Oh, heavens, George, it was only a matter of a few miles between Pembroke and Ferring, and the horses were so sweet-tempered. Besides," she threw back her head, a challenge in her eyes, "I've driven for years!"

"You'll break your neck someday, Alexandra!" George warned.

This grim prediction affected Alexa not a jot. With consummate sweetness, she reminded her brother that during the past seven years he had been predicting one or another dire fate to befall her.

"Once, I believe, you foresaw a future for me as a faro dealer in some gaming hell!" Her eyes twinkled. "And I can only thank my stars that you did not see me taking up residence in *other* establishments I am much too virtuous to mention."

This jest nearly set George off again, but fortunately Maria, a vision in pink satin, just then entered the room, stopping dead at the sight of Alexa.

"Alexa!" she exclaimed at once, running to her. "Can you be here already? And I was not even informed! What a wretch you are! When did you arrive?"

"Not yet an hour ago," Alexa said, hugging her affectionately. "George has been pointing out the impropriety of my driving myself here, and I wish you would persuade him that for once I am in the right. After all, country conventions are supposed to be less stringent than ways in town. And I vow I felt perfectly free to drive myself about in London." Laughter sprang again to her eyes. "I fear, dear Maria, that George considers me sunk beneath reproach, and I must rely on you to restore my reputation with him!"

Maria gurgled helplessly. "Oh, Alexa, you are always so droll. I vow George thinks you splendid, just as I do!"

At this naive utterance, both brother and sister looked askance at each other.

"That might be doing it too brown," Alexa said with a mischievous smile, "if you'll forgive my sporting cant."

However much Mr. Eiseley would and did deplore such expressions from the lips of females, Mrs. Eiseley was more than inclined to forgive her sister-in-law this lapse and much more, for a genuine fondness existed between the two ladies.

Maria, unlike George, took shy pleasure in having such a dashing relation, delighting in reading about Alexa's many triumphs in the columns of the *Morning Post* and the *Gazette*. The one hope she had secretly nourished, that Alexa might one day marry happily, had been so far thwarted. No lady was more highly courted than Alexa, but no female was more adamant against the marital state.

"It has been an age since I've seen you," Alexa said, drawing Maria down onto the couch next to her. "How is Baby? I suppose he has at least a tooth or two by now? How backward of him if he does not!"

Maria, laughing, assured her that Baby had several teeth, which he put to good use when provoked.

"He sounds like a nephew after my own heart," Alexa said cheerfully. "What have you been up to this morning? Out purchasing a new bonnet? It is charming."

"Oh, no, this is an old hat!" Maria said, touching the wispy confection on her head. "And I am glad that you like it. Actually," her face sobered slightly, "I have been visiting Lady Donaldby. Do you remember her?"

"Too well," Alexa replied, shuddering. "And I do hope you don't count her among your intimates, for while I was determined to be the perfect guest for a se'nnight and try to love those you love, that might be too ambitious a task. As I recall, you love practically everyone!''

Her sister-in-law uttered a quick disclaimer. ''I certainly don't love Mrs. Borthwick, who was one of Lady Donaldby's guests today and is such a dreadful prattle box. Only, of course, Lady Donaldby hadn't told me she would be there and had already invited me, and it would have been uncivil not to have gone.''

Alexa could not help smiling at this recital. ''It's very well for you to go, then, but I hope I shan't have to spend many hours with them.''

''Oh, no. And I shan't either. I don't like that Mrs. Borthwick. She has the most peculiar stories to tell.'' She blushed a little under Alexa's swift scrutiny.

''They have upset you!'' Alexa cried out. ''Vicious tabbies. If they dared to say a word against you I shall slay them. Or George shall,'' she added, generously including her brother in this threat.

Maria hastened to reassure Alexa. ''They said nothing untoward about me. Actually,'' she confessed, ''it was you. Mrs. Borthwick has a sister—Mrs. Nettles is her name—and she told her the queerest tale about you and Lord Winslow being seen alone this morning at Pembroke after spending a night together.'' A blush spread over her cheeks. ''I knew it could not be true, but still it was so disagreeable a tale!''

George had been rendered silent at his wife's entrance into the room, but now roused himself from his stupor.

''Maria,'' he demanded autocratically, ''what did you just say?''

Maria blinked and made a dutiful attempt to repeat her statement, but the laughter of the third member in the room made it impossible for her to be heard.

''Me and Winslow!'' Alexa gasped between whoops. ''Oh, no! It is really too stupid. I shall give a monkey to see his face when I share this story with him.''

Her brother, his cheeks flaming red, stood over her. ''Share the story with him?'' he demanded in an outraged voice. ''Don't be such a shameless creature, Alexa. And I'll be dashed if I can see why you're in whoops. It's not the least bit funny. Haven't you any sense of conduct?''

Her hazel eyes danced as she made no attempt to stifle her giggles. ''None at all, my dear George, as you so frequently inform me.''

His cheeks filled and deflated. ''Alexa, I must insist you tell me at once if any part of this appalling tale is true!''

''George, don't be idiotish!'' Alexa protested. ''You shall give yourself a fever of the brain if you're not careful. I haven't seen Winslow since we met at least a month ago at Lady Jersey's ball in London. And I daresay it is just like Mrs. Nettles to make such a ridiculous mistake, for she is notoriously shortsighted and so vain that she won't wear spectacles. It wasn't Winslow I took leave of this morning but his nephew, Mr. Leigh Denning. Are you perchance acquainted with him?''

George, who had been somewhat mollified by his sister's first remarks, now went as rigid as his collar points. ''Winslow's *nephew*!'' he ejaculated, his jowls heaving. ''Do you mean that the heart of this abominable tale is true? That you spent the night under Pembroke's roof with a man?''

Alexa's eyes narrowed. ''Come now, George . . .'' she said in a rallying tone.

''Of course the servants were there, but still, Alexa—''

''Actually,'' she divulged, resigning herself to another explosion, ''the servants weren't there. I sent them ahead to Bath, for I'd planned on going there after my stay with you was completed, and I wanted the house opened. There was no reason to keep them at Pembroke.''

At her words, her brother choked. ''No reason? Alexa, I've warned you repeatedly about flouting convention so willfully, and just look at the result. Your reputation lies in tatters.''

Alexa blinked. ''Leigh is only a lad. And there was nothing the least bit sordid about his seeking shelter under my roof during a driving rainstorm. I couldn't throw him out into the cold and wet, now could I?'' From the glazed expression on her brother's face she realized the futility of logic. ''Oh, very well, George, you shall have the truth. I spent a night of wild abandon with that young man. In fact I seduced him!''

"Alexandra!" George thundered.

Even Maria was betrayed into a nervous titter. "Alexa, you didn't, now did you?"

"Of course I didn't," she exploded, "but George appears willing to believe the worst of me no matter how untrue!''

"I wonder how you can jest when you are compromised," her brother said thickly.

A brief silence fell over the combatants in the room. "I am *what*?" Alexa asked, dumbfounded. "No, pray don't repeat it. You shall send me off again, and the servants shall undoubtedly think me demented. How can you be such a slowtop, George," she railed. "Compromised, indeed! I have told you that nothing happened at Pembroke. Don't you believe me?"

"Of course he does," Maria said loyally before her spouse could speak.

"What I believe is beside the point," George said with some dignity. "Mrs. Nettles has set the tale about. The damage is done whether you like it or not. You are compromised. I shall take steps to speak to young Leigh Denning!''

Alexa's first impulse was to laugh at such an outrageous idea, but one look at her brother's face and she realized that he was fully prepared to undertake so cork-brained a notion.

"And just what do you intend to do to poor Leigh?" she asked. "Call him out? I don't think that shall answer, for even though he is a trifle green, Winslow had a hand in his education, and the earl is alleged to be a good shot. And at your age, George, you shouldn't start dueling! Furthermore," she swept on, "if your goal is, as I fear, that Leigh do what is termed the honorable thing, I tell you now that I have no intention of marrying a mere child. So you shall only succeed in making yourself look ridiculous. Besides which I don't know where Leigh is or could be found, and now," she turned to Maria, "I wonder if I might go up to my room, for I am rather fatigued from my trip."

Mrs. Eiseley, recalled to her duties as hostess, at once led Alexa up the stairs and into the pink bedchamber, which had always been reserved for her use. Ordinarily Alexa would have praised Maria on the new curtains and the rose-colored wallpaper, but she found that her quarrel with George had upset her more than she had thought. In truth, her head throbbed. Compromised, indeed! Was there ever such a brother? Maria, instinctively realizing that this was not the most propitious moment to enjoy a comfortable cose with Alexa, tactfully withdrew. Alexa inhaled a breath, enjoying the reprieve of solitude. This state, however, lasted only a few minutes, for the door flew open and Penny was upon her in a trice.

"Aunt Alexa, how famous! I came the instant I could," Penny said, speaking, laughing and hugging her aunt in an excess of emotion. "I knew you wouldn't fail me and would come to my rescue."

Alexa, returning the embrace, drew away to observe her niece. At sixteen, Penny stood between girlhood and womanhood, with blond hair tied back in braids and two enormous gray eyes, which always reminded Alexa of a fawn's.

"For a victim you don't look starved or beaten," Alexa said affectionately. "I daresay no one has been cruel to you. And if you think you can gammon me into believing that sweet little Maria has been bullying you—"

"Oh, no, of course she wouldn't," Penny said, collapsing in giggles on the bed. "Maria wouldn't know how to be cruel to anyone. But she and Father treat me as though I were a child, and I'm not. I'm sixteen! And you promised that when I turned sixteen you would sponsor me in the ton, for you know how Papa dislikes town life. And I vow Maria is just a little frightened of taking me to grand balls. I know I couldn't have a better sponsor than you, for you know everyone!"

"Not everyone, my dear," Alexa said, trying to dampen Penny's excitement. "I daresay there are a few notables I am unacquainted with."

"Then they must be cits or mushrooms! Why, even Papa says that you are feted more than any female has a right to be. And I don't think your quarrel with him today shall alter that opinion any."

Alexa glanced at her niece, who was lying on the bed. "Did you overhear the quarrel?"

"Yes, but I couldn't help it!" Penny protested, rolling over on her stomach. "Papa's voice *carries*."

Alexa trilled with quick laughter. "So it does, my dear."

"What was it all about, Aunt Alexa?" Penny asked naively, propping her hands on her fists. "I couldn't hear the details, but I could tell Papa was on his high ropes."

"It was nothing to signify."

"I just hope it doesn't get in the way of our plans," Penny said, accepting this easy evasion.

Alexa's brows rose. "Our plans?"

"You did get my letter, didn't you?" Penny asked. "You must have if you came here to rescue me. I thought we could go to Bath together, since you said at Christmas that you planned to open up your grandfather's house there. And I'm sure if you told Papa and Maria, they would consent for you to show me a little of Bath society."

"So that is what our plan is," Alexa said, an ironic gleam in her eye. "I own it is sound enough . . ."

"Aunt Alexa, you can't fail me now!" Penny implored, adopting the tragic air of an orphan. "I have no one else!"

Alexa laughed. "I can see that you have been reading too many of those circulating romances again. If you did overhear your papa just now, you must know that I am in his black books. It would not do to start teasing him now about taking you under my wing, for he'll think it a rather ramshackle wing indeed."

"Pooh!" Penny tossed her head back, "You make too much of your quarrel. Papa is always that way. Maria shall coax him out of the sulks soon enough, and if you dislike asking him, I shall do it myself."

"No!" Alexa's reproof was gentle but firm. "Don't breathe a word of this plan to anyone. George is certain to object even more strenuously if he discovered the whole notion of going to Bath originated in the head of a sixteen-year-old fed on lending library novels."

"If you say so, Aunt Alexa. Perhaps it is forward of me to

ask you to take me to Bath. Possibly you might not like to take charge of me.''

"Now you are talking like a peagoose! I am not adverse to taking you to Bath. It shall do us both a world of good. It's just that I must know the reason why you are so wild to get away from here. You seemed troubled in that letter, and while I don't mean to poke my nose into what doesn't concern me, it seems like more than just the usual vexatiousness of being tied to a schoolroom, odious though I know that can be. Is it possibly Baby?'' she asked delicately.

"I suppose he has something to do with it,'' Penny said, hanging her head. "You mustn't think I don't like him, Aunt Alexa, for I do. Even though he seems rather small, and it is queer that Maria and Nurse should go into raptures at every move he makes. It's just that things are not the same here anymore.''

"No, of course not,'' Alexa said, pressing her shoulder lightly. "And I suppose George is very absorbed in the baby, too, and not as available to you as he used to be?''

Penny's head shot up. "You think I'm jealous.''

"Not at all,'' Alexa said mildly, her eyes searching Penny's, "but I do think that if you remain here much longer you well might be.''

"Then you do understand,'' Penny said gratefully. "I knew you would.''

"Yes, and I'm resolved that we shall go to Bath. I also understand that I have only an hour until dinner, and I shan't risk another setdown from George so soon after coming to cuffs with him, so you must leave or I shall look positively hagged at dinner!''

At this Penny burst into giggles, but she took her dismissal in good form and departed.

A half hour later, Alexa sat in front of the mirror, her thoughts far away from the beguiling reflection of herself dressed in an elegant jaconet muslin opening over silver satin.

Under normal circumstances she would have swept Penny off unhesitatingly to Bath without a moment's delay, but these, she reminded herself, were not normal circumstances. She grinned wryly at herself. She was, after all, compromised!

The thought brought a smile to her eyes, and she resolved to prove the lie of that absurd tale by appearing totally indifferent to the whole preposterous tale.

Three

Despite the best intentions of the two families, the tale of Miss Eiseley's compromising position did not die down. If a malicious sprite had himself handpicked Mrs. Nettles and Mrs. Borthwick, he could not have selected more willing accomplices in mischief making. For twenty-four hours the two sisters had tirelessly repeated the tale. If several key points in the story were in error—Mrs. Nettles still stoutly insisted that Miss Eiseley's companion in sin was his lordship the earl of Winslow, swearing that she would know his great, multicaped driving coat anywhere—they remained unflagging in their diligence in repeating a tale that became more and more embroidered with each telling.

Since Winslow did not count Mrs. Nettles or her sister among his acquaintances, the tale did not reach him firsthand. It did, however, reach the ears of his boon companion, Major Archibald Jayneway, whose usually placid demeanor underwent a swift metamorphosis, and he lost not a moment in heading straight for Winslow Park, catching the earl still lingering over a late breakfast.

"Have a little something, Archie," Winslow urged his visitor and gestured generously toward the sideboard heaped with breads and muffins. "You look as though you could use some nourishment."

"Not hungry, thank you," the major said distractedly, running his thick fingers through his sandy-colored hair. "Sebby, I must speak with you."

Winslow chewed mightily and swallowed. "Thought we were doing that!"

"This is serious."

The earl looked up with concern. It was not like Archie to betray such agitation at any time, particularly so early in the day. He was in a pelter about something, Winslow deduced as he sipped his coffee.

"Fire away, then," he said calmly.

The major, given this opening, stared down at his hands for a moment, uncertain as to how he should begin. "Sebby, just how particular are your attentions to Alexa Eiseley?"

The earl wiped his mouth with a napkin. "I should think not particular at all. We're friends, of course. Known her from the cradle. Charming lady—that goes without saying. And she has a slew of suitors only too eager to marry her." He glanced meditatively over at his friend. He had never known the major to evidence such curiosity in females before. "Why? Are you dangling after her?"

Jayneway, as confirmed a bachelor as the earl, recoiled visibly from such a notion.

"Good God, no!"

Winslow could not resist a smile and a clap on the major's shoulder. "Then why are you so intrigued with Miss Eiseley?" he demanded.

"Because that revolting Borthwick creature has been spreading lies about you and her."

Winslow raised his eyebrows a fraction of an inch. "Lies about me and Miss Eiseley?"

The major nodded.

The earl laid down his fork carefully. "What is he saying?"

"It's not a he. It's a she," his friend replied. "More's the pity, for if it were a man I'd just call him out!"

"It must be serious to tempt you to duel, Archie," Winslow observed. "Come now, out with it! What is the creature saying?"

The major hesitated and then blurted out the rest of his information. "She has concocted some wild tale of you compromising Alexa. Claims to have seen the two of you at Pembroke early one morning and swears it is you on account of that driving coat you are so devilishly fond of wearing. And you needn't bother to tell me it's a hum, for I know that. And I also know you ain't a loose screw as to resort to such vile tactics if you were dangling after Alexa, which you say you aren't!"

The earl heard him out with surprising patience. "When did you hear all this?"

"Some hours ago," the major reported with a grimace.

Conscious now of his dwindling appetite, Winslow pushed his plate away. "She is actually going about saying I compromised Alexa?"

The major shook his head. "She doesn't actually say it, Sebby. She ain't that touched in the cockloft. She merely hints at it in the most odious way possible, batting her eyelashes and claiming that she knows naught but what she saw with her own two eyes, which was you taking leave of Alexa the other morning at Pembroke. Everyone in the area knew Alexa had dispatched her servants to Bath and didn't have her abigail about."

"Well, I'm obliged to you for bringing it to my attention," the earl said slowly. "I've not had time to gad about. Been busy, as you may deduce, getting ready for Leigh and my impending guests."

"Yes, I had heard you were doing it up for him," the major sympathized. "But won't it be devilishly awkward now, Sebby? What with this ugly story afloat?"

"I shall take steps to scotch it," Winslow promised. The major, assured that his friend would do just that, departed, leaving the earl to mull over a course of action. Who would have dreamed that he would figure in Leigh's folly merely because the boy aped his style in fashion? Dratted driving coat, indeed. Loath though he was to meddle in the lad's affairs, it seemed imperative now that he take a hand in things.

With this thought fresh in his mind, he went into the hall, where he found young Leigh just descending the Adam staircase. The night's sleep had restored a little color to the lad's cheeks, but it had worked no such beneficial wonders on his wits. He still doggedly insisted that he must make a clean breast of things to Miss Fornhurst on her arrival, and nothing would dissuade him from doing otherwise.

"But you have nothing whatever to confess!" Winslow expostulated at one point, repressing the justifiable urge to shake some sense into the lad.

"Then I shall have nothing to fear," Leigh replied with the earnestness of youth.

Winslow tried a different tack. "Do you love Miss Fornhurst, Leigh?"

"Oh, Uncle Sebby, how can you even ask that!" Leigh implored. "Have you never seen her?"

"I believe I have glimpsed her upon occasion in London," Winslow acknowledged, watching him closely.

"Then you must know what an enchanting creature she is," Leigh said, his eyes shining. "I know I fell under her spell within seconds of meeting her at Almack's, and when I saw that she might possibly return my feelings . . ." His voice trailed off, unable to do justice to the full tide of his emotion for Miss Fornhurst, much to the relief of his uncle, who had been rendered a trifle nauseated by Leigh's few words on the topic.

The lad was totally and utterly besotted. That much was clear. Winslow's own reading of Miss Fornhurst's character was slight, but he would have wagered anything that if Leigh did carry out his skittle-brained scheme to confess all, a scene such as that which a Kean or Siddons might relish would soon ensue under his roof! And by God that would not do!

Sustaining himself now with the recollection that Miss Fornhurst and her family were not due to arrive until the end of the week, he resolved to settle the problem.

"What do you have there?" he asked now, his attention drawn to something in his nephew's hand.

"A letter to Miss Eiseley," was the explanation. "Actually, it's an apology for embroiling her in this fix."

Winslow put out his hand. "I plan to see Miss Eiseley this morning at Ferring. I shall be happy to deliver it, if you like."

Leigh's face brightened at once. "Oh, would you, sir? That would be so much better. You must tell her how dreadfully sorry I am."

"Indeed I shall. Perhaps together Alexa and I can smooth this path over."

Leigh relinquished the letter to the earl and gave no further thought to how this path smoothing might be accomplished. His uncle, however, had mulled over the situation carefully, and a half hour later, riding toward Ferring on Caesar, his great black stallion, he pondered anew the dubious merits of a scheme which had taken root during Major Jayneway's visit and which he planned to lay before Alexa. While some, including the earl himself and undoubtedly Alexa, would call it the most chuckleheaded plan in Christendom, it was the only way he could see to stop the tale Mrs. Nettles was bent on circulating and at the same time keep young Leigh from divulging all to Miss Fornhurst.

As Winslow made his way toward Ferring, Alexa sat on the Egyptian couch in her brother's Ivory Saloon all but transfixed by her morning caller. The Viscount Cawly, known in London circles as a pleasant enough gentleman and one of her more persistent suitors, had pretensions to dandyism, which was attested to this morning by his Chinese red frock coat, cherry-colored waistcoat and cardinal breeches. This raiment, Alexa ruefully acknowledged to herself, quite cast her half dress of green gauze in the shade.

Cawly, however, had more in mind than clothing, judging by the way he clasped her hands to his bony bosom and murmured, "Poor, poor Alexa. I came the instant I heard."

"Heard what?" she said, totally baffled.

The viscount touched a forefinger to his thin lips. "Not a word of the sordid tale shall pass these lips."

"Lord Cawly, I must ask you to stop speaking in riddles!"

"That's the spirit," he said encouragingly. "Such pluck even in the face of adversity. Almost any other lady of my acquaintance would be prostrate with mortification by now, but not you! I hope I can assist you with your problem. In fact I'm sure I can. I shall marry you."

Alexa had been watching her visitor with a bemused expression on her face, but at his words she gasped audibly.

"You shall *what*?"

A broad smile spread over the vacuous face in front of her. "Marry you. And you needn't thank me."

"*Thank* you!" she exclaimed as she realized that her hands were still clasped in his and snatched them free. "Pray, why should I thank you, Lord Cawly?" she asked stiffly.

The viscount was momentarily startled by her change in demeanor, but he soon recovered his élan. "Why, for restoring your good name, of course, Miss Eiseley," he said, wetting his lips.

"My good name is in no need of restoration, sir," she said dangerously.

"No, of course it isn't," he said hastily. "But still you must see that marriage to me is the answer. I know you have refused my offers in the past, at least five times in as many years, but I shan't hold that against you. And I give you my solemn oath that I shall never hold your unfortunate predicament with Winslow against you once you are my wife!"

With Winslow? The light at last dawned, and Alexa's brow cleared. So that was what lay behind Cawly's surprise visit and the renewal of his offer. And just when she had hoped that she had finally discouraged him! Never had she judged the viscount's intelligence to be of the first order, but she had assumed that he would treat the story as a mere *on-dit*. Since he did not, she wondered, what must her other acquaintances make of it?

"Alexa?" The viscount waited, not a little confused by the conflicting emotions flitting across her face.

"Lord Cawly," she said, returning to earth, "I must once again decline your kind offer. That odious tale you no doubt heard is mere tittle-tattle."

Surprise registered on the viscount's fair cheeks. "Then you and he were not . . ." He paused delicately.

"I would not scruple to deny such an obvious falsehood," Alexa replied, conscious that her own cheeks were flaming wildly. "Suffice it to say that I have not seen Winslow for several weeks and have no expectation of seeing him any time soon."

Any hope that Viscount Cawly might be persuaded to believe in her innocence went by the board moments later when Winslow himself strolled into the Ivory Saloon just as Cawly rose to leave.

Alexa's mouth dropped open at the sight of her visitor looking as elegant as usual in a well-cut coat of cinnamon superfine, ecru waistcoat, flawless cravat, tan breeches and high-polished top boots.

"Winslow," she gasped.

Cawly turned as well. "I would not think that you would dare to show your face here, Winslow," he said, obviously intent on taking up the cudgels on Alexa's behalf.

"My dear Larry, if your next words to me are to insinuate that you wish to give me the thrashing of my life, I advise you that that threat has no bark left in it. Miss Eiseley's brother has already informed me of those intentions. He didn't appear willing to endure my presence under his roof."

"That comes as no surprise to me." The viscount sniffed. "You would be unwelcome under my roof, too."

The earl looked singularly unaffected. "How fortunate, then, that we are not under your roof at the moment."

"Miss Eiseley." The viscount turned toward Alexa. "If you desire me to remain here, you have only to say the word."

"Oh, heavens, no!" Alexa exclaimed. "I mean," she went on as his brows knitted into a frown, "you must not linger away from your very pressing affairs on my account.'' Her sense of humor came to the foreground. ''I assure you I am perfectly safe under my brother's roof.''

The viscount did not appear wholly convinced at this, but he nevertheless withdrew, leaving the earl to deal Alexa a quizzing look.

''What a pompous jackanapes he is. And you, my dear, 'perfectly safe under my brother's roof,' indeed!''

His perfect mimicry sparked another laugh. ''I couldn't help it, Winslow,'' she said, collapsing in helpless laughter on the satinwood sofa. ''If people shall talk as though they are in a melodrama, I can only follow suit.''

The earl deftly folded his lanky frame into the seat next to her. ''What was Cawly doing here, anyway?''

Her eyes twinkled good-naturedly. ''If you must know,'' she said demurely, ''he was offering to reestablish my good name!''

Winslow let out a bark of laughter. ''The good name that I am rumored to have caused you to lose?'' he asked ruefully.

She lifted her head quickly, reading comprehension in his blue eyes. ''So you have heard that ridiculous tale as well,'' she said with a sigh.

He nodded. ''Prior to which Leigh confessed all to me, and while I had hoped that I would have no need to come the ugly with the lad, if you are truly reduced to marrying Cawly because of this entanglement, I shall never forgive the lad.''

Alexa was thoroughly bemused. ''Then you shall be relieved to know that I have declined the Viscount Cawly's very chivalrous offer.''

His eyes affectionately traced the merriment on her lovely face. ''You are taking all this lightly for one who is sunk beneath reproach, Alexa.''

''Yes, I know,'' she retorted gaily, ''which I suppose shows a sad want of character in me.'' Her face sobered slightly. ''I'm not saying it's not irksome, Sebby, for of course it is. And if Cawly heard of it and you as well, Mrs. Nettles must be having a very busy time of it, indeed!''

His brow furrowed. "I believe she has assistance from another quarter. A female relation of some sort. Detestable pair of prattle boxes!"

While wholly agreeing with him, Alexa could not help inquiring about his reaction to the news. "Confess, Winslow. Were you not in whoops when you heard that people were saying that you and I—"

"My emotions were many," the earl acknowledged dryly. "But whoops, I fear, were not among them. I suppose George has been taking it badly?"

Her eyes rolled heavenward. "No more than usual. And I do hope he didn't plague you, for he knows quite well I sheltered Leigh and not you."

The earl became suddenly alert. "That reminds me I have something for you from that addled nephew of mine." He searched his coat pockets and handed her the note. "He wrote it this morning. I fear you'll find it overly long and undoubtedly illegible. I was to deliver it to you with all manner of profuse apologies."

Alexa sighed as she opened the letter. "Poor Leigh. To be embroiled in such a bumblebroth must be utterly bewildering to him."

"Yes, it has even affected his wits. He is determined to confess all to Miss Fornhurst, the young lady he had planned to offer for."

Alexa drew back, her lively face filled with dismay. "Sebby, he must be funning! Pray, what is there for him to confess? Nothing whatever happened between me and your nephew."

The earl opened his enamel snuffbox. "Your assurances to me are quite unnecessary, Alexa," he replied blandly. "I have absolute faith in you. But do read the note."

Obediently, she scanned the lines, which were, as the earl had promised, difficult to decipher. Midway through her perusal a frown appeared on her own brow, and when she finally put down the letter she was shaking her copper tresses. "Foolish, foolish boy. Is he desperately in love with Miss Fornhurst?"

"So it would appear," Winslow said, turning from his

scrutiny of a glowering Eiseley ancestor on the drawing-room wall. "According to Rowena, the lad clapped eyes on the Fornhurst chit during some rout party in London and quite lost his heart. He's been mooning about ever since, giving every sign of one nursing a grand passion. Besides which," he added in a plaintive tone, "if he's not in love, I wish to know why I have had to put up with all the botheration of this betrothal party. What did he say in his letter?"

"He offers me matrimony," Alexa divulged, "and so heroically, Sebby! With a divorce, of course, to follow in a year's time. Can you even think how idiotish such a match would be?"

The earl took another judicious pinch of snuff. "It does boggle my imagination," he agreed. "Shall I tell Leigh, then, that you have declined his offer?"

She nodded, tapping her fingers lightly against the letter. "But kindly, if you please, Sebby, for he is young, and he appears to think he is doing me a great service!" A faint tremor nearly overset her. "Good heavens, two offers in one morning. First Cawly and now Leigh."

"And you have declined them both," he pointed out.

Her eyes narrowed. "Surely you didn't think I would consent to either as a way out of this fix!"

His smile was gentle. "No, indeed, I had rather hoped that you would consent to become betrothed to me."

Utter silence greeted this bombshell. "What did you say?" she asked finally, trying to make sense of the enigmatic expression on his face.

"I hope you'll become betrothed to me," the earl repeated patiently, as though to a slow child. "Since I am the one rumored to have caused your problem, I deem it only fit that I help to solve it."

Alexa rose and paced the floor. "Don't be daft, Sebby. You can no more wish to marry me than I to marry you!"

Since the earl considered himself something of a matrimonial prize, her vehement reaction to the only offer he had ever made caused him a moment's pique. But it swiftly passed.

"That is hardly the manner in which a gently bred female

ought to decline a gentleman's offer," he said in a voice of mild reproof.

Her eyes softened. "Well, I am sorry. But I seem to have spent all my civility declining Cawly's offer, and the only emotion left me at this moment is to wonder if you are foxed."

He winced. "Do hear me out, Alexa. I quite agree that the notion sounds absurd. But this whole situation is that! And if it had happened to anyone else, the two of us would be laughing ourselves silly over it, wouldn't we? As it is, the tale has foisted the craziest of situations upon us."

"Even so—"

"And," he continued, undaunted by her interruption, "the thing of paramount importance is to restore our good names. I assure you I have been as woefully wronged as you."

"I know," she agreed. "But, Sebby, I don't wish to marry anyone, not even such a specimen as you!"

He bore this apparent slight with unfailing good humor. "Yes, I know. But do you think you should dislike just being betrothed to me?"

"It amounts to the same thing!" she exclaimed.

"Indeed it does not," he countered, taking her hand. "I agree that neither of us is so enamored of marriage, are we? But we might still contrive to be engaged and give the lie to the story that way."

She hooted. "Give the lie, Sebby? That is an air dream. We'll be confirming the tale."

"We will stay engaged until the story dies down," he explained, paying her no heed. "And it shall die down as soon as there is another rumor for Mrs. Nettles to spread about. Then, as is your privilege as the female, you may cry off."

"And that shall undoubtedly give rise to all those odious rumors again," she pointed out skeptically.

He shrugged. "Perhaps not. Time is a great healer. Mrs. Nettles will have found a new tale to twist to her satisfaction. You shall have had ample opportunity to review Cawly's offer and make him happy, or any of your other beaux. Just a friendly suggestion, no need to rip up."

"There is also no need for a bogus betrothal," she said gloomily. "I shall go away to the Continent."

"And leave me behind branded a *blackguard* for ruining you?" he demanded. "Not for the world! You forget that I am embroiled as deeply in this as you." His tone softened a little. "Alexa, do but consider the fix we are in. Through no fault of ours, our names are being bandied about in quite scurrilous fashion. And I don't care for that. My mother in Brighton might get wind of it. And you have George to worry about. And then there's Leigh! If we pretend to be engaged, that shall prevent him from making an addled confession to Miss Fornhurst. We'll preserve his happiness at least." He paused, noticing some sign of weakening in her for the first time and quickly pressed his advantage. "Do think of the lad, Alexa."

"Oh, drat you, Sebby!" she exclaimed, flinging wide her hands. "It was my thinking of Leigh that landed me in this coil. I should have let him catch his death of cold in the storm. Very well. We shall pretend to be engaged. Pretend, mind you," she warned him strictly, "for I have no real intention of marrying you."

"Nor I of marrying you," he retorted affably.

"Now then, when shall we announce it?"

"As soon as possible," he replied without a moment's hesitation. "There is just one thing, Alexa. Do you think you might act as though you really did wish to marry me? I know it is a good deal to ask of you after all you have been through, and you needn't appear *totally* besotted with me, but . . ."

"I believe my acting will pass muster when the situation arises," Alexa replied dismissively. "We shall have to concoct some tale about our attachment and how it came about."

The earl cocked his head to one side. "I see no reason why the truth shouldn't suffice."

She stared at him. "What truth?"

"That we are old friends," he said blandly, "and Cupid caught us unaware. Our love, er, bloomed. Where was it we saw each other last? Lady Jersey's dreadful party, wasn't it?

And that ever since we've been fighting it, but it finally burst out of control.''

"Good Jupiter," Alexa ejaculated. "I suppose it shall have to do. And now, my dear, beloved Sebby, we might as well begin by telling George the happy news!''

Four

Any qualms Winslow may have entertained about Alexa's ability to play her role disappeared as they entered her brother's library. Blushing prettily as any female on the wings of love might, Alexa led the earl forward hand in hand. Mr. Eiseley's intellect was by no means superior, but it was sufficient for him to grasp the essentials of the moment, particularly when he was assisted by his sister's radiant countenance and the quizzical smile of Winslow himself.

"My word, Alexa," he murmured as he pushed his stout form out of a chair, "do you mean that you and Winslow here . . . ?"

She nodded, smiling.

"Well, well, first rate, my dear," he said, pecking her dutifully on the cheek. "And Winslow, fancy that! Who would have thought it? Old chum I always thought you said he was," he said as he crushed the earl's hand in his clammy paw. "What will Maria say when she hears?" George babbled then caught himself up short. "My word, Maria! She'll be heartbroken if she's not here.'' He hurried over to the bellpull and gave it a sharp tug. A footman was soon dispatched to find Maria and escort her back to the library.

Ten minutes later, Maria appeared, carrying a basket of roses, which she had been happily cutting when her husband's urgent summons had reached her. For a moment she stopped dead, alarmed at the sight of her spouse drinking what appeared to be champagne at such an early hour of the day.

The reason behind his apparent lapse in character was quickly established, and Maria tearfully admitted that the occasion of Alexa becoming affianced to the earl was an event worthy of champagne.

''Now, Maria, don't be a wet goose!'' Alexa laughed and handed the basket of roses to George. ''One would almost think you didn't wish me to marry!''

''But I do,'' came the tearful rejoinder. ''Indeed, it was the one wish of my heart, Alexa. Often did I pray that you would find just the right gentleman, and now you have! I'm so happy I could burst.''

Maria's words came so evidently from the heart that Alexa felt a momentary twinge of guilt. She did not relish deceiving her gentle sister-in-law.

''Some champagne, Mrs. Eiseley?'' Winslow asked, rescuing Alexa from what he perceived was a ticklish situation.

His ploy worked. Maria happily brushed aside her tears and took the glass he offered her.

''George,'' she said, prompting her husband, who was still standing with the basket of roses in his hand, ''we must have a toast!''

Mr. Eiseley roused himself willingly, placed the roses down on his mahogany desk and wished his sister and her husband-to-be much happiness.

''And now,'' George said, laying aside his glass with a flourish, ''when shall the wedding be? And where shall it take place?''

His words caught both Alexa and Winslow unprepared.

After a swift exchange of glances, however, Winslow rose to the occasion.

"At the moment, such details are beyond us, George," he said with a charming smile. "My mother shall, of course, have no little say in the matter."

"Yes, of course she shall," Maria agreed, her eyes beginning to mist again. "Only think of you married, Alexa! How grand you shall look."

"You plan to sell Pembroke, I suppose?" George inquired, shifting rapidly from wedding plans to estate matters.

Alexa put down her champagne glass. "Sell Pembroke?" she asked in astonishment. "Why should I?"

George looked surprised. "Oh, I don't know. I'd presumed you would sell it. After all, Winslow has his estate not so very far away. Odd to keep two houses in such close locations. I know of several gentlemen who might be interested in buying it from you. Pay a good price for it."

"I am not selling Pembroke." Alexa's reply was firm and augmented by the mulish set to her chin. "Aunt Mary left Pembroke to me, and if you think I shall sell it to a perfect stranger . . . And I do hope you shan't set the word about that it is for sale, George, for it isn't."

"Come, come, Alexandra!"

"Your sister is very attached to Pembroke." Winslow broke into the family skirmish. "I happen to think that whatever the oddity, George, we might contrive to keep both houses for now." He rose. "I must be off."

"I shall see you out, Sebby," Alexa said quickly, adding in an undertone when the two of them approached the front door, "After all, it stands to reason, since I am so besotted with you."

His grin broadened as they went out into the open air. "Does George always call you Alexandra in that grating fashion?"

"Only when he is vexed," she said with a sigh.

He looked at her thoughtfully, and his expression was frankly curious. "Having second thoughts?" he asked as he picked up the reins of his mount.

She considered the question for a moment and gave her head a definite shake. "No! But you must own it felt awkward to be accepting such felicitations knowing it all to be a sham. And"—her tone was wry—"I hadn't fully realized my situation in life was so desperate as to have little Maria praying nightly for my conversion from the ranks of spinsterhood!"

Winslow chuckled along with her. "I should think that any number of gentlemen would have ably assisted your sister-in-law in such a task."

"Prettily said, Winslow," she replied.

His lips curved up in a smile. "I mean it."

She turned away from him quickly to hide her confusion. "I just hope Maria shan't be too dashed down when it all comes to naught."

He continued to smile down at her. "Who knows? Perhaps it shan't."

She felt suddenly anxious. "Winslow, I have no wish to marry you!"

"I know that!" he said dampeningly. "However, you might find being betrothed to me enjoyable enough to wish to undertake it with one of your other beaux—Cawly, for instance. No, perhaps not him. Then Langly or Montcalm." To her surprise he named two of her other London suitors. "They may stand you in good stead. Till then, of course, I must lay claim on you." He had picked up her hand as they spoke and now he touched it lightly to his lips before she could utter a protest.

"Camouflage," he explained. "In case your little sister-in-law is still spying on us from that upstairs window."

She laughed as he mounted up. She could not, in good faith, protest such easy familiarity, but she did not like to encourage it either. It was one thing to treat Sebby as an old friend. It was quite another to have him as her betrothed, and she wondered fleetingly what she had gotten herself into.

She stood for a moment, watching his tall figure on horseback disappear from sight, then she gave her head a tiny shake as though to clear it and stepped back toward the house. An involuntary smile came to her lips as the upstairs curtain flitted hastily back in place.

Before she could fully contemplate on the audacity of the situation she had undertaken, Maria came down the stairs in a rush, so full of plans and schemes for the wedding that Alexa did not have the heart to inform her that she and Winslow had more or less settled on a long engagement.

Winslow, on the way back to Winslow Park, felt all the pleasure of having rescued Leigh from the folly of his years and having repaired Alexa's reputation and his own. Thinking of Alexa as Caesar carried him along the road, he wondered why she had not yet made a match. It certainly could not be for lack of opportunity. She was the most courted lady of his acquaintance. Odd, then, that she had never shown the slightest inclination to marry any of her plentiful suitors.

Perhaps, he mused as the wind blew briskly against his face, he would have a chance to discern the reason during his bogus betrothal to her and might later suggest to the more worthy of her beaux the proper steps to win her over.

The earl's mood of self-satisfaction lasted until he reached the environs of his estate, where he soon discerned a traveling chaise halted at his front door. Another minute passed as he recognized the slender form of his sister in an aqua riding habit. The newcomers surrounding her would be the Fornhursts. But they weren't due for at least another two days. Intrigued, he urged Caesar forward.

"Sebby, there you are!" Lady Rowena's voice was gay as her brother approached. "And just in the nick of time. The Fornhursts have only just arrived. Aren't you going to welcome them?"

This reminder was unnecessary, for the earl had already dismounted and was bowing to both Mrs. Fornhurst and her daughter, then shaking hands with Mr. Fornhurst.

Mrs. Fornhurst, pale and trembling-eyed, did little to return the earl's civil greeting, being rather too absorbed in bemoaning the dreadful jostling associated with being transported hither and thither in the traveling chaise. Jenkins, rising to the occasion, finally persuaded her to lie down in a small anteroom to recover from what appeared to be a shattering migraine.

The love of Leigh's life, Miss Fornhurst, had inherited her mother's pallor and delicate features but had, thankfully, not succumbed to a migraine. Her nemesis was carriage sickness, a situation unfortunate enough to cause her to pay no heed at all to Leigh's halting words of welcome as she all but dashed upstairs to the safety of a bedchamber.

The only one of the family unaffected by the trip appeared to be Mr. Fornhurst, stout, gray-haired and with the reputation of being the greatest bore in London. Receiving a frantic appeal for help from Lady Rowena, Winslow took command of this guest, leading him into the blue drawing room to sample his prized Madeira.

To his astonishment, Fornhurst tossed down the liquid, pronounced it tolerable and then proceeded to down an additional three glasses, leaving the earl to wonder what would be the fate of any Madeira his guest pronounced more than tolerable!

The wine, combined with the afternoon heat, made Fornhurst rather more garrulous than usual, but by his fourth glass of Madeira, he owned to some fatigue, and the earl led him to a library couch to enjoy a solitary doze.

Freed at last from his duties as host, Winslow went off in search of his sister and found her with her son in his grand saloon, firmly ensconced on a French chair, and convinced that he had caught a chill.

"Good Jupiter, Ro," Winslow implored, throwing up his hands to the rococo ceiling, "don't start quacking the boy. You'll turn into one like Mrs. Fornhurst herself. You never showed such concern about Leigh's chills before!"

"What an unnatural parent you make me out to be, Sebby!" Lady Rowena replied with mock umbrage. She smoothed her honey-colored curls. "I worried a good deal about Leigh's health, although I own I never took the particular pains that Mrs. Fornhurst takes with Miss Fornhurst's well-being." She sighed and stared moodily up at one of the chubby nymphs painted on the ceiling. "I daresay I have been remiss in allowing Leigh to grow up quite *ignorant* of all the dread ailments he might possibly die of.''

The earl's guffaw sparked an answering peal of laughter from her, much to the annoyance of her only son, who informed both his mother and uncle with a hauteur that would have done credit to Mr. Brummell that naturally Mrs. Fornhurst would be concerned over Miss Fornhurst's well-being.

''Her constitution is delicate.''

''Yes, of course it is,'' Lady Rowena replied at once.

The earl, growing rapidly bored by the topic of the Fornhursts holding sway in the Grand Saloon, inquired about his brother-in-law's absence.

''I thought Oswald meant to join us here.''

''Ozzie,'' Lady Rowena replied in judicious accents, ''is nursing a sprained ankle. Nothing could have been more stupid. He was just stepping out from White's and lost his balance and was forced to come home in a chair, which was so *lowering* to someone who dotes on sport the way he does.''

''Is the injury serious, Mama?'' Leigh asked with quick concern.

''Not at all.'' Lady Rowena waved away the very idea. ''And I don't know if you could precisely call it an injury. However, the upshot of the matter is that Ozzie remains in London to bully the servants into looking after him. I must remember to write him that I reached here safely lest he worry. And now.'' She pushed her husband and his ankle resolutely out of her mind. ''Where were you, my dear brother? I thought you had made good your threat to desert me in my hour of need.''

''I was paying a visit on Alexa Eiseley,'' he informed her, leaning an elbow against the mantelpiece and gazing at her appraisingly. ''She is at Ferring with her brother George.''

Lady Rowena clapped her hands. ''Good! I've been racking my brains trying to think how we shall even begin to entertain our guests. Alexa shall be the perfect answer for our little parties and excursions, and although her brother is a trifle prosy, his new wife is rather sweet. You must induce them to come here often, Sebby, but pray don't tell them about the Fornhursts lest that scare them away!''

"Mama!'' Leigh ejaculated, outraged by his parent's frankness concerning the family of the woman he loved. ''You speak as though you disliked the Fornhursts.''

His mother stared at him as though at a worm found on a dinner plate. "What an ungrateful boy you are, Leigh!'' she scolded. "Would I have plagued your uncle to have opened up his establishment to us if I disliked them? A rather *peevish* creature that would make me and so disobliging to poor Sebby, who would much rather be in Scotland with his grouse.''

"Salmon,'' her brother replied.

"And as far as the Fornhursts are concerned,'' Lady Rowena continued, undaunted, "I don't really know them, so I can't say whether I like them or not. And while in perfect truth they appear to be somewhat weak, constitutionally speaking, I have no serious objection to them as in-laws.''

"Would you object to having Alexa as an in-law, too, I wonder, Rowena?'' Winslow asked quickly before Leigh could get a word in.

Lady Rowena rose and stood perfectly still. Her blue eyes were wide with disbelief. "Pray, what does that mean, Sebby?'' she demanded.

His eyes glinted appreciatively. "Precisely what it sounds like! Alexa and I reached an understanding this morning.''

"If you're roasting me, Sebby, I shall slay you,'' she warned, shaking her fan under his nose.

He prudently removed the weapon from her grasp. "Don't be a peagoose, Rowena. As a matter of fact, I popped the question to Alexa this morning.''

Her eyes searched his face. "And she accepted?''

"Why shouldn't she?'' Winslow asked, a little vexed at his sister's reaction. "I'm not Bluebeard!''

"No, of course you're not,'' she soothed quickly. "He, you must remember, had *several* wives, while you have had *none*. Until now, it would appear. It's just that I am in amazement. Alexa Eiseley!''

The earl stirred uneasily. "Yes, Rowena. Alexa Eiseley. Do you have something against her?"

Lady Rowena came out of her trance. "Don't be idiotish!" she commanded, reclaiming her fan and plying it energetically. "Who could object to Alexa? So highly courted! I'll have you know that Lady Sefton once divulged in strictest confidence that Alexa might have been a duchess if she wished. And you say you have captured her heart?"

"Something like that," Winslow replied, taking care to avoid her too inquisitive eyes.

"Of course, you have known her forever," Rowena continued with a frown. "That must count for something, particularly nowadays when people are so prone to fall in love at the drop of a glove, and most of them so ineligibly. And yet never once did I see you pay her the slightest attention except that which always exists between childhood friends. And I vow I've never seen her cast out the slightest lure to you. Pray, how did it all come about?"

The earl conducted a rapid search through the recesses of his memory. "Lady Jersey's ball," he said at last and with some relief. "We danced together there and it all came to a head. You are pleased, I hope?"

"No, not a bit," she said with a roguish gleam in her eyes. "Of course I'm pleased, you gudgeon. Let me have all the details."

"I have told you all the details," Winslow said, a trifle nervous at her persistent questions and apparently inexhaustible curiosity. Beads of sweat formed on his brow, and he wiped them away with a handkerchief. "We've been good friends for years, and at Lady Jersey's ball I was emboldened to think it might be something more."

His sister's face lit up. "Sebby, never tell me this is a love match? My dear, this gets better and better. Is that why you had no strenuous objection to opening up Winslow Park for us? You must have known that it would be only a day's ride to Pembroke and rather closer to Ferring. How clever you are. To have won Alexa's hand is a feather in your cap. I'm sure Mama shall say as much when she hears the news."

Jolted by this announcement, Winslow worked quickly to

forestall his sister's natural tendency to play town crier. All he needed in addition to Leigh and Rowena and the Fornhursts was his mother descending on him.

"I'd liefer tell Mama the good news myself, Rowena," he said firmly.

"Oh, very well, if you insist, Sebby."

"I do. And now I must speak to Jenkins about dinner," he said, deciding to beat a hasty retreat.

He had reckoned, however, without Leigh, who exited the Grand Saloon on his heels.

"Uncle Sebby, I must have a word with you," the younger man cried out.

Muttering a silent oath, Winslow turned. "A word about what, halfling?"

"About your marrying Miss Eiseley, of course!"

The black frown so seldom seen by any of Winslow's intimates descended on his brow as he peered down his nose at his nephew.

"My dear Leigh, you forget yourself," he said in his most autocratic manner. "I don't believe I need ask your permission to wed Miss Eiseley!"

Leigh turned a furious red. "I know that. I'm not such a nodcock. But do you really expect me to swallow that twaddle you sold Mama about how you always meant to offer for Miss Eiseley?"

"It's not twaddle," Winslow retorted, throwing himself with as much abandon as he possessed into the totally unfamiliar role of an ardent lover. "While you may not have realized it, the attachment between Alexa and me is of long duration. I had long nourished hopes that she might consider my suit, and today she did. But why must I stand here explaining myself to a nursery brat like you . . . !"

He walked farther down the hall, trailed by Leigh.

"If you had a tendre for Miss Eiseley, I should have thought that you would have offered for her a long time ago," Leigh said, pursuing the topic like a dog does a bone. "She's been out for years."

"Those of my generation prefer a more leisurely pace to

courtship than those of yours,'' Winslow pointed out with crushing pretension.

''Then you're not sacrificing yourself for me?'' Leigh asked uncertainly.

Winslow sighed. ''My dear boy, however fond I may be of you, I would not sacrifice myself on the altar of St. George's for you or anyone else! And now if I were you, I'd put all thought of your predicament concerning Alexa behind me. There is no reason to dwell on it further, nor to make a full breast of things to Miss Fornhurst, who is looking quite knocked up as it is. Do you get my drift, lad?''

Leigh, being a highly intelligent young man, not only got his uncle's drift but agreed that it would never do to overset Miss Fornhurst, whose state of health was always somewhat ticklish.

As the days passed, Leigh settled down to paying court to her. But in this effort he was momentarily stymied by Miss Fornhurst herself, who, emerging a trifle wan but victorious from her battle with carriage sickness, proved to have no great interest in riding, picnicking and the other amusements the country and Leigh offered.

Five

Lady Rowena lost not a moment in welcoming Alexa into the family. So warm was her greeting that the recipient of these good wishes once again felt the twinges of guilt that deceit always brings upon those unacquainted with the habit. For Rowena, her visits to Alexa were the only agreeable part of her first week at Winslow Park. The Fornhursts were living up to her brother's grim prediction of their being dismal houseguests.

Leigh's attempts to amuse his beloved met with continued indifference from Miss Fornhurst and outright hostility from her mother, who seemed inclined toward the belief that Mr. Leigh Denning wished her daughter to contract a fatal chill in the country air.

The earl might have been diverted by it all had he not been obliged to undergo a similarly disagreeable task with Miss Fornhurst's other parent, who, unlike most members of his sex, showed no predilection for hunting or riding. Fishing he termed a colossal bore, and he was left to wile away the many hours of the day dispensing unasked-for advice to his host concerning the proper management of estates. Since Winslow prided himself on running his estates quite ably—a fact well known to all in the district—such advice did not set well in his dish.

He was complaining about it at length one morning to his sister, who had been fortunate enough to make her escape from Mrs. Fornhurst's bedside and who had been startled at the sight of her brother's buckskin-clad figure in the sitting room.

"Good God, Sebby, come in quickly and shut that door!" she commanded, looking desperate in a morning gown of dove gray crêpe.

"In hiding, Ro?" he asked, looking wickedly at her even as he complied with her request.

"Do you blame me?" she asked sourly.

"No. By the by, just how long a penance are we in for?"

Lady Rowena lifted a supplicating hand. "I can't recall. Not that long, I should hope."

Her brother fixed his eyes on her face. "I warn you, if they stay much longer than another week I shall go to Brighton and join Mama."

"That would be desertion."

"If I stay any longer, it shall be murder," he said grimly as he stretched out in his top boots, a new purchase from Mr. Hoby. "When I think of the way you foisted this insufferable situation on me! Didn't I say in London that it would come to no good?"

Lady Rowena pursed her lips. "Nothing is more intolerable than someone saying I told you so. And how was I to know they would be such dreadful bores? Anyway, I have been grateful to you for bearing up under Mr. Fornhurst. For I know how trying it must be to listen to advice, particularly since you never listened to advice from any quarter—not even mine or Mama's. And if you are tiring of Fornhurst, perhaps you would rather undertake the entertaining of his spouse while I try a hand toward amusing him."

"That won't wash," Winslow said, shifting his legs slightly. "But I must own that coping with an invalid, even one who only imagines she is one, would be preferable to coping with a bore.''

Lady Rowena emitted a scornful laugh. ''That is easy enough for you to say,'' she replied with some bitterness. ''But when I think of the hours I have sacrificed handing that woman tonics and vials, and fetching mustard plasters for her chest, and opening and then closing windows—for either she thinks the room too drafty or too warm—I vow I could collapse myself.''

Her brother looked totally unmoved by such a threat. ''If you turn invalidish now, Rowena, you shan't get an ounce of sympathy from me. This whole affair was your doing!''

''How can you be so perfectly horrid as to keep harping on that!'' she said miserably. ''Besides, you know perfectly well I had only Leigh's happiness in mind.''

''Speaking of which.'' Winslow shot her a quick glance. ''How is the lad progressing with the fair Miss Fornhurst?''

Lady Rowena sighed noisily. ''Better, I hope, than either of us is progressing with her parents. One can't help *feeling* for the boy, Sebby, for it is difficult. If Miss Fornhurst would attempt to be amused, I daresay it would make a world of difference. As it is, she dislikes walking lest she catch a chill, and I know she's never been taught to ride, so we may as well scratch that. She doesn't play cards and has no skill at either chess or backgammon. Reading is alleged to be bad for her eyes. You see the poor boy's situation!''

''She must talk, one would presume,'' Winslow said, not unsympathetic to his nephew's plight.

Lady Rowena's delicate nostrils flared. ''Of course she talks. But perhaps a listener would rather wish she didn't. For in that respect she is too much like her mother, carping about one thing or another.''

The earl stared at the tambour frame Lady Rowena had been working on. ''I deem it nothing short of a miracle that Leigh could ever have been smitten by her in London,'' he pointed out.

''Don't be a simpleton, Sebby!'' Rowena looked cross. ''During the Season in London, he saw her only at balls, where she would be amused, and he saw only her beauty, which even I must own is considerable. And, of course, her aunt brought her out and her wretched parents weren't there to lend their disagreeable presence." Her words came to a sudden halt as she stared out into space. "That's the thing, Sebby!" she said, emerging from her trance.

Winslow stared at her as though in a fog himself. "Her wretched parents?"

"No, stupid! A ball! I have been trying to think of a way to amuse them. We shall give a ball. What is today?" she asked impatiently. "Monday, is it not? We shall have it Friday evening. I shall invite some of the families nearby, and you shall be sure to invite Alexa and her brother's family."

The puzzlement had not faded from Winslow's face. "Rowena, are you undertaking the ball to honor the Fornhursts?"

"Don't be daft," she pleaded. "I'm undertaking it to keep from driving myself to Bedlam." She noticed that he had already risen and was edging toward the door. "Pray, where do you think you are going? We have a hundred things to discuss about the ball. The menu and the invitations . . ."

"You can do all that without me," Winslow assured her blithely. "I had thought of paying a call on Alexa."

The one advantage to being thought violently in love, Winslow thought as he went down the marble staircase, was that no one in his household, not even his sister, thought it the least bit peculiar if he deserted his guests in order to make love to Miss Eiseley. And, given the quality of his guests, he had paid almost constant homage to his betrothed.

The object of these daily visits had herself been somewhat overwhelmed by their frequency, for she could not help thinking he was doing it a trifle too brown. She quizzed him about this dogged devotion as they walked in the Shakespeare gardens that afternoon at Ferring.

"I had not expected you of all people to dance attendance on me, Sebby," she said, looking quite gay in an apricot muslin walking dress hemmed in a pattern of flowered lace. She carried a matching sunshade and twirled it absently.

Winslow's eyes were warm. "It pains me to have to admit it, Alexa, but I have an ulterior motive for seeing you. The Fornhursts!''

Her soft laughter wafted out in the summer air as they strolled side by side down the steps. ''Are they still as vexing as ever? And how is Rowena bearing up?''

''For the moment, nobly,'' the earl answered. ''But if she is asked to find another gum plaster for Mrs. Fornhurst, I shan't answer for her conduct.'' He led her over to a stone bench, the better to admire the sunlight glinting in her hair. ''Rowena never suffers fools gladly and only a herculean effort on her part has kept her temper under control thus far.''

Alexa smiled. ''Do you think if I went over to visit I might be of use?''

''I would not subject you to that,'' he objected at once. ''Within seconds of your arrival, you would be obliged to take up attendance on Mrs. Fornhurst on her daybed.''

''But I wish to help.''

''You are helping now,'' he said, looking her in the eye. ''You are my escape!''

''So I deduce,'' she said with a severe look. ''But I must confess that George and Maria have an entirely different view of the matter.'' She chuckled softly. ''They are utterly convinced that I have captivated you, putting these daily calls down to my fatal charm.''

''Is the situation here still awkward for you?'' he asked, smiling affectionately at her.

''Oh, no! Mrs. Nettles has been thoroughly scotched. And no one this week has dared to repeat her slander to me, so I find my situation much more comfortable than I ever thought possible. Indeed, I am inclined to think a betrothal infinitely more amenable than I used to think it might be. But perhaps that is because I know this one shan't last long, and I've never had difficulty in speaking my mind to you.'' She tilted her head up to him slightly. ''But I do own that Maria and George do praise you so much, particularly George, who never hoped that I would be sensible enough to attract such a notable prize as you!''

He winced. ''Alexa, do try for a little conduct! You are making me blush!''

Her eyes widened with laughter. "I am sorry, my lord, but I speak the truth. Luckily I didn't know beforehand what awe George has always held you in. Your consequence with him is enormous."

"My dear child, what shocking things you say to me. Enormous consequence, indeed." His mouth curved in a smile. "Instead of passing on your amiable brother's quite undeserving compliments to me, I suggest you attend to more pressing matters such as this." He held out a small present to her.

Surprised and curious, Alexa opened the proffered gift, stunned to find herself gazing at a ruby and diamond bracelet. The lovely jewels danced intoxicatingly in the sunlight. It had, she realized with a sinking heart, all the look of a family heirloom.

"I hope you like it," Winslow said, taking it out and putting it on her wrist. "The setting is a bit old-fashioned."

"Oh, no," she protested, "the setting is beautiful. But I cannot accept this from you."

He stiffened momentarily. "And why not, may I ask?" he said in tones that were decidedly grim.

"Oh, dear." A stricken look came into Alexa's eyes. "Pray don't get on your high ropes. It is the most perfect of bracelets, and I don't like refusing it. What female would? But I cannot, under the circumstances. Do but consider that our betrothal is nothing but a hoax, so there is not the slightest need for presents such as these. It must be worth a goodly sum of money."

"No doubt if the jewels were paste, you would have no compunction about accepting them?" he drawled. "And you mistake my intentions, Alexa. The gift is not in honor of our betrothal. It's a bribe."

"A bribe?"

He nodded. "You must promise to wear it Friday evening when you come to Winslow Park with your amiable brother and his wife. Rowena," he sighed, "has hit upon the perfect idea for entertaining our guests. I don't consider it so perfect myself, but since I am merely her brother, I don't count. We are giving a small ball at Winslow Park. An idiotish affair it

will be, but presumably this will give Leigh the chance to
view Miss Fornhurst in her glory again."

Alexa eyed him with some curiosity. The note of dissatisfaction in his voice had not passed unnoticed. "You don't
appear pleased at the prospect of Leigh offering for her,"
she observed.

He grimaced. "Of course I'm pleased. That's the whole
point to our situation, you must remember—to grant Leigh
the peace of mind to dangle after the Fornhurst chit.
And while I don't precisely begrudge being engaged to
you . . ."

"You always did have such distinguished manners, my
lord," she said demurely.

He grinned. "I do draw the line at entertaining the family
all summer long. So if Leigh would just pop the question,
I'd be eternally grateful."

Alexa's face turned thoughtful. "But Sebby, you needn't
try to bribe me. I shall be glad to go to your ball and to bring
George and Maria with me." She hesitated a moment.
"And do you think I might also bring Penny, my niece? She
is sixteen and while not precisely out, I have great hopes for
her. Indeed I promised to undertake her come-out next year
in London, and we had thought of going to Bath later this
summer, just the two of us. But that is a secret."

"Go to Bath?" he inquired faintly. "You at Bath, Alexa?
Impossible!"

"No, it's not so impossible, you odious creature," she
retorted with a laugh. "And it shan't be that tiresome, for I
have an old friend there, Bronwyn Finch. And it will give
Penny the opportunity to try her wings before she sets out
for London. Why do you look so surprised?"

He shrugged, as much from the question as from the bee
buzzing noisily about his ear. "I suppose because most engaged ladies do not desert their fiancés to undertake the
launching of a niece in Bath."

"Good heavens, we both know our engagement is nothing but a hum," she pointed out. "And there is no need
whatever to dance attendance on one another. Besides, I
promised Penny long ago and see no reason not to keep the

promise. My grandfather's house in Bath shall be available for our use. Who knows, by then you and I might not be betrothed!''

''You don't mean to keep me on a string a second longer than necessary, do you?'' he observed acutely.

A faint chagrin spread over her face. ''Have I offended you?'' she asked frankly, looking into his blue eyes.

He shook his head, already regretting his brief pique. ''No, and by all means do bring little Penny to the ball, and if you will wear the bracelet . . . ?''

His request was more of a command, but Alexa did not refuse it. She felt she more than owed it to him to comply with the request—not that she meant to keep the bracelet!—and it would be fun to wear for one evening. After another half hour in the garden spent chatting about the habits of his guests, the earl left, and Alexa returned to her bedchamber still wearing the ruby bracelet.

She had not been in the bedroom long when Penny entered and immediately exclaimed over the earl's bracelet, begging leave to try it on her slim wrist.

''Is it not the most elegant thing you have ever seen, Aunt Alexa?'' she cried out.

Alexa smiled. ''Quite.''

Penny danced over to the window and held her hand up to the sunlight. ''I think Winslow is the best of all your beaux! He is always so civil to me. And he is the most tremendous swell, is he not?''

Alexa let out a peal of laughter. ''You had better not let your darling father hear you say that about the earl. Tremendous swell, indeed. Where do you pick up such deplorable language?''

''How grand you shall be when you marry him,'' Penny went on, undeterred. ''Not that you are not already grand, but only think you will be a countess.'' Dreamily, she took the bracelet off her arm and handed it back to her aunt. ''He must love you a good deal.''

The truth, had Alexa spoken it, would have greatly surprised the very romantic Penny, so Alexa forbore comment on this point and instead informed her briskly that Winslow had come by to invite them to a ball on Friday evening and that if she were very good she might come along with them.

At the news of this treat in store, Penny's eyes lit up, and she flung both arms about her aunt. "Oh, Aunt Alexa. Thank you. I know I have you to thank for it. And why you can continue to be bothered about my silly problems when you are engaged to the earl I shan't know."

"You are quite welcome, my dear," Alexa said, extricating herself from her niece's suffocating embrace. "And I don't think your problem silly at all." Or at least, she amended to herself after Penny had gone off on a whirl-wind of excitement, no sillier than her own problems!

The earl had willingly abdicated all responsibility for the ball on Friday to his sister, informing her that since it was her idea she could bring it to fruition. Lady Rowena was not entirely displeased by her brother's actions, since she felt privately that male assistance in such matters turned out to be more hindrance than help. Since no one, not even Mrs. Fornhurst, could think her unfeeling if she chose to be no longer at that lady's beck and call, she became pleasurably absorbed with all the details of the ball and was soon up to her ears in flowers, musicians, menus and the guest list it-self.

Absorbed in squiring Mr. Fornhurst about several of the farms on his estate, Winslow had not concerned himself with whom his sister might choose to invite to the ball until Friday morning. A question from Fornhurst as to the exact number of guests expected prompted the earl, for curiosity's sake, to seek out the list of names. The sight of one brought a slight pucker to his brow, and he went off to find his sister.

His search brought him to the small parlor which served as her headquarters for the ball preparations and where she reposed, fittingly enough, on a small daybed in a pearl white muslin dress, gathering her strength for another skirmish in her battle with Henri, Winslow's toplofty Parisian chef.

"Sebby!" she greeted him warmly. "The very person I've been yearning to see and the only one that Henri will listen to. Do you think it too early in the year for turtle soup?

Such is Henri's opinion. But the Fornhursts are partial to it. And should we have a baron of beef or shall that be too coming of us?''

Winslow stripped off his York tan gloves and waved away both the turtle soup and the baron of beef.

''I understand Cawly and Montcalm are coming to the ball.''

Rowena put the menu aside, her battle with Henri temporarily forgotten. ''Do you have some quarrel with them?'' she demanded. ''I suppose it was some horrid masculine falling out. They didn't perchance beat you at Gentleman Jack's?''

''No, of course not,'' came her brother's testy reply.

''Well, I should hope not!'' Rowena declared. ''You are supposed to be one of Jack's prize pupils, or so Leigh tells me. And I wish you will not encourage him to take up that sport.''

She brought herself back to the topic at hand. ''Why are you quarreling with my inviting Montcalm and Cawly? Montcalm's uncle lives not very far from here, and I heard the nephew was visiting. He is always the perfect gentleman—Montcalm, I mean, not the uncle, who can get peevish when he is in his cups. And Cawly is a slowtop but congenial.''

''If one's taste runs to fops,'' Winslow observed.

His sister narrowed her eyes speculatively. ''I hope they shall divert Mrs. Fornhurst. They are successful with ladies, you must know.''

''Are they, indeed?'' the earl inquired frostily.

''Why, yes,'' Lady Rowena said naively. ''I own that Alexa herself was once thought to entertain a tendre for the colonel.'' She paused, noting the saturnine expression on Winslow's face. ''Good Jupiter,'' she exclaimed, ''is that why you are so skittish about Montcalm? Oh, no, Sebby, my dear. It won't do. I vow it is positively *Gothic* in this day and age to hold such a grudge. Just because Alexa was prone to dote on him before is no reason to look so murderous! You have won her.''

''Just how many of Alexa's other suitors have you felt

obliged to saddle me with this evening?'' Winslow inquired acidly.

Lady Rowena looked surprised. "Well, I don't know," she said truthfully. "There is Birmingham, who used to like her a good deal. And Hopkins as well, but he dangles after any female he sees."

"And he shall probably continue to dangle after Alexa," the earl said, looking so grim that his sister was seriously alarmed.

She laid one hand on his arm. "Sebby, just because Alexa is to marry you is no reason that she may not have other friends. Custom dictates today that a married woman may even avail herself of the comfort of a cicisbeo or two!"

"I am thoroughly acquainted with that custom," her brother retorted, "and as far as I am concerned it shan't be the custom in my house. But," he relented now, "I suppose it's too late to prevent Montcalm and the rest from coming tonight."

"Indeed it is," Rowena said frankly. "If you had told me about these freakish whims earlier, I could have scratched them off, but since the invitations are dispatched and they have accepted, they shall think it uncivil of us if we bar the door to them. So I hope you shall endeavor to appear pleasant when you see them tonight." Her eyes flitted across her brother's handsome face as though searching for something.

"You know, Sebby," she said, watching him intently, "one would almost think that you are jealous of Alexa's other suitors, but surely that must be absurd, since you are betrothed to her, are you not?"

"Most assuredly, Rowena, I am," he replied cordially and with that Parthian shot left her to ponder anew the vexing problem of turtle soup.

Six

"*Good God, not again,*" Winslow muttered as he stood in the midst of his dressing room wearing the white, frilled shirt, buttoned waistcoat, black pantaloons and silk stockings that constituted evening dress for a gentleman.

As he spoke, he stripped off the neckcloth, which had once again failed to match his standards of perfection, and flung it down to join the other failures littering the carpet.

"I have never had the least difficulty before in tying a simple cravat," he muttered to James. "Why do I find it so trying now?"

The valet, standing implacably and holding out yet another linen cloth, murmured a soothing rejoinder. He was a bit unnerved that the *Trône d'Amour* could be called simple even by so noted an expert as the earl.

Much to the relief of both men, the fifth neckcloth fell into place without difficulty, and with this task at last completed, Winslow donned the black, swallow-tailed coat James held out for him. No one seeing the emergence of his tall, elegant person would have had a clue as to just how much care he had taken with his toilette, except perhaps his sister, who, while tending to the inevitable last-minute crises which had arisen both upstairs and down, had been privileged to hear several veiled oaths emitted behind the earl's dressing-room door.

Lady Rowena was a dotingly fond sister, but she was not blind to her brother's faults, chief among them, she felt, a predilection to giving orders to everyone about him. His alliance with Alexa had caught her by surprise, for she never dreamed to see such sense in him and had once gone so far as to lament to their mother that Winslow would sooner offer marriage to a ballerina than to any eligible female.

Alexa's own role in the proposed match perplexed Rowena as much as her brother's. Why should a female who had once turned down a duke suddenly wish to marry Sebby? Something, she'd go bail, was amiss, and it vexed her beyond reason that she had no way of discovering what it could be.

As she applied the finishing touches to her dress, a flowing lime green gauze over an underdress of matching satin, perfectly accentuated by an emerald necklace clasped about her slender neck, she formulated and rejected several pet theories about Winslow and Alexa. Perhaps, she told herself, she would learn more about their sudden romance at tonight's ball. Satisfied with this plan, she picked up her fan, gave her hair one final pat and went out into the hall just in time to intercept the earl on the stairs.

Her greeting checked his progress, and he turned, holding up his quizzing glass to survey her finery.

"Well, well, Rowena. First rate. A pity Ozzie isn't here to appreciate it."

"Thank you, dear Sebby," she replied, preening happily for a moment. "And you are looking quite the top of the trees yourself. Such sartorial splendor. You put Brummell to the blush. It wouldn't have anything to do with cutting out Colonel Montcalm now, would it?"

"Rowena," her brother said dampeningly, "sometimes you can be such a corkbrain."

Laughing, she tucked her hand in his arm, and together

they made their way into the Long Saloon, where they had only enough time to quaff a single sherry with the Fornhursts and Leigh. Within minutes of the last swallow of sherry, the first of the carriages could be heard arriving, and after that it was as the earl put it to his sister: a never-ending parade of bibble babble as their guests trekked up the stairs.

As the host of the ball, his station was next to Rowena at the top of the stairs, and he did his duty shaking hands and growing more acutely bored with each minute. The sight of Alexa in a long-sleeved gown of ivory lace with red velvet trimming on the bodice checked Winslow's ennui and took his breath away. She mounted the stairs with her brother's family, and she was the most exquisite lady in the gathering. The ruby bracelet he had given her sparkled on her slender arm.

"Good evening, my dear," he said with unexpected warmth, carrying the hand she extended to him to his lips, a gesture that took her by surprise. "You are looking charmingly, as always."

"Thank you, my lord," she replied, conscious of her heightened color and the indulgent smiles of George, Maria and Rowena. "You know my brother and sister-in-law," she said quickly to hide her confusion. "And this is my niece, Penny."

Penny, looking like a doe about to be shot, dipped a quick curtsy to their host, who kindly passed her on to his sister.

"A taking thing," Winslow murmured, still keeping Alexa's hand in his. "She must take after her aunt."

"You shall turn my head with all your flummery, Winslow," Alexa retorted.

He lifted an enigmatic brow. "It's not flummery," he stated firmly and might have gone on to exchange more words on the topic, but he was being hastily summoned by his harassed sister. With unexpected reluctance, he allowed Alexa to pass on into the grand ballroom, where, he wagered grimly to himself, she would shortly be inundated with requests for her hand for the dances to come and idly cursed himself for not having put in his own request some days previous.

On this point, Winslow need not have teased himself. This evening, Alexa was far more concerned with finding partners in the ballroom for Penny than for herself, a circumstance that Colonel Montcalm, a resplendent figure in his regimentals, took exception to when he strolled up to her a half hour later.

"The whole purpose of a ball is to dance, Miss Eiseley," he reminded her with a smile nearly as dazzling as his uniform.

"I know," she agreed readily. "But really I am supposed to be looking after Penny."

"At the moment your niece is enjoying the attentions of several gentlemen in the younger set." Montcalm gave a nod with a well-chiseled jaw. "And her father appears to be keeping an eye out for her. You needn't hover about her as well. She shall do splendidly."

"Do you really think so?" Alexa asked eagerly. "This is her first ball, you see."

"All the more reason for you to act as you usually do," he observed wisely. "And when, Miss Eiseley, did you ever sit out a dance at a ball?"

Since her love of dancing was well known in London, she could not dispute this and at last gave in and followed him out into the quadrille. Montcalm was always an able partner, and she soon relaxed, enjoying the flow of music and the accompanying rush of blood to her head. The colonel was not her only partner that evening, for almost immediately he was followed by Cawly and her other admirers, and in this comfortable fashion the first few hours of the Winslow ball drifted by.

Unfortunately, the evening had not passed quite so comfortably for Winslow. By the time he had had his fingers crushed by the last of his arriving guests, he was tired and hot and vowing never to grant another favor to Rowena as long as he lived. At long last he relinquished his place on the stairs and slipped away to the grand ballroom, which was adrift with the scent of flowers and the steady beat of music, desiring nothing more arduous than the occasion to speak a few words with Alexa.

But he had to find her first! On the face of it, this seemed a simple enough task, but he soon learned differently. All about him couples whirled madly, laughing and chattering like magpies. He could not take a step forward without being immediately swept back, usually into the bosom of a turbaned matron only too happy to see him and make him better acquainted with a daughter, niece or other female relation.

When he finally did snatch a glimpse of Alexa, he almost wished he hadn't, for she was dancing and looking totally enchanted by her partner, Colonel Montcalm!

Muttering an oath about the custom of allowing gentlemen to attend parties in regimentals, Winslow deserted a dowager in the midst of her recitation about her niece's many accomplishments on the harp and strolled over to the chair Montcalm was leading Alexa to.

"Enjoying yourself, Alexa?" Winslow drawled.

At the sound of his voice, Alexa turned, surprised to find his grim-faced visage at her elbow.

"Oh, Sebby! There you are," she said softly. "How tedious it must have been for you to shake all those hands. You know the colonel, of course?"

The two men exchanged bows, the earl's rather stiffer than the colonel's.

"May I have the honor of this waltz, Alexa?" Winslow asked.

A stricken look came into her eyes. "Oh, dear. I'm very much afraid that Captain Myers has this dance, Winslow. Would you take another waltz, perhaps later in the evening? He asked me at least twenty minutes ago, and I see him coming toward me now."

"Far be it for me to prevent you from doing your duty toward one of your admirers, Miss Eiseley," the earl returned with icy courtesy and a look that spoke volumes, and stalked away.

His reaction left Alexa speechless for a moment. Surely

Winslow could not expect her to throw over the captain? But why else should he have flown into the boughs?

The stormy scene did not go unnoticed by several others in the ballroom, including Mr. George Eiseley, who complained petulantly to his patient wife that Alexa would find some way to ruin the excellent match fate had thrown her way; Lady Rowena, who began to speculate more and more about the curious attachment between her brother and Miss Eiseley—if attachment it was; and Major Jayneway, who sought out his old friend in the refreshment room in a vain attempt to cheer him up.

"I don't need cheering up," Winslow said, looking as sulky as a bear. "What I need is a drink. What is this vile stuff, anyway?"

"Lemonade, I believe," the major said, taking a cautious sniff of the glass in his hand. "And why do you complain? 'Tis your ball, after all, and your refreshments."

The earl emitted a hollow laugh. "Touché, Archie. I believe in my library I've left a bottle of Madeira which thus far I have managed to hide from Fornhurst. Care to join me?"

Since the major was of the opinion that lemonade, no matter how worthy a drink, was far inferior to the earl's Madeira, he made haste to join his friend in the book room.

"What's amiss, Sebby?" he asked, watching the earl cross the room to the bottle and pour a healthy dose of the liquid into a crystal glass.

"Nothing. What makes you think anything is amiss?"

"You have that hunted look on your face," the major replied affably. "About the eyes. Saw it the night you called Simmons out. You wouldn't be anticipating doing the same to Montcalm or Cawly now, would you?"

The earl snorted. "Damn puppies."

"Oh, they ain't puppies," the major demurred, taking an approving sip of the Madeira. "Montcalm is even longer in the tooth than you or me. But he's still uncommon good-looking, or so the females I know say. Never could cotton with their tastes."

The earl took a large swallow of his Madeira but appeared

to find no liking for it. "His good looks are of no interest to me. It's his dancing I object to."

The major spluttered into his glass. "His *dancing*? I say, Sebby. Rather freakish reason to hold a fellow in dislike. Not as though he had a poor seat or drove like a whipster."

"He was dancing with Alexa, Archie!" The earl was betrayed into impatience.

Struck by the vehemence in his friend's tone, the major's affable face clouded over. "Well, I don't see the harm in it myself, Sebby. This is a ball, after all, and dancing is quite the order of things." He paused as the frown grew even more pronounced on his friend's brow. "Bless me for a gypsy, I think you're jealous," he said, slapping his knee.

"I am no such thing!" Winslow answered punctiliously.

"Poker up all you want," the major said, unconvinced. "I know the signs. Don't forget I was present at Lady Heathcoate's that evening when Caro Lamb herself threw that scene over Byron."

The earl fixed a baleful eye on the major. "If you are confusing me with Caro Lamb, Archie, there is no hope for you. And I believe you have had entirely too much Madeira!"

The major laughed away the intended insult. "Whether you know it or not, Sebby," he said as he rose to his feet, "you are jealous. And over Alexa!"

"Don't talk fustian rubbish," Winslow snapped. "I've never been jealous over any female in my life nor have I dangled after one."

"Nor have you been engaged to one," Jayneway said mockingly as he headed for the door. "But there is always a first time, isn't there, Sebby?" he asked and left, chuckling loudly to himself.

Winslow stared fixedly into the fire that crackled only a few feet from his chair as though some clue to the riot of emotion he felt could be deduced in the orange and red tongues of flame. Jealousy, bah! It couldn't be that. Pray, what was there to be jealous about? He had no real vested interest in Alexa, nor she in him. They had made that plain from the start. Friends, yes, but no more than that. And, he

thought, stiffening in his chair, she was as good as reminding him of that by dancing with all her different beaux.

A muscle twitched in his jaw as he sketched those suitors
one by one in his mind's eye. Men of rank and wealth, yes,
but a rather pasty-faced bunch, and he would have thought
Alexa immune to their superficial charms. Not, he reminded
himself again, that it mattered a jot to him.

"Good heavens, Sebby, here you are!"

His sister's voice summoned Winslow from his reverie.

"You are missing your ball," Rowena scolded as she
came into the library.

"I was under the impression that it was your ball, Rowena," he replied.

Ignoring his churlishness, she took him by the arm. "You
are missing a heartwarming sight. Leigh has actually coaxed
Miss Fornhurst to dance, and now I see what had smitten
him earlier in London, for she does dance divinely."

Winslow greeted this news with relief. "Does this mean
he is popping the question?"

"Well, I don't think he shall offer for her tonight, but perhaps by tomorrow. I have been thinking of leaving them the
perfect opportunity. You and I shall accompany that
wretched Mrs. Fornhurst to that fair she has been yearning
to see, and don't, I beg you, say no, Sebby, for I shan't tolerate her company unassisted."

He stared absently at her. "I am always at your disposal,
Rowena."

She smiled fondly at him and squeezed his arm. "You are
a good brother. And you needn't look so innocent, for well I
know that you shall hold this over my head as long as I live.
As long as I am not obliged to fetch that woman another
poultice, I am willing to endure anything, even your thun-
dering scolds. But why do we prattle of such dismal things
when a ball is under way?" She had led him out into the
hallway and turned now with a curious gleam in her blue
eyes. "I haven't seen you dance once this evening, Sebby."

He scowled. "The only woman I would dance with won't
have me as a partner," he remarked acidly.

She gave an amused smile. "If you refer to Alexa, it does

appear that she is the belle of the ball. One would think she wasn't even betrothed to you, informally, of course,'' she said hastily as a sound rather close to the gnashing of teeth escaped from the earl's throat, ''what with Montcalm being so persistent in his attentions. But do ask her again, Sebby, civilly, and she shall undoubtedly save a dance for you.''

It had been Winslow's intention of doing precisely that, but when he passed through the ballroom doors again and his eyes fell on Alexa's laughing face, with the colonel's only an inch or so away, these intentions took a turn for the worse. Montcalm was just a bit too sure of himself and his success with Alexa. And he should not be allowed to conduct his flirtation in such a brazen way. If Alexa didn't see fit to stop it, he certainly would!

He pushed his way across the floor toward them, rudely breaking into their conversation and demanding of Alexa the waltz now being danced.

''My dear Winslow.'' Montcalm lodged a faint protest even as he took an involuntary step back at the earl's glare. ''You may be the host of this affair, but your manners—''

Winslow fixed his eyes challengingly on the colonel's jutting jaw. ''I am dancing with Miss Eiseley. Any objection, Montcalm?''

''As a matter of fact, yes—''

''Pray don't disturb yourself,'' Alexa interposed quickly in order to squelch what looked to be an uncomfortable scene between the men on either side of her. ''I promised to keep a waltz for Winslow earlier this evening, Colonel. And I am glad, sir, that your duties as a host have not caused you to forget it.''

''My memory is not half as bad as it's reputed to be,'' he informed her and led her out into the waltz now playing.

Alexa felt little pleasure in dancing with him. He moved stiffly without his customary grace and skill and at one point did not seem much inclined to even speak to her. Could this be the man Lady Jersey had once described as the most civil gentleman London boasted?

Exasperated and puzzled by his continual frostiness, she demanded to know why he was in the hips.

"In the hips?" Winslow repeated, looking down his nose at her. "You are mistaken, Miss Eiseley, I am not in the hips."

"Oh, no?" she scoffed. "Then you give a fair imitation of being in them, sir. And why am I suddenly reduced to being Miss Eiseley again, if I am not in your black books? There is no denying what is writ so plainly on your face. But what prompts this vexation? Unless it's due to the dance you sought earlier, which I had promised to Captain Myers. But truly I could not help that."

He swung her expertly on the floor. "Nor, I suppose, could you help any of your other dancing partners?" he asked cuttingly.

Alexa's head whirled. "Are you vexed because I am enjoying myself by dancing tonight?" she asked in astonishment. "This is a ball, is it not?"

"I need no reminder of that," he replied arctically. "But perhaps you need a reminder that you are supposedly engaged to me."

She studied him for a moment. "Are you accusing me of impropriety, Winslow?" she asked coldly.

He was not prepared to go that far. "No," he answered, "merely of some indiscretion."

"Indiscretion!" She did her best to keep her voice low, but it caught in her throat. "So that is how you see me! I have been flinging myself at everyone's head, is that it? Or is there someone in particular whom I have pursued in such a hurly-burly fashion?"

"I have not called you hurly-burly," Winslow said acidly. "But perhaps your conscience compels you toward such a spirited defense!"

"My conscience!" Color flooded Alexa's cheeks, and the urge to box her partner soundly on the ear nearly overcame her. "You may not have accused me of anything, my lord," she said, keeping a firm grip on herself, "but I should have to be a dolt not to see what your odious hints entail. Your insinuations are rude and unconscionable! Furthermore, you have no right to chastise me for my behavior in any arena. Our engagement is one of form only."

"Our engagement may be of form to you and me," Winslow said with a tight smile, "but while my sister and your brother consider us all but betrothed, you shall have to appear more the thing!"

Alexa gritted her teeth. "I have never been accused of rag manners before, Winslow, except perhaps by George, who is odiously starched up, and you are as bad as he!"

Not a moment too soon, as far as Alexa was concerned, the music ended, and without waiting for Winslow to escort her off the floor, she departed in a high dudgeon.

He was without doubt the most insufferable man she had ever known! To be accused of acting in a coming fashion merely because she had stood up for a few dances with old friends. The injustice irked her beyond patience.

She was still brooding over it a half hour later when Penny skipped up to her. "Aunt Alexa," she said gaily, "isn't this the grandest party?"

Resolutely, Alexa thrust her own problems out of her mind and smiled at the girl's enthusiasm. "The grandest?" she teased. "I shall have to think about that for a moment. I have perhaps attended one or two squeezes a shade grander, for there are no royal dukes present tonight."

"I don't care," Penny declared, flown with the excitement of her first grown-up ball. "I'm sure I've never seen such beautiful ladies and such handsome gentlemen, and I'm sure I could never have gone through the evening without you."

"Me?"

Penny nodded. "When I got too unbearably nervous, I would merely look at you and contrive to do the same."

Alexa laughed ruefully. "Perhaps you shouldn't, my dear, for there are some who claim I evidence a sad want of conduct."

"How absurd! Who could have said such a thing? Whoever did it must be a coxcomb. I vow everyone is talking of you this evening."

This naive utterance caused Alexa to flinch slightly. Had Winslow been right? she wondered. Were people actually calling her a flirt?

Penny's next statement pulled her from her air dream. The earl had invited the younger Miss Eiseley to stand up with him later that evening, a piece of gallantry Alexa had not expected. She was acutely aware of the honor Winslow was bestowing on a girl temporarily removed from the schoolroom. Odious though it was for her to admit, Winslow's consequence was enormous.

She watched him weave his way toward them for the appointed dance and vowed silently that if he so much as uttered a syllable to her about proper conduct, she would give him a setdown he'd long remember.

The occasion for such hostilities did not arise, for Winslow merely bowed coolly toward her—as though to a chaperone!—and led a blushing Penny out into the dance. There would be no keeping Penny in the schoolroom after this, Alexa thought wryly to herself as she watched the two figures dance away.

As for her own situation, she was fully determined to show Winslow exactly what came from issuing commands to her. Far from retreating demurely to her chair the way she supposed he deemed fit and proper, she proceeded to dance every dance right up to the end of his ball, pausing only to sample the turtle soup that had so engrossed Lady Rowena in the supper room. By the time they returned to Ferring, Alexa was fagged to death and collapsed on her bed.

Wearily, she undressed, blew the candle out and drew the coverlet over her shoulders. But though the evening had ended, not so her sense of ill usage. Each time she thought of Winslow, she felt a growing dissatisfaction. Clearly, she told herself as she stifled an enormous yawn, she must put an end to the whole charade of a betrothal. But how? She fell asleep still mulling over various solutions to the dilemma. But when she woke the next morning she had the answer. She would take Penny to Bath!

Seven

Alexa's first opportunity to put her plan into action came at breakfast with Maria. Over amicable chatter about the Winslow ball and steaming hot chocolate sipped from china cups, she inquired about Penny and soon learned that the young lady in question had been returned to the schoolroom, where she had continued to rail unceasingly against the injustice of her young life.

"Aunt Alexa, have you ever heard of anything so *barbarous*?" Penny demanded, flinging down a history book when Alexa appeared to investigate the situation firsthand. "What use is history, anyway?"

"Not the use that balls are, I suppose?" Alexa quizzed, picking the volume up from the Wilton carpet.

Penny flushed, turning as pink as her muslin dress. "They would put me back here."

"Yes, I know, and so distressing for you," Alexa sympathized. "But perhaps we can do something about it. Do you feel like coming to Bath with me? It shan't be as fashionable as last night, mind," she warned as Penny's face lit up. "As

72

a matter of fact, Brighton has far eclipsed it as a fashionable watering hole."

It was plain, however, that to Penny any watering hole was preferable to her schoolroom. "Oh, Aunt Alexa, yes, yes, yes," she proclaimed, throwing her arms about Alexa's neck and threatening to strangle her with joy. "Do you mean that Father has said yes?"

"Your father does not know a thing about it," Alexa said wryly as she steeled herself for the battle ahead. "But he will in a very short while."

Although Alexa's plan was swiftly accepted by Penny, it was not so cordially endorsed by George, who took no pains to hide from his sister his belief that she was becoming a ramshackle chit.

Alexa gurgled with laughter. "Good heavens, George! You are the only soul who would call me a chit at all. Do prepare yourself for a shock, my dear brother. I was five-and-twenty at my last birthday and am no doubt considered to be at my last prayers. And I'm not ramshackle, just a bit foolish now and then, which I daresay we all are. Now do, pray, give my plan some thought before just pokering up and saying no."

"I don't need to think about it," George retorted, picking up his copy of *Gentlemen's Magazine*, which he had been endeavoring to read in the Ivory Saloon before his sister had burst in. "The whole notion is idiotish. You and Penny in Bath. Hah!"

"I don't see what is so idiotish about it," Alexa said reasonably. "You saw yourself how she conducted herself last night and did you proud."

George looked momentarily rattled. "I didn't say she hadn't."

"Well, then," Alexa went on in the same reasonable voice, "can you really expect her to remain happy in a schoolroom after sampling the delights of last night? She'll be miserable and shall undoubtedly contrive to make you miserable as well."

"If so, I'll blame you," George answered with a nod that

caused his jowls to tremble. "It was your idea to take her to the Winslow ball."

"But I shan't be here to blame," she pointed out airily. "I'm going to Bath, either with Penny or without her. I do, however, think you should let her come along, for she is not a little chit anymore but very nearly grown up. And since her heart is set on making her come-out next season in London, I do think she should try her wings in Bath for a month or so."

George cast an august eye on his sister, who was looking absurdly youthful herself in a high-waisted lemon frock. "Don't be daft, Alexa. Penny isn't going anywhere. Neither are you, come to think on it. You're engaged to Winslow. He won't have you jauntering about the country!"

Satisfied that he had scored a notable hit, he again retreated into his magazine, only to have Alexa pluck it out of his hands and toss it aside.

"I hardly see how my taking Penny in hand for a few weeks could be considered jauntering about, George."

"Winslow won't have it."

"Winslow won't have a thing to say about it," Alexa answered, betraying a flash of temper for the first time that day.

George sat up in the curricle chair looking stunned. "Not a thing to say? What fustian! Of course he must have something to say about it. The man's engaged to marry you, ain't he?"

For her answer Alexa smiled, a gesture not entirely lost on her brother. He had seen that look on her face more than a few times in his life, and it boded no good.

"Alexa," he said, looking thoroughly alarmed, "you aren't planning to cry off now, are you? Freakish sort of behavior, that would be."

"I am not concerned with my engagement to Winslow at the moment, George, but rather with my removal to Bath. I do intend to leave here tomorrow, and I give it to you that Penny shall be happier with me than with mooning about her schoolroom. So think it over and give me your decision soon, for I mean to set off while the weather holds."

George was by no means satisfied with this state of events, but he finally agreed with Maria's admonition, delivered in their private rooms, that Alexa was no doubt right about Penny being shut up in the schoolroom, and he gave reluctant permission to his daughter's removal to Bath. He also made one last attempt to speak to Alexa about the earl, dispatching his wife to do the deed for him.

Alexa had just ordered her portmanteau packed and corded when Maria entered her bedchamber, and a mischievous expression stole over Alexa's face.

"Poor Maria," she said at once. "George has sent you up to me, has he not?"

"Oh, n-no, Alexa," Maria stammered. "That is . . . well, I would have wanted to see you before you left, anyway."

Alexa took pity on her sister-in-law's confusion. "To be sure. And I would have wanted to see you and tell you how heartily I enjoyed seeing you and visiting with you and to promise that I shall take good care of Penny."

"Oh, I know that!"

"What is it, then?" Alexa asked, patting the bed. "You are not worried that Penny shall fall into mischief, are you?" She searched her sister-in-law's face. "There are only a few people in Bath in the summer to begin with."

"Oh, Alexa," Maria had finally screwed her courage to the sticking point, "don't you think you should tell us what to say to the earl when he comes calling?"

Alexa looked surprised. "What to say? Well, I suppose nothing whatever shall suffice."

Maria's mouth dropped open. "But my dear, we must say something!"

"Perhaps so, but I don't think a speech is necessary. I've left a letter, which he may read if he calls, but I can't predict when that shall be, for he's flown into a dreadful pet with me."

Maria looked more and more stricken. "How irksome. But do not take it to heart, Alexa, for that is in the nature of lovers' quarrels."

Alexa recoiled visibly at such an addled notion. "Good

God, Maria! This isn't a lovers' quarrel. In fact we are not—'' She swallowed her next word, lovers, and adroitly inserted quarreling. ''At least I am not. I've long planned on taking Penny to Bath. I promised her at Christmas, don't you remember? Winslow knows about it, for I told him about it myself, and I don't think it shall come as any great shock.''

From the mulish look on Alexa's face, Maria knew better than to press her, and she finally departed, leaving Alexa alone. The next morning, accompanied by Penny, who could hardly stand still for the excitement of it all, Alexa handed her portmanteau into the carriage, kissed Maria and George good-bye and commanded one of her brother's grooms—for nothing would induce that gentleman to allow his daughter and sister to roam the countryside unattended—to put the horses to.

Within minutes of setting off, Alexa felt her spirits on the rise. Ever since her arrival at Ferring, she had been feeling a distinct case of the dismals, a circumstance which had as much to do with George as with her strange betrothal to Winslow. Now, for the first time in weeks, she was doing exactly what she wished—beholden to no man, be he brother or would-be husband. She felt almost giddy with the excitement of once again being on her own.

The miles flew by as she answered the myriad questions Penny threw her way. Finally, however, the young girl succumbed to the lull of the carriage wheels and fell asleep, leaving Alexa to indulge in the luxury of her own thoughts.

Her good spirits continued unabated as the carriage took the turn for Bath and traversed the streets, stopping finally at the tall, stately town mansion on elegant Milsom Street. Although fatigued from the trip, Alexa felt her heart leap at the sight of the familiar house that she remembered so clearly from her own girlhood. Now it gleamed and sparkled its welcome to her, and she congratulated herself on her wisdom in sending the servants ahead to open it up. Moreover, there was no brother lurking within to advise her as to just what she could or could not do with herself!

* * *

Within a few days, the two ladies had settled into their new home. In fact, Penny grew quite accustomed to all the delights that Bath offered, from the Royal Crescent to the Circus and Assembly Rooms, not to mention the Pump Room, which was the only fashionable place for invalids seeking the waters.

Acceding to Penny's request one morning, Alexa drove her carriage across the Pulteney Bridge, and together they watched the river Avon flowing swiftly below them. A quick turn about the Spring Gardens was next, and then it was back over the bridge and on to Queen Square, where Alexa's good friend Mrs. Finch made her home these days.

Bronwyn Finch, a widow, was a friend of Alexa's from the time they had been children. As young ladies they had come out together, and while Alexa had disdained marriage, her friend had accepted the hand of the dashing Captain Harry Finch, who, within six months of the wedding, had been slain at Salamanca.

By a stroke of good fortune, Bronwyn had her younger sister, Courtney, staying with her for the summer and, within minutes of meeting her, Penny had found a bosom bow.

"They shall do very nicely together upstairs," Bronwyn said complacently, settling herself into a Trafalgar chair. She tossed her raven head back, and her dark eyes flitted across to her friend. "That leaves us free for a comfortable cose. My dear Alexa, how do you go on? One hears the most alarming rumors!"

Alexa, in a peacock blue morning dress, gave her head a rueful shake. "I daresay you have! And the truth is even more alarming."

"How intriguing," Bronwyn said, settling back to enjoy the chat that would ensue. "Well, my dear, I am all ears," she said and recommended that Alexa waste not a moment in putting her to rights immediately.

While Alexa was regaling her friend with the news of the rather startling betrothal she had undertaken with Winslow, the earl himself was tending to his duties as a reluctant host.

Contrary to Lady Rowena's expectations, Leigh had not yet put his fate to the touch, and his uncle no longer blamed him. What he did wish to know was just how much longer he would be obliged to tolerate the Fornhursts.

"Yes, they do eat so, don't they," Lady Rowena admitted with a sigh one morning. "Perhaps if we provoked them into a quarrel they might leave."

"At this point I am willing to try anything!" A note of exasperation had crept into Winslow's voice, and Rowena glanced up in quick alarm.

"I shall do it," she said hastily. "For if you provoked them, Sebby, it might come to a war! And that shall never do!"

Lady Rowena did not provoke a war. She merely turned an increasingly deaf ear to the plaintive entreaties of Mrs. Fornhurst, who became piqued when her invalidism went unappreciated. What was the use of a sterling performance on the couch without an appreciative audience? Since there could be nothing more vexing to one of her temperament than to be ignored, she lost not a moment in informing her spouse that the amusements of the country had palled and ordering him forthwith to return to London.

"And now that that is done," Winslow said to Rowena after the Fornhursts had departed and they were relaxing in his drawing room, "I wish to know why you even bothered to invite them here." He turned, surprising a look of repressed merriment on his sister's lively face. "By all rights you should be dashed down because Leigh isn't marrying the daughter." The truth suddenly dawned. "Good God, Ro. You didn't want Leigh to marry her, did you?"

"Of course not," she replied, squirming under her brother's piercing eyes. "I am not such a fool."

"This whole plot of yours, turning my home upside and down. Causing me to put aside my plans for Scotland! Rowena, I could wring your neck!"

She wriggled a shoulder. "Perhaps it does seem dreadfully forward of me, Sebby."

"*Forward!*" His voice was grim. "It was more than forward! It was unconscionable!"

Lady Rowena did not appear too distressed by her brother's outburst. She heard him out complacently, picking a thread from her French cream muslin gown. "But really, Sebby," she pointed out when he paused, "what else would you have me do? You saw yourself how *ineligible* the match would be. I saw it at once, not that the Fornhursts don't have respectability and standing, for of course they do, but such a want of dash through them all." She sighed. "Poor Leigh would never have been able to tolerate such a dismal family. Only of course he was bedazzled and couldn't see it for himself."

"Then I fail to see why you didn't do your mother's duty and point out his folly to him and leave me and my estate out of it."

Lady Rowena eyed him with the natural superiority of an older sister. "That," she said scornfully, "would be the most skittle-brained notion yet. Had I done anything so ill advised, Leigh might have risked an elopement. That, I assure you, is the consequence of mothers who point out the flaws of the gentlemen or ladies their sons and daughters fall in love with."

"And Ozzie?" Winslow asked, continuing to pace the length of the room, his sense of ill-usage undiminished. "I suppose he doesn't have a sprained ankle back in London at all!"

Rowena looked shocked. "But of course he does, Sebby, I wouldn't lie about such a thing."

A laugh escaped him. "Who dreamed up this charade?"

"Actually it was Mama's idea," Rowena confided. "She saw even before I did that Leigh was taken with Miss Fornhurst and knew that once he was away from London he would see that they wouldn't suit. Mama is long acquainted with Mr. Fornhurst. In fact, Sebby, she told me once that he had conceived a tendre for her when he was no older than Leigh and behaved like a perfect mooncalf."

"Our mother's tendres may be of interest to you, Rowena, but not to me," Winslow said testily. "And give me leave to say that I have been woefully used. When I think of what I had to endure on Leigh's account: not only the Fornhursts but my betrothal to Alexa—''

''Alexa?'' Lady Rowena pounced on this name with alacrity. ''Pray, what does your betrothal with Alexa have to do with Leigh?''

Inwardly, Winslow cursed his slip. ''Nothing,'' he said. ''It was a mere trick of the tongue. I take it that since the Fornhursts are gone, you won't be remaining here?''

Lady Rowena replied quickly in the negative, advising him that she and Leigh had every intention of returning to London to tend to Oswald's ankle.

''And you, Sebby?''

He smiled, thinking already of the salmon to be enjoyed in Scotland.

''Scotland!''

''Scotland, is it?'' she asked incredulously. ''But what about Alexa? Surely you don't mean to leave her high and dry?''

Except for an enigmatic curve to his lips, Winslow vouchsafed no reply. But high and dry was precisely where he did plan on leaving Miss Alexa Eiseley. Now that Leigh's involvement with Miss Fornhurst was at an end, there was not need to continue his bogus betrothal to Alexa. And he was quite certain that she would be as relieved as he was when he told her.

The earl's arrival at Ferring that afternoon cast that household into a state of high fidgets, extending even so far as to the head of the house himself, who had been hastily summoned to deal with his sister's earl. George, who had been avidly dreading the meeting with Winslow, hemmed and hawed now at the earl's request to see Alexa.

''The thing is, Winslow, you can't,'' George said at last, beads of perspiration popping up on his brow.

The earl lifted an eyebrow before remembering that he had not endeavored to mend the tiff suffered on the night of his ball. He smiled encouragingly at George.

''I know I must be in her black books, George, but if you would tell her I am desirous of speaking with her, I shan't take up too much of her time. I know what I say shall be of interest.''

''I'm sorry, Winslow,'' George said gruffly, ''but she isn't here. Told her myself how it would look if she went racketing about. But she has a maggot in her brain. Never did pay me any attention!''

Winslow searched the other man's face. George was looking strangely pale. ''Do you mean that Alexa is no longer staying with you? Has she returned to Pembroke?''

''No, blast her! She's gone to Bath and taken Penny with her. I couldn't say no to that, because the chit would cry and beg that she wouldn't be imprisoned in a schoolroom, as though I were a gaoler!''

With difficulty Winslow strove to untangle Alexa's part in the story from her niece's.

''Do you mean that Alexa has gone to Bath with your daughter, George?''

''Yes.'' George emphatically bobbed his head up and down. ''And I almost forgot this. She wasn't so skip-brained after all.'' He held out the note Alexa had left behind. ''She left this for you in case you called.''

Puzzled, Winslow broke the seal and perused the few lines. It was enough, George noticed, to cause a black frown to descend on his lordship's noble brow.

> *Winslow,*
>   *I am taking Penny to Bath. If you are still in the hips about my outrageous behavior the night of your ball, you have my permission to consider our betrothal at an end. I daresay it shall come as no great loss to either of us, shall it?*
>
>   *Alexa*

''Alexa also ordered that this be returned to you,'' George said when the earl finally glanced up. He was holding out the ruby bracelet Alexa had worn to the ball. For a long moment, Winslow did nothing, then, with a slight twist to his lips, he picked it up, bowed and rode off, looking, Mr. Eiseley later confided to his wife, for all the world like one about to do murder.

George was not far off the mark in this assessment. Upon reading Alexa's note, Winslow was beset with a totally unfamiliar emotion: anger. It was the outside of enough to be given his congé in such an uncivil fashion by any female. Was he no better than a servant to be dismissed out of hand? And after saving her reputation!

A small voice within him broke in at this point, dutifully reminding him that he had intended to break the engagement himself, but this only made him more infuriated. She had stolen a march on him. Permission to consider. Permission. No great loss.

Reaching Winslow Park, he flung the reins down to his groom and stamped into the house, nearly colliding full tilt with Lady Rowena, who had come out to see what all the commotion was about.

"Good gracious, Sebby," she said, catching her balance. "What is amiss? You look as though you've seen a ghost."

"Nothing is amiss, Ro. Except that I have made a slight change in my plans for the summer. I am not bound for Scotland after all."

"Indeed?" Lady Rowena was all amazement. "And after all the time you spent moaning and groaning about the salmon you were missing. Where then do you intend to pass your time?"

"In Bath!"

"Bath?" she shouted up to him in disbelief as he mounted the stairs. "Are you jesting, Sebby? Pray, what is there for you to do in such a dreadful place?"

"I shall do what everyone else does," he returned grimly. "I shall take the waters, of course!"

The earl departed for Bath in a high flush of anger, but by afternoon his temper had cooled, helped in no little part by a thunderstorm that caused him to wait for two hours in a damp and overcrowded posting house. By the time he made the turn toward his destination, his anger had given way to fatigue.

Thanks to General Cathcart, a rather doughty military gentleman who was a friend of his mother's and had been a habitué of Bath for decades, Winslow did not have to think twice about having a roof over his head. The general had extended the earl an offer to stay with him several times in the past, implying that it would be a personal insult if he found out later that Winslow had ever been in Bath and had failed to stay with him.

Since Winslow had borne with the company of the foolish Mr. Fornhurst for so many days, he meticulously reviewed the general's foibles. Finding nothing that would form an impediment to taking him up on his hospitality, Winslow proceeded up Milsom Street and over to Pulteney Street. He had no difficulty gaining entrance, for the butler who answered his knock recognized him from previous engagements with Cathcart and had no compunction in escorting him to the blue drawing room.

Winslow, trailing after him, had half expected to find the general, grizzled and gray, waiting there. He was completely astounded to find instead a pale, young specimen of a man with a violet neckcloth knotted about his throat occupied by reading verse to a lady at least thirty years his senior, a lady moreover whom Winslow had not the slightest difficulty in recognizing as his very own mother!

Eight

Several minutes elapsed as the countess, shrieking like a banshee, hurled herself across the room and onto her son's bosom. She then bounced free to bustle her poet friend, Mr. Hormfeld, and his verse out of the general's drawing room, explaining that as she had not seen her son in several weeks, she must by necessity have a long cose with him.

"Alone," she added when the poet fluttered a mild protest.

With that task behind her, she uttered a sigh of relief and stepped back across the Wilton carpet toward the earl, her tiny figure not quite topping five feet, and her silvered hair dressed à la Sappho, a beguilingly youthful style.

Winslow watched her maneuvering with a fascinated eye. Although delighted as always to see his mother, he had thought her in Brighton enjoying the fashionable set of the Prince Regent and was puzzled to find her now in Bath under General Cathcart's protection.

"Mama," he said as she led him by the hand to one of a

pair of matching velvet-backed chairs encircled by a carved Chinese screen, "what are you doing in Bath, and particularly in General Cathcart's residence?"

"Well, I haven't been *seduced*, if that is what worries you," she replied with a saucy smile.

He grinned back at her. "That does relieve me, ma'am. Although poetry, I recall, has been rumored to win many a female heart!"

Lady Winslow barely repressed a shudder. "Only a gentleman who has not been obliged to listen to twenty stanzas of such vile stuff could scruple to say such an idiotish thing. Pray don't think me *unfeeling*, Sebby. I could, I suppose, listen with perfect composure to a sonnet or two, but Mr. Hormfeld insists on penning odes." Her nose wrinkled. "Odes, I ask you. Do you know just how many stanzas there must be in such things?"

"Too many, it would appear," Winslow said with a quivering lip. "But just who is this fellow Hormfeld and how is he here? He's not staying with you, I see."

"He is a poet," the countess announced.

"A poet," Winslow echoed. "I see; that explains everything. And where is your host?"

She looked up, surprised by the question. "If you mean the general, as I suppose you must, he is in Brighton with Prinny playing whist, and not for chicken stakes! And while I have nothing against cards, for I am not Quakerish, it does seem rather lacking in character for them to be forever obliged to risk such excessive sums on the turn of a card!"

"I've often thought the same thing myself, Mama," Winslow replied, not taking his eyes off her. "But no more nonsense, my dear. How do you come to be in Bath?"

"I began to feel a trifle out of sorts," Lady Winslow confessed at last. "Nothing to signify, so you needn't start treating me like a doddering old lady. But it was enough to make me think of coming here to take the waters in the Pump Room in peace and quiet. That, you must know, is never possible in Brighton, what with the hordes of people Prinny attracts even now when they dislike him so. So when I confessed as much to General Cathcart, of course he insisted on my using his residence for as long as I wished, which I must say is excessively civil of him.''

''And how long have you been here?'' the earl asked, stroking his chin with a forefinger.

The countess thought a moment. ''About a se'nnight.''

''And are you feeling better?'' he asked, an anxious look in his eyes. ''For if not, I shall find the nearest doctor and bring him here at once.''

The countess waved away his alarm. ''I am perfectly stout. And I do feel it is not the waters so much, merely that I had begun to feel a trifle bored in Brighton. Bath seems ever so much more agreeable!''

Her statement, as the earl took pains to point out, now bordered on heresy for any lady of fashion.

''And,'' he added, ''I fail to see the attractions here.''

She shot him a quizzing look. ''Indeed? Then why, may I ask, are you here?''

''Touché, Mama,'' he said with a laugh. ''But it so happens I have personal matters that draw me to Bath, and I hoped to avail myself of the general's hospitality. You shan't throw me out on my ear?''

She choked on a laugh. ''No, indeed. By the by, how are the Fornhursts doing? I suppose they have quitted Winslow Park, for even you cannot be so rag-mannered as to come to Bath, pressing affairs or no, while they remain behind.''

''Mama, you are incorrigible,'' he chided sternly, not taken in by the innocent face across from him. ''And Rowena takes after you! To talk of *my* being rag-mannered when the two of you foisted that impossible family on me in the first place!''

Laughter bubbled up from the countess's throat. ''Well, my dear,'' she said as she struggled to speak, ''you have always been considered the strong one in the family. No, don't scold. It reminds me of your great-uncle Henry, and you know what an old stickler he was! Dare I hope that Leigh is safe from Miss Fornhurst's clutches?''

''Safer than you appear to be from your poet!'' Winslow announced. ''And give me leave to say I never expected to see you listening so complacently to such . . . drivel!''

She gurgled again more helplessly than before. "He is young, and although his verse is quite bad he may yet improve. Who knows what Byron wrote when he was just a callow youth?"

"I don't," the earl informed her, "and I don't much care. Just, for heaven's sake, don't encourage that fellow."

Lady Winslow drew back. "I don't encourage him, Sebby. In fact I've come close to being abominably rude to him."

"Now that won't wash. You could not be abominably rude to anyone."

"I suppose not," she said ruefully. "But I came close to it with Mr. Hormfeld when he would arrive tonight and sit there," she indicated the chair he had taken with her hand, "reading verse to me when anyone could see I was wild to leave. I was just on my way out when he arrived."

Alerted by this statement, the earl noticed for the first time that his mother was sporting an elegant gown of exquisite yellow satin flecked with lace at bodice and hem and a cashmere shawl about her shoulders. Too much finery for the mere entertaining of a poet.

"In fact," Lady Winslow went on, "I was almost tempted to take him to the party, for it is not a formal affair, and perhaps he might meet someone more inclined to favor his verses. Someone younger, perhaps, and more appreciative of his efforts; but fortunately you routed him, and that is much better, for I'd as lief go with you as Mr. Hormfeld."

Smiling, Winslow shook his head. "I should love nothing more than to be your escort, Mama, but not tonight. I fear I am fagged to death, and I don't think I shall be of much use dancing attendance on you. But don't despair! It may not be too late to call your poet back. Shall I dispatch a servant to scour the streets for him? He may be lingering nearby waiting patiently for a glimpse of you."

The countess went off on another peal of laughter. "Odious, odious boy. And anyway he wouldn't come back. Poets are devilishly sensitive to any slight. Indeed I may have lost him forever." Her face brightened at the thought.

"Are you sure you shouldn't like to come with me, Sebby?"

"Quite sure, Mama. All I desire for the evening is a bite of supper, and then I shall fall into one of the general's vacant beds."

"What a pity. I know you would enjoy this evening so much. There is someone of particular interest to you who shall be there."

He gazed idly across into her blue eyes, so very much like his own. "Is there, Mama?" he asked politely. "Pray, who would that be?"

"Why, your fiancée, of course, dear Sebby. Alexa Eiseley!"

Stunned by this blithe announcement, Winslow stared, aghast, at his mother's beaming face. Somehow she had learned of Alexa and the bogus engagement. But how?

Nettled, he dipped into his snuffbox. "I suppose Rowena wrote to you?" he asked.

"No, as a matter of fact she did not. Or perhaps she did," Lady Winslow said, wrinkling her brow in thought. "But since she would have sent the letter on to Brighton I would not have seen it. No, I had the good fortune to run into Lady Markham. A goosish creature as a rule but quite reliable in her facts. While I was in the Pump Room last week she came over to congratulate me, saying that George Eiseley— she is a connection of the family—had finally found a husband for his sister, which, I must own, is putting it badly, for Alexa never lacked for any suitors! And I am convinced her dreary brother had nothing whatever to do with things. But I am undeniably pleased that you won her over, Sebby, for I have often wished you to marry. Not," she reassured him at once with a maternal smile, "that I consider you so wild or with so many Cythereans under your wing."

"Mama!" He was betrayed into a protest.

"One has to be realistic, after all," the countess replied large-mindedly. "Fortunately, you never dabbled that much in the muslin company, which was a great relief to me and must be, I'm sure, to Alexa."

The seeming ease with which his mother linked his name

with Alexa's did not bode any good as far as Winslow could see, and he wondered if the two ladies had already been exchanging confidences in Bath.

"Have you seen Alexa?"

"Not yet, my dear," his mother responded. "That is why I am bound for Mrs. Finch's tonight. She is giving a party for that sister of hers, and since Alexa is a bosom bow of hers, she is certain to be in attendance this evening along with her little niece. I thought it the perfect opportunity to welcome her into our family." She gazed over at her son, who wore a somewhat glazed expression on his handsome countenance. "Are you certain you won't change your mind, Sebby, and come with me? It would be such a surprise for her."

"It would at that, wouldn't it," the earl agreed, emerging from his brief reverie, an ironic gleam quite pronounced in his blue eyes. Recollection of a certain letter in his possession clinched the matter for him. "Do you know, Mama, I am feeling rather less fagged, and if you can delay your departure another twenty minutes to allow me time to change, I shall be more than happy to escort you to Mrs. Finch's."

At the house on Queen Square, Alexa smothered a yawn discreetly behind the edge of a delicate Chinese fan and endeavored to remember just how a chaperone ought to behave at a ball. If this, her first venture into Bath society, was any omen, taking Penny under her wing might ultimately lead to her undoing. Turning her head to the far corner, she again glimpsed the sea of chattering young girls sitting on chairs scattered about the ballroom, and despite her gown of apricot spider gauze, she felt as old as Methuselah.

"That shall never do," Bronwyn said, sidling up to her friend.

"What shan't do?" Alexa demanded of her hostess, who herself appeared to good advantage in a burgundy crêpe gown with scattered flowers along its skirt.

"That look of yours," Bronwyn quizzed. "I saw it as plain as day from across the room. Need I hazard a guess?

You've been feeling the interminable weight of your years tonight, am I right?''

Alexa laughed. "Yes, but how . . . ?''

"Because I felt much the same, escorting Courtney here in Bath," Bronwyn explained as her eyes swept meditatively over her guests. "Perhaps I should have tried to get a better assortment of people. They all seem so young, but this is Bath, not London. One can't expect to find the cream of the crop here. I daresay everyone over the age of twenty-three is acting tonight as a chaperone.''

"Not quite," Alexa corrected. "I saw Major Jayneway just before he stepped into the card room.''

"Poor Archie! I do wish the company were more enlivening for him. I myself have never seen the fascination in cards. However, I warned you ahead of time the party was for Courtney and not for me. At least we have adequate refreshments.''

"So I have discovered," Alexa answered, idly plying her fan. "Any number of the young sprigs dangling after Penny have sought leave to bring me refreshments. Nourishing the dragon, as it were. Perhaps I ought to follow Archie's lead and retire to the card room for the duration.''

"Now that shows how little acquainted you are with the hazards of chaperonage," Bronwyn retorted. "For while you are closeted away playing whist, I'd give you odds your precious Penny will find herself in the briars somehow or another. And it is so nettlesome to be summoned from a card room to cope with a disaster, particularly since you will be in the midst of your first splendid hand all evening and that shall leave you even more cross and ill-prepared to handle the calamity under way.''

Alexa laughed merrily at the picture her friend had described.

"You have persuaded me that my station is by Penny's side, and while I have you here at mine, tell me, who is that young tulip she is dancing with?''

Bronwyn directed a keen eye at the young man Alexa had singled out. "Mr. Harrison Kitteridge. That's Thomas Kitteridge's youngest. A pity he is the younger son, but he is uncommonly good-looking—or would be if he didn't have that thing looped about his neck!''

Happily, the music being vigorously played kept Mr. Kitteridge from hearing this scorching indictment of his neck-cloth.

"And that boy dancing with Courtney?" Alexa queried.

"Lady Hackett-Jones's grandson," Bronwyn replied promptly. "Gideon Ramsey is his name. An agreeable sort of chap. Actually, I'm rather gratified that his grandmother showed up as well tonight. Although she can be a bit of a tartar, she dotes on the boy. You know she is a boon friend of Sebby's mama?"

"I didn't, and pray don't bring *him* up," Alexa pleaded.

Bronwyn gave her a crooked smile. "And why not, pray? Are you regretting that shabby treatment you dished out to him?"

Alexa's head shot up, and she looked her friend in the eye. "Of course not! And it wasn't so shabby."

"Oh, no?" Bronwyn scoffed. "It was the height of propriety, I suppose, to cry off in a letter?"

"I didn't cry off," Alexa replied with crushing pretension. "I merely told him that if he wished to end things I wouldn't stand in his way. I have no doubt he was heartily relieved to do so. And the letter wasn't written so badly!"

"I hope not for your sake, Alexa," her friend replied in a much altered tone, "for here comes your spurned earl along with his mama!"

Vainly hoping that Bronwyn was roasting her, Alexa whirled around just as Lady Winslow entered the ballroom. Waving gaily to several of her acquaintances, the countess made a beeline for Alexa's corner of the room, accompanied every step of the way by her cool and elegant son. A mad desire to flee the room nearly overcame Alexa. But both mother and son barred her line of flight, and it would be, she reasoned, an act of cowardice to duck into the card room now.

"My dear Alexa!" There was no time for further thought as the countess swept Alexa into a heartfelt embrace. "My dear, nothing could give me more pleasure than seeing you here, dearest future daughter-in-law!''

Alexa, struggling to catch her breath, gasped at being addressed so by Winslow's mother.

"My dear Lady Winslow," she murmured, unable to think of anything to say. What was there to say to such a greeting?

The countess pressed her hand tightly between two of her own. "My dear Alexa, you must try and call me Mama. I know how difficult it can be, but after all your mama has been dead some dozen years, so it might not be so difficult for you as for others!"

"Dear countess, you are all kindness—"

"You are to be my dear Sebby's bride!" the countess proclaimed. "How else should I act?" Put in mind now of her son, she stared at him. "Sebastian, are you going to stand there like a simpleton or are you going to greet Alexa?"

"I was merely allowing the tide of your feelings to run its course, Mama, before inflicting mine on Alexa, who looks to have borne with enough emotion for one day," the earl replied. He took the hand his mother was not holding between hers and kissed it lightly. "Delighted to see you, my dear."

Now that that was over the countess took command again. "I have been telling Sebby that we must sit down soon, the three of us, and make plans."

"Plans?" Alexa echoed, finally regaining custody of her hands. "Plans for what, pray?"

The countess's eyes widened. "For your wedding, of course."

"I told Mama that she must needs discuss everything with you," Winslow drawled, hugely enjoying the discomfiture on Alexa's face. "I know nothing of such matters."

"Very true," the countess agreed. "And while I don't mean to be meddlesome, I do think we should set the date at least. Here it is July. Quite a horrid month for a wedding, and August is only a little better. September is nicer, but I shouldn't like to wait till September, do you? Fortunately, I still have the guest list from Rowena's wedding somewhere about. Several of the people on it have died in the meantime, but we shall go through that thoroughly enough, never fear. Do you remember Rowena's wedding, Sebby?'' she asked as he choked on a laugh. ''You were only ten at the time.''

''Alexa,'' Bronwyn said, taking advantage of the countess's nostalgic turn of mind, ''I do think I see Penny looking for you.''

If Mrs. Finch had done nothing previous in her life to earn her the distinction of being a friend, she had fully earned this epithet now. Gratefully, Alexa excused herself from her impending nuptial arrangements and walked over to Penny, who was informed by her beleaguered aunt that she looked as though she had a toothache.

''A toothache?'' Penny expostulated. ''Aunt Alexa, what are you talking about? Oh, this is Mr. Kitteridge.''

The young man at her side, in the throes of suffocation from his enormous cravat, bobbed his head at Alexa.

She smiled at him. ''I wonder if I might have a word in private with my niece, Mr. Kitteridge.''

''Good heavens, Aunt Alexa, what is the matter?'' Penny demanded as they drew away. ''You look positively demented.''

''I suppose I do, and I can't help it!'' Alexa replied. ''Winslow is here with his mother.''

''Is that the countess?'' Penny asked, turning to peek over her shoulder. ''She looks sweet.''

''She is sweet,'' Alexa said distractedly. ''Penny.'' She grasped her niece by the wrist. ''Do you think you shall dislike having a toothache that much?''

Her niece recoiled. ''I should think so. I loathe such things.''

''Yes, I know how disagreeable they can be. It shall only be a pretend toothache, my dear.''

''Pretend toothaches in my experience are every bit as disagreeable as real ones, Miss Eiseley,'' a voice intruded urbanely.

She jumped. Winslow stood at her elbow.

''Why don't you leave Penny in the hands of the young

gentlemen just pining to admire her and allow me to waltz with you?''

"Waltz with you!'' she exclaimed hotly. "I'd sooner—''

"Not in front of the children,'' he murmured, cupping her elbow and propelling her around the dance floor. "Mrs. Finch is a good friend of yours. Very tidy the way she extricated you from that little scene with Mama.''

"What do you mean by telling your mama we were to be married?'' Alexa hissed as they danced.

"I didn't tell her anything,'' he retorted, spinning her so that she was rendered a trifle breathless. "She had it straight from Lady Markham. A relation on *your* side, I believe?'' he asked goadingly.

"Only through marriage,'' Alexa muttered hatefully. "But why didn't you just tell your mother the truth?''

He peered down his nose and into her hazel eyes, which were now flashing lightning bolts at him. He found it oddly endearing. "Tell her that I had contracted a marriage merely as a hoax?'' he inquired. "Mama would think me bosky and quite without principle. And while I don't particularly care what others might think of me, I do care what my mother thinks.'' He waltzed her toward one end of the ballroom then started back toward the other.

"Didn't George give you my letter?'' she asked, the lightning bolts subsiding somewhat.

"Letter?'' he asked blandly. "Oh, yes, I believe so.''

Alexa had had enough. "Winslow, did you even *read* it? Don't let's peel eggs at such a time. I told you in the letter that it would be best for all if our engagement ended.''

He chuckled. "Your memory is faulty, Alexa. Actually, you said if I wished to end the matter, you had no objection to make. But it would have been such an awkward muddle if I had done the thing just then. After all, George was watching me like a hawk as I read the note. And I couldn't just say you had had second thoughts about our wedding. He'd be bound to think you freakish!''

"Oh, bother George!'' Alexa exclaimed, resisting the urge to kick her partner in the shin. "As though he doesn't already think me freakish. You must know, Winslow, that I have no wish to marry you.''

"Of course I know that," he said crossly. "You've said as much throughout our engagement. But you'll allow me, I hope, the courtesy of deciding how to end it.''

"Very well," she said, giving ground reluctantly. "But it must be soon.''

"Don't worry. Perhaps later in the week we can have a rousing quarrel. It shouldn't be too difficult. We always seem to be coming to cuffs of late.''

She fell silent, momentarily abashed. "I suppose you thought my letter cowardly.''

His smile spoke volumes.

"And I suppose it was," she continued in a chastened tone but rallied instantly at his needling look. "You were much to blame, Winslow! Telling me how a betrothed lady ought to act.''

"I beg your forgiveness, Alexa," he said blithely, looking anything but repentant. "Playing the part of your fiancé I found myself carried away. It shan't happen again.''

"Good," she said, satisfied on this point and turning her mind to another. "Now, who shall tell your mama the truth?''

"I shall, I suppose," the earl said ruefully. "And I don't much look forward to it either. She shall be devastated, for she seems quite taken with you. I own to becoming a trifle bored at having a litany of your qualities and virtues read aloud to me continuously.''

Alexa laughed. "Dear Lady Winslow. Are you certain you can handle telling her when the time is right?''

"Nothing shall be easier," he said airily as the waltz came to an end. "Let's go over and talk to her now." He led her through the thick of the crowd and glanced about him in confusion. "Where the devil did she go to? I left her here. . . . Ah, to the right, with Lady Hackett-Jones!''

"Here they are!" The countess beamed fondly at their approach. "The very ones we were speaking of. Lady Hackett-Jones only this minute was commenting on how excellently matched the two of you were for the waltz. And I could not help divulging that she might wish to keep an eye out in the *Gazette*."

"In the *Gazette*?" Winslow echoed, frowning. "What do you mean, Mama?"

"Why, for the announcement of your betrothal, of course," the countess said with a sunny smile. "The instant Lady Markham told me the news, I dispatched a notice to the newspaper. And why, pray, do the two of you look so *surprised*?"

Nine

"*I thought you told me this betrothal was nothing but a hum?*" Bronwyn demanded as she draped a handkerchief, dipped in her favorite lilac water, on the brow of the prone figure on her four-poster bed.

"It is a hum," Alexa muttered, lifting a despairing hand to her forehead. "What is this?" she asked. "It smells!"

"French perfume," came the reply. "The latest cure for the migraine, and you needn't scruple to tell me that was the merest pretext, for I have cut my wisdoms. And I'm certain Winslow has as well. Lie still!" she commanded as her friend twitched convulsively at the mention of the earl's name. "You need something to calm your nerves before you venture downstairs again."

"My nerves do not need calming," Alexa replied. "Or at least they wouldn't, if not for Winslow! When I think of him smugly standing there, smiling at me and his mother, I . . . I . . . could slay him!"

"I'd sooner slay Lady Markham," Bronwyn said, taking

a practical view of the matter. " 'Twas she who told the countess about your engagement to Sebby."

Alexa considered the matter. "You're right," she said, nodding. "I'll slay Lady Markham *after* I dispose of Winslow."

Laughing, Bronwyn sat down on the edge of the bed and begged her friend to be serious.

"I am serious!" Alexa retorted. "Only what shall I do about that wretched notice in the *Gazette*?"

"There is nothing that can be done," Bronwyn replied oracularly. "It's water under the bridge now. But I thought you had cried off from Sebby in that letter you left behind at Ferring. How comes it that you are still engaged?"

"He chose to ignore it!" Alexa said, sitting up, one hand still clamped to her brow. "He says he couldn't tell his mama when she had only heard the news and was so in alt by it. We had intended to break up later in the week. But that notice in the *Gazette* thrusts a spoke in our wheel for certain."

Bronwyn's face turned quizzical, then thoughtful. "Do you think Sebby knew about the notice the countess sent in?"

"No, he looked almost as surprised as I was. Drat that announcement. How can we cry off now?"

Bronwyn patted her hand. "There is no need to adopt any tragic airs, my dear. If worse does come to worst, you could just marry him!"

Alexa pulled the handkerchief from her brow and rounded on her friend.

"Bite your tongue!" she ordered. "I marry Winslow? I shan't be browbeaten into accepting such an insufferable situation!"

"I wouldn't call it insufferable," Bronwyn said frankly. "And don't be a goose, Alexa. Sebby is an earl after all and alleged to be as rich as Golden Ball. Oh, I know that doesn't signify with you, since you have your large fortune, but he is also devilishly good-looking and quite amiable as a rule. And I've always understood the two of you to be firm friends. So why should you suddenly rip up at the notion of marrying him?''

''Because it's absurd!'' Alexa said, the mulish look coming back to her face. ''Friendship is one thing, marriage quite another.''

Bronwyn shrugged. ''Well, his mama seems to think you are the very bride for him.''

Alexa groaned. ''Was there ever such a female as Lady Winslow?'' she asked. ''Not that she isn't a pet, and so wild to have him married that it doesn't surprise me that she has clasped anyone respectable to her bosom.'' She heaved a sigh and stared distractedly at the ceiling. ''Bronwyn, this fix is none of my doing. I should have left young Leigh out to catch his death of cold. I must remember to do so the next time. And do stop laughing at me,'' she said crossly, ''and tell me what I should do!''

''I haven't a clue,'' Bronwyn answered cheerfully. ''I vow it's almost as good as one of those amateur theatricals where one never does *know* just how things will turn out until the very last minute. A pity we don't know any playwrights between us. Poets, yes, but never a playwright when you really need one. He might at least supply ideas worth following—''

''Bronwyn,'' Alexa wailed, ''this is my *life* you are prattling about.''

''Yes, but do try and look on the bright side,'' her friend implored. ''At the very worst, as I said before, you might find yourself married to Sebby.''

''Do oblige me and stop bringing that up! I have no desire to marry such an aggravating, high-handed man.''

Bronwyn, in justice, could not let such a statement pass unchallenged. ''You might turn up your nose at him, Alexa, but I know a full dozen females who would snap him up at the drop of a handkerchief!''

''Then they are most welcome to him,'' came the cordial rejoinder. ''And, speaking of handkerchiefs, I've had quite enough of this one. Any more of this scent, and I shall have a migraine for certain.'' She handed the cloth to Bronwyn and swung her legs off the side of the bed. ''Much as I'd like to, I can't stay here all night. I must find Penny. Whether she knows it or not, she has the toothache, and that is final!''

"You might be doing it too brown with the family ailments," Bronwyn advised as she disposed of the offending handkerchief in a basin. She dried her hands on a towel and uttered a quick exclamation. "My dear, you can't go downstairs like that!''

Alexa looked down automatically at her ball gown. "Why not, pray?''

"Because you look radiant as always, and only an utter fool would think you've just recovered from an attack of the migraine. Do try and look *hagged* for once in your life!''

At the sheer absurdity of her friend's admonition, Alexa burst out laughing, but she did her best to appear weak and wan when she finally drifted down the stairs with Bronwyn. Young Miss Eiseley, when informed for the second time in the same evening by her aunt that she did indeed have the toothache, felt with a wisdom beyond her tender years that perhaps she did at that and agreed that it would be better to leave the party and nurse the toothache back at Milsom Street.

The countess watched them leave the ballroom with real regret, promising to dispatch a footman the next morning with a recipe for the draught that had cured her last toothache in a trice.

"And I hope, Alexa," she said, a worried frown puckering her brow, "that your headache will be better by then.''

"I'm certain it shall be, ma'am," Alexa reassured her. "Bronwyn bathed my temples with lilac water and already I feel more the thing.''

The countess beamed. "Good! Then you shall feel up to taking tea with me tomorrow afternoon. Sebby and I can have a comfortable cose with you then. It is always so difficult to chat in a ballroom, but over tea we can begin to make plans.''

Alexa had a grim foreboding of the type of plans Lady Winslow wished to concoct but was driven to the wall and reluctantly agreed to have tea with mother and son. Smiling at her answer, Lady Winslow gave her a peck on the cheek while the earl announced his stalwart intention of seeing Alexa and Penny off in their carriage.

"Did you know anything about the notice in the *Gazette*?" Alexa demanded under her breath as they made for the door.

"Do you take me for a flat?" he responded acidly. "I wasn't even aware that Mama knew anything about us until earlier this evening. It took the wind out of my sails, I'll have you know. Can't think how it's ditched me."

Alexa stared at him speechlessly as they stepped out into the biting wind. "Ditched *you*?" she demanded. "What of me? Oh, why do we quarrel over that when I daresay we are both ditched. We can't delay telling your mama the truth any longer. And it must be done before my afternoon tea with her."

"I know, yet dash it all, it shall make her deuced unhappy! How the devil did we land in such a fix?"

With what the earl termed scorn unworthy of a lady, Alexa reminded him that the whole besotted notion was his to begin with.

"You should have talked me out of it."

"I believe at the very first occasion I told you it was stupid and nonsensical," she replied frigidly.

"Yes, well, I only dreamed it up to assist you," he said, distracted by this reminder.

"Don't let's come to cuffs now, Winslow," Alexa hissed, nodding at the gawking Penny, who was a step behind them, which put a swift end to their hostilities. "I hope I can rely on you to correct your mama's mistaken ideas about us."

"I shall do my best," he said as the carriage, not a moment too soon, approached Bronwyn's front door.

Some minutes later, safely ensconced in the carriage seat, Penny turned a worried face to her aunt. "Aunt Alexa, what were you and Lord Winslow arguing about?"

Alexa was brought up short by the question. "Nothing important, my dear," she said, hoping Penny would be fobbed off.

"If that's true," her niece went on, undaunted, "I don't see why I must have the toothache!"

Her aunt chuckled. "You are right. At the very least, you deserve an explanation." She paused to mull over several stories she could relate to her niece. "It's just a stupid misunderstanding. Winslow and I have agreed we shouldn't suit!"

"Shouldn't suit?" Penny asked, aghast. "Do you mean that you aren't going to marry him?"

"Something like that," Alexa said warily. "And now, my dear, tell me all about your Mr. Kitteridge."

Penny, however, was not about to be led off on a tangent. "Why have you decided not to marry Winslow?" she asked. "And does his mother know? And only think what Papa will say!"

"Lady Winslow doesn't know, more's the pity," Alexa replied, "and never mind your papa. Come, goose. There's no need to look so tragic. I assure you Sebby hasn't broken my heart, and I haven't broken his. In fact, we were on the road to the most amicable of partings, except that his mother had gleaned the news from Lady Markham and she—the countess, I mean—had dispatched an announcement to the *Gazette* concerning the match. So you see, the matter is now rather awkward for all concerned. But"—she managed a rallying tone—"Winslow has promised me to tell his mama the truth, so I daresay we shall soon resolve things."

Penny chewed on a lip. "Was it his jealousy?"

Alexa stared at her through the shafts of moonlight filtering into the carriage. "His what?"

"His jealousy! Was that what caused the breach between you?"

Alexa laughed. "Good heavens, what put such an addled notion in your head?"

"At the ball he gave," Penny replied. "I could see then that he didn't much like your dancing with Colonel Montcalm or Viscount Cawly or any of your other beaux."

"I'm sorry to disappoint you, Penny," Alexa said firmly, "but Winslow is not the least bit jealous of me, nor am I of him. We have reflected on the matter and have merely decided to end our attachment. Now, that's more than enough talk about him for one evening. Do tell me about that young Mr. Kitteridge!''

The earl had had every confidence that he would speak to his mother about his bogus engagement to Alexa, but he found each attempt to broach the topic with her meeting with failure. During the first half of their return journey to Pulteney Street, he was obliged to endure another recitation of the virtues of Alexa Eiseley, a topic he was rapidly growing bored with.

"Really, Mama,'' he expostulated when the countess paused to inhale a breath, "you make her out to be a horse!''

"Sebby!'' His mother laughed. "What an absurd thing to say.''

"I beg your pardon,'' he responded stiffly. "But I have been endeavoring to get a word in, and you do nothing but go on about Alexa.''

She turned a quizzing face up at him. "Is that why you have that positively hunted expression in your eyes?'' she mused. "It puts me in mind of the time you were screwing up your courage to tell me that you had broken one of my prize Ming vases in the parlor. Of course, you were only ten at the time.''

"Mama . . .'' he said in a voice of abject desperation.

She smiled at him. "Am I being a prattle box, my love? How foolish of me when I can see you have something you are bursting to tell me. Is it about Dowager House?''

The earl was taken aback. *"Dowager House?* Good God, no! What the devil put that dungeon into your mind?''

"Your wedding,'' she replied. "It is only natural that after your marriage you might wish me to take up residence there.''

"Mama! You don't like that gloomy dungeon any more than I do. You have your own home in London, and for as long as you wish it. Not that you are ever there longer than a month,'' he teased, "you do gad about so!''

She looked up with evident relief. "Well, then I am

happy I shan't have to put up there just yet, but if that's not what you're pining to tell me, what is?''

Her clear blue eyes turned expectantly to him, and Winslow, with a heroic force of will, forced himself to face them.

''Mama, did you really send an announcement about my marriage to Alexa to the *Gazette*?''

''Why, yes, of course I did,'' she said patiently. ''My dear, that is the very place where such betrothals are announced. I daresay because you are male you do not understand fully how such things are done. What a stroke of fortune that I am here to advise you.''

The earl, who would sooner call his mother's presence other things than a stroke of fortune, hastily ran a finger between his cravat and shirt points.

''Mama,'' he began, but he got no further, as the countess took the lead again.

''All betrothals are first announced in the *Gazette* and the *Morning Post*,'' she instructed him, then halted suddenly. ''Good Jupiter, I've forgotten about the *Morning Post*! I must draft a notice for it when we return to General Cathcart's and have it delivered immediately to London.''

''No, by heaven, don't do that!'' the earl cried out in abject alarm.

The countess's eyes narrowed in sudden suspicion at his vehement reaction. ''What an extraordinary thing to say, Sebby. You appear uncommonly agitated this evening.''

Gazing at her dear little face inches away from his, Winslow realized it was now or never. ''Mama,'' he said, plunging in before his courage could ebb, ''I don't know how to tell you this, and I daresay you shall be shattered, but my engagement to Alexa is at an end.''

His bombshell fell sadly flat. ''Don't be silly, my dear.'' The countess tapped him dismissively on the wrist with her fan. ''You've only gotten betrothed to her. Pray, how could it come to an end so quickly?'' She searched his face meditatively for a minute. ''Now that I think of it, the two of you were exchanging heated words during that one waltz together. I hope you didn't quarrel.''

''Yes, we did!'' the earl exclaimed, grasping at this straw

as though it were a log and he a drowning man. "It was the most horrid quarrel imaginable. At one point she called me a stupid coxcomb, and I called her . . . Well, you don't need to know that. The crux of the matter is our betrothal is at an end!"

Lady Winslow chuckled long and heartily. "A stupid coxcomb, is it? My dear, what did you do to set her off?"

"I can't remember," the earl said, not entirely pleased by his mother's show of levity.

"Then it can't have been that serious," she pointed out, holding on to his arm as their carriage rolled over a poor patch of road. "For a moment you actually had me worried. But you can't end a betrothal simply because your bride-to-be happened to call you a stupid coxcomb. Sometimes," she confided, "men do behave that way. I distinctly recall telling your father so whenever we quarreled."

"Even so, Mama, this is different," Winslow insisted stoutly.

"Of course it is," the countess soothed, "but one quarrel is not the end of things. I daresay all lovers must quarrel. It is in the nature of things. And that's what makes reconciliation such fun. Now"—her tone turned brisk—"the very first thing you must do tomorrow shall be to dispatch flowers to Alexa."

"Flowers?" he expostulated. "Why in heaven should I do that?"

His mother sat back against the velvet squabs and stared at him. "Don't you want to win her back?" she asked sharply.

"Yes, of course," Winslow muttered, taking upon his reluctant shoulders the totally unfamiliar burden of a spurned suitor, "but—"

"Make it the largest bouquet possible," his mother said, reflecting on the matter, "roses, I think, unless you know of her particular favorite." A quick look at her son's stormy countenance told her he hadn't a clue about Alexa's preference in matters floral. "And," she continued, not discouraged by his stony look, "you shall pen her a pretty note of apology."

"A *what*?" he ejaculated thickly.

"An apology, which shall clinch the matter of your forgiveness."

The earl made another attempt at severing relations between himself and Alexa. "You are very kind to recommend such a course of action, Mama. But I fear the matter is beyond such easy rectifying."

"No one says it shall be easy, Sebby," Lady Winslow replied, exasperated. "I daresay you don't know how to apologize properly to a lady. But that is a fault shared by all of your generation. In any case, I am here to advise you on such critical matters."

"I fear all your advice, splendid as it is, shall be in vain," the earl protested doggedly as the carriage clattered over the cobblestones. "Alexa has her mind firmly set against me."

The countess did not appear persuaded by her son's comments. "I daresay you may have behaved badly, Sebby, but I have never known Alexa Eiseley to be narrow-minded. And I wonder what you did to set her back up. You say the quarrel was over something so trivial you can't even remember it. I do hope it wasn't over some other female!"

"Good God, Mama!" Winslow said, shaken to the core.

An apologetic smile flitted across the countess's face. "Well, I am sorry, Sebby. I didn't really think you such a loose screw, but why else would Alexa take such a firm stand against you?" She clung to his arm again as the carriage careened around a corner. "I don't need to know all the details of your quarrel. I shall speak to her on your behalf tomorrow at tea. I'm sure I can persuade her to forgive you."

"I'm not so certain, Mama."

The countess was known for her amiability and tolerance, but she had reached the end of her patience with her son. "Sebastian!" she said in a tone that always reduced him to the status of a schoolboy. "All this pessimism is most unlike you. Here you have the lady of your dreams within an amesace of St. George's Hanover Square and all you will do is prattle about how she won't have you and your uncertainty of winning her back. Do you mean to let her go without a fight? Rather pudding-hearted of you!''

"Yes! No! I mean—dash it all, Mama—I don't know what I mean now,'' he expostulated, feeling utterly frustrated.

The countess, observing the signs of one in the throes of love, patted him forgivingly on the cheek.

"No, of course you don't, my dear boy. Such are the ways of Cupid."

Just in time Winslow bit back an angry retort. He made however one final attempt to set the matter straight.

"Mama, it's not as simple as it appears to be."

"Yes, I know,'' she said complacently, "but do stop all this weary gloom and tell me: Shall we have your wedding in August or September?''

The next morning as Alexa, in an ivory muslin day dress, sat lingering over her morning coffee and a plate of hot buttered muffins, Walter, the footman, staggered in carrying two enormous bouquets of red and yellow roses, each one nearly as tall as himself.

"They came just now, miss, along with this,'' he said, puffing from his exertions and offering her two notes on a silver tray.

She plucked one of the roses from the bouquet and inhaled its heady fragrance. The scent caused her senses to spin slightly. Then she scanned the first of the two notes and almost immediately erupted in giggles.

Unfortunately, there was no way for Alexa to fully appreciate receiving an apology from the earl, particularly since she had no way of knowing they had quarreled or that the countess herself had dictated every word of the message while her scowling son had applied quill to ink.

The laughter continued to bubble up as Alexa reread the note, hugely enjoying such gems of self-censure as "ridiculous stupidity'' and "error of my ways.'' What on earth had gotten into Winslow?

As she laid one note aside and reached for the other,

Penny came into the morning room and stopped dead at the sight of the roses filling the room.

"Who sent them, Aunt Alexa?" she demanded, skipping over to smell the flowers.

"Winslow," Alexa replied with a smile.

"The earl!" Penny burst out. "Fancy that. He must be trying to get back into your good graces. Will you be seeing him again?"

Alexa, who had been reading the second note, which contained the cure for the toothache, looked up distractedly at her niece.

"What did you say, my dear?"

"I asked if you would be seeing Winslow again," Penny said impatiently.

Alexa frowned. "I suppose so. I am having tea with his mother, so he is bound to be somewhere underfoot." She handed Penny the cure for the toothache with a mischievous grin. "This, I believe, is for you. It's Lady Winslow's recipe for the toothache. You cannot have forgotten that, I hope?"

"But I can't swallow this," Penny protested as she perused the cure, which seemed to be a good deal worse than the ailment. "It sounds dreadful."

Alexa laughed. "That probably means it shall work."

Penny buried her head in the roses. "Do you still think you shan't suit?" she asked.

"What did you say, my dear?"

"You and the earl!" Penny emerged from the flowers. "Just see how he has gone to such lengths of sending you the roses. It would be cruel to dash his hopes. Can't you patch up your quarrel?"

"I'm afraid the quarrel is beyond the patching-up stage," Alexa replied firmly, and then, brooking no arguments, she swept Penny off to decide in which part of the house the roses would look their best.

Ten

Promptly at two o'clock, Alexa, a vision of loveliness in a pelisse of palest Prussian blue and a matching walking dress, arrived at Pulteney Street to take tea with Lady Winslow. Ushered into the Green Saloon, decorated with a dozen austere portraits of the general's military forebears, she found the countess, a study in lavender, presiding prettily over a tray of teacups with no trace of the earl anywhere about the room.

"I dispatched him to the library," Lady Winslow explained, enfolding Alexa in a scented embrace. "A mother can do that, you know," she added with an impish smile. "He shall stay there until I ring for him."

"Is he in your black books then, ma'am?"

The countess shook with genial laughter. "Heavens, no! Sebby, I confess freely, has every part of his father's charm. I never ever had the heart to scold him even as a boy. I suppose I spoiled him," she said reflectively. "But not horridly so, I hope. And he is not so arrogant a creature. At least several of my acquaintances tell me he is always so civil when they meet in the street, which does me great credit, of course. Not"—she sighed—"that I had much to do with that. However, all gentlemen, even the most civil, do get irascible at times—at talk of weddings and particularly their own. This morning, for instance, I merely inquired whether we ought to invite his second cousin Bertram to the wedding, and it was enough to put him into the sulks. He could never abide Bertie, who is, I must own, a bit of an April squire."

A pause in this recital ensued as the countess handed her guest a teacup. "Take this and sit here," she directed, patting the sofa on which she sat. "It is General Cathcart's favorite blend, and I am determined to drink it all up, which will make him cross as crabs when he discovers it. You must assist me in this task, for then I could say with a clear conscience that the fault was not mine alone." She sipped her tea for a moment and gazed across at Alexa. "Actually, my dear, I had another private wish: to speak to you without Sebby looming about. It's this horrid quarrel."

"What horrid quarrel?" Alexa asked innocently.

Lady Winslow arched an eyebrow. "Have you forgotten about it so soon?" she exclaimed with a tinkling laugh. "I felt he had exaggerated, but you know men! They shall make a Cheltenham tragedy of anything! And I do hope you don't think it coming of me to broach the topic, for I promise you I'm not the type of mother forever poking her nose into her son's affairs, or even her daughter's, for that matter. And you may ask Rowena when next you see her!"

"Of course I don't think any such thing of you, Lady Winslow," Alexa replied, a bit confused by the countess's words. She had never considered Sebby's mother to be queer in the attic before, but what was she babbling about? "I'm afraid, however, that I'm in a bit of a fog about this quarrel you refer to."

The countess put down her cup and knitted her brow. "Didn't you have a horrid quarrel with my son?" she asked point-blank.

"Did he say so?" Alexa parried, feeling her way gingerly.

"Indeed he did." The countess's vigorous nod sent all her curls aflutter. "Oh, he fought shy of it at first and merely hinted at it in the most roundabout way last night until I was forced to ask him straight out what he was trying to say. And then he revealed that he had come to cuffs with you on some issue and that it had ended with your calling him a stupid coxcomb."

"Good heavens," Alexa said a trifle unsteadily. "How *uncivil* of me."

The countess waved away her apology. "Oh, I'm quite convinced that he had worse coming to him. Men are the most impossible creatures," she confided with the conspiratorial air of one divulging a state secret. "And you must not think badly of Sebby for confiding in me, for he was desperately convinced that he had lost you. Indeed he did nothing but prattle on about how the engagement was lost until I told him not to be so pudding-hearted and suggested that he make it up to you by sending you the roses. I do hope you liked them, my dear, for he had not the least notion of the flowers you favor. And since gentlemen today never know how to compose a letter of abject apology, I had to pen that for him. I hope together they succeeded in winning forgiveness."

"The roses were lovely, ma'am," Alexa said at once. "And truly I have never read a prettier apology."

"Good, good." Lady Winslow sat back on the velveteen sofa, a pleased look on her face. "I knew you could not be so odiously starched up as to hold one tiny quarrel against him!"

"Well no, of course not. It's just that . . ."

"My dear," the countess pressed on, "you needn't bother to thank me for taking a hand in all this. I am only too pleased to help. As I told Sebby: what are mothers for? Although you may not remember, having lost yours at such a tender age." She blinked back tears. "She was one of my bosom bows, you know, Alexa."

"Yes, I know," Alexa said softly, much touched.

"And," the countess continued, "nothing could be more

provident than to have her daughter and my son linked in matrimony.''

At the mention of matrimony, Alexa choked on her tea, and Lady Winslow obligingly patted her on the back.

"Dear Lady Winslow, you are very kind to say such things to me,'' she said when she had recovered her powers of speech, "but the matter is by no means resolved between your son and me.''

The countess looked momentarily stricken, then a mischievous gleam came into her blue eyes.

"Of course not, my dear,'' she said, emitting a soft chuckle. "It is infinitely more rewarding to have an apology delivered in person, is it not? Shall we conspire and make poor Sebby grovel a trifle? I know it is heartless to say such a thing being his mother, but I am female!'' She gave the bellpull a vigorous tug. "This shall bring the miscreant out.''

"Oh, no, don't do that!'' Alexa cried out in alarm, but it was already too late. The countess rose, a tiny picture of good humor.

"I shall take myself off, never fear, and leave you two to make up in private. But mind I shall only allow you ten minutes to extract all manner of promises for good behavior from him. Then I shall make my return.'' She gave Alexa a fond smile and departed merrily, murmuring "Stupid coxcomb'' and chuckling to herself.

As soon as she had gone, Alexa sank back wearily on the sofa. Make up in private? Quarrel? Just what had Winslow told his mother? Before she had time to dwell further on the matter, Winslow, in a coat of sea blue superfine and matching kerseymere trousers, stalked into the Green Saloon, his nostrils flaring.

"Where is my mother?'' he demanded, seeing Alexa alone.

"Gone, my lord. She thought it best to allow us some private moments to stage our reconciliation.''

He had been advancing into the room but halted at her words. "I should have known you would spoil everything!''

Alexa flushed with indignation at the injustice of such an

accusation. "Spoiled what, pray?" she demanded. "I don't even know yet what Banbury tale you told your mother. How could I, from what little she divulged? And your abject apologies didn't shed any light."

"Don't mention those apologies," he stormed back at her. "She wrote the thing for me."

"So I have been informed."

Her honeyed tone prompted another glare from the earl. "I always thought you had more sense, Alexa. Didn't you wish me to break the news to her about us? That's what I did, after a fashion."

"Winslow, if you do not sit down and explain everything to me at once, I shall go into strong hysterics."

"To match your migraine attack of last evening?" he asked solicitously.

"Bother my migraine! Sit!" To her surprise, he obeyed. "What did you tell your mama?"

Under this blunt attack, the earl colored slightly but made a notable recovery. "I couldn't tell her we had concocted the whole affair as a sham. Instead I said we had quarreled and you had thrown me over. That way she'd be satisfied that we had broken it off. Only she began to suggest ways I could woo you back." A flicker of disgust crossed his face. "She even encouraged me to send flowers and to write that curst letter."

"And you obeyed?" A note of exasperation crept into her voice.

"What else could I do?" he demanded, put on end by her failure to appreciate his situation. "I had to act as though I wanted you back, didn't I?"

Alexa threw her hands up to the ceiling. "Why didn't you just tell her I wasn't the right sort of wife for you?"

"How could I say such a thing, with her tallying up a list of your virtues daily. I'm getting deuced aggravated hearing how sweet-tempered, intelligent, charming, gracious, not to say beautiful, you are!"

She could not help laughing at his glowering face.

"What is so amusing?" he asked crossly.

"Nothing." She stifled her giggles. "It's just that I have

rarely heard such wonderful compliments delivered in so reluctant a manner.''

"Don't be a minx," he retorted, but his tone softened. He ran his fingers through his hair. "Did you tell Mama you forgave me the quarrel?"

"When she left the room that was her impression," Alexa acknowledged.

She expected more Sturm und Drang, but to her surprise the earl absorbed this blow philosophically.

"We'll have to contrive something else. Perhaps another quarrel?"

Her gaze was stern. "I don't doubt, Winslow, that you are accustomed to quarreling every second with your acquaintances, but I am not. And I should hate to be thought so quarrelsome by your mama. Why did you even need to invent a quarrel in the first place? You could have said I was too tall or thin or sensible or flighty, and cried off."

"And have Mama haranguing me about it for the rest of my life?" the earl asked. "Need I remind you that she thinks you a paragon among women?"

"Poor, poor Sebby," Alexa soothed. "But in truth I bore much of the same treatment from George. He could not get over my excellent choice in gentlemen."

"In which case I fully appreciate why you left Ferring for Bath."

"Let's be clear on one point," Alexa said firmly. "I am not about to marry you."

"Good Jupiter, I know that even if my mama doesn't."

"But she must," Alexa insisted. "And I think the sooner the better, lest we find ourselves at St. George's! You must prevail on her to listen to you."

The earl shook his head. "You have forgotten, Alexa, that I had my attempt at telling Mama the truth last night and I made a mull of it, receiving for my efforts a lecture on my ill-formed penmanship and the constant deploring of my generation. Apparently, we gentlemen now can't hold a candle to those of my father's generation. I believe it's your turn at telling Mama the truth."

Her eyes never wavered from his. "I never knew you to be such a coward, Sebby."

"Not to mention a stupid coxcomb," he said with undiminished affability, "but the roses took care of any names you might call me."

Just as Alexa was about to utter a scorching indictment of men too spineless to do their duty, the countess reappeared in the doorway, wearing a sunny smile.

"My dears, is the breach fully healed by now?" she asked, gaily stepping in before coming to a rigid halt. "Sebby, whatever are you doing on that chair? You should be on the sofa, next to Alexa. Yes," she nodded as he reluctantly obeyed her, "that is much better. To think of you being in such a quake last evening. I told you Alexa was broad-minded."

"Indeed you did, Mama," Winslow agreed. "I can only bow to your greater understanding of your sex."

His mother beamed at them both. "Have some tea," she commanded, "and then let's talk about your wedding."

"Mama," Winslow choked.

"I suppose we can put off for now deciding just whom we should invite," she acknowledged, paying no heed to her son, "but I think it essential to decide just where it shall be and when. Here it is, almost the tail end of July, and August practically upon us."

Alexa, aware that Winslow's courage was wilting fast in the face of his mother's assault, decided to take the bull by the horns.

"Lady Winslow," she interjected, "I think it only fair to tell you—"

"Do you have a great many people to invite, my dear?" The countess turned an inquiring eye her way. "That is always the case for a bride! But you needn't worry. We shall fit them in somehow. If necessary," she said, making the grand gesture, "I'll even sacrifice Cousin Bertram!"

"That is sweet of you, ma'am," Alexa said, doggedly bent on her course, "but still—"

Lady Winslow reached out and cupped Alexa's chin, silencing her. "My dear child, for my son's bride nothing could ever be enough. I can confess now to having been somewhat alarmed in the past at having such a confirmed bachelor in the family. And it delights me no end that he had the wit and the good luck to offer for you, and that you saw fit to accept him. I know you have scores of admirers in London, and I am just so proud of the two of you I could burst! So eminently suited! So charming a pair! What more could any mother ask for?'' She dabbed at her eyes with a handkerchief. ''Pray, don't think me a watering pot! But you wanted to tell me something, Alexa?''

Here loomed the perfect opening! But how could anyone tell the countess that all her hopes for her son were naught but an air dream? One look at Lady Winslow's guileless face and Alexa felt her resolution drain away. It was impossible, just as Winslow had warned it would be.

''No, ma'am,'' she said softly as she avoided the earl's mocking eyes. ''I did not wish to say anything except to thank you for your kindness in welcoming me.''

As Lady Winslow smiled beatifically, Alexa sat back, trying her best not to notice the superior smile decorating the face of Lady Winslow's only son.

A distinctly nuptial air settled over the three occupants of the drawing room during the next half hour, an atmosphere finally shattered by the arrival of the countess's favorite poet, bearing, it seemed, another labor of love in his grubby hands. This ode, Winslow surmised from the distance, was at least two dozen stanzas in length.

The earl's second encounter with Hormfeld proved no more rewarding than his first. Daylight had worked no miracles on the poet. With his hair all about his face and a coat that he had probably slept in, Mr. Hormfeld appeared even more simianlike than the earl had at first supposed. Watching the poet bow over his mother's hand, Winslow took the opportunity to leave.

''For I know, Mama, how you must treasure Mr. Hormfeld's odes and will wish to hear them in private!''

''And I must go, too, Lady Winslow,'' Alexa said, following Winslow's cue, only too glad to beat her own retreat. ''Thank you for the tea and the chat.''

"Dear Alexa, I shall see you soon again, I hope," the countess said, pressing her cheek warmly against the other woman's. "Do you plan to attend the Hackett-Jones affair?"

"I'll be bringing Penny."

"Wonderful! I shall attend as well. It might be a trifle boring, but at least there is always whist!"

Together, Winslow and Alexa exited the Green Saloon.

"Don't say a word," she warned as they went down the stairs.

He turned, an affable smile on his handsome face. "Say what, Miss Eiseley? I am too much a coward to say a word at all, remember?"

She grimaced. "I was all prepared to do the thing. But your mama had such a look on her face. It would have been like kicking a puppy. But you must tell her, Sebby! Somehow or another!"

"I know," he muttered. "The longer we put it off, the more of a Chinese puzzle it becomes."

"She has us practically marching down the aisle of St. George's together," Alexa pointed out. She halted abruptly on the stairs, almost causing him to trip over her. "Winslow, I have it! The way out of this coil."

"Do you, by God? Well, speak!" he urged.

She choked on a laugh. "You must marry someone else!"

The excitement drained from his face, to be replaced by utter bafflement. "I must what?" he demanded.

"Marry someone else," she repeated calmly.

The earl stood on the stairs, staring at her as though she belonged in Bedlam.

"Alexa," he chided, "you're foxed—and from tea no less!"

A fresh attack of giggles overcame her. "I am not," she declared finally. "And do pay attention, Sebby. Surely your mama couldn't expect me to marry you if you were already leg-shackled."

"I suppose not," he acknowledged faintly. "I believe

even Mama would realize the legal difficulties of such an endeavor. But your idea is absurd.''

''Why?'' she asked, tilting her face up to his. ''You must be prepared to marry some time in your life. Only think of your title going to waste. And should you need any assistance in finding ladies of quality, I shall be glad to introduce you. Although,'' she said pensively, ''Bath is rather thin of company now.''

For several moments, Winslow leaned against the polished banister, bent nearly double with laughter.

''Alexa,'' he said, wiping his streaming eyes, ''you are outrageous and so is this idea.''

''Why?'' she demanded. ''You must realize you are not so disagreeable to some ladies. In fact, Bronwyn was telling me only last night that there are a full dozen who would snap you up in a trice, and she couldn't think why I was so stupid as to spurn you.''

The earl took his spurning without a blink. ''I don't want to marry anyone,'' he announced.

''That is disobliging of you, Sebby,'' Alexa said reproachfully. ''Here I thought it the perfect answer to our troubles. For your mama has been so excited over the prospect of a wedding that it seemed a shame to cheat her out of that spectacle. Are you certain you shan't wish to rethink the matter? And have you given a moment's thought to Bronwyn herself? She's quite the best of persons, good-tempered, very pretty and so kind. She's been married before, and I'm sure she shall make any man a splendid wife.''

''I'm sure she shall,'' Winslow said cordially, ''but do give over broaching that idea to me. You can't have considered the consequence of such a jingle-brained notion. You would be jilted!''

This aspect of the situation sobered Alexa momentarily. ''I suppose I would. And that would be unpleasant, for people would be bound to talk, but I suppose it would be better—''

''Than to marry an ogre like me?'' he finished for her with a lift of his autocratic brow.

"Now, Sebby, how could you think I would say anything so uncivil?"

"You don't need to," he replied dryly. "And I'm only glad that dear Mama isn't at hand to hear you spurn me so shabbily, for she dotes on me so." He flicked her cheek with a careless finger. "Like it or not, Miss Eiseley, for the time being you and I *are* engaged!"

An hour later as Winslow sat in the general's book room pondering a way out of his entanglement with Alexa, his mother burst in.

"Really, Sebby, how could you have been so heartless as to leave me with that Mr. Hormfeld? Such desertion in my hour of need!"

"How now, Mama," Winslow replied, a smile playing around his lips, "you know that propriety dictates a gentleman absent himself when his mama is being made love to by another, *particularly* when the other is a poet!"

The countess shrieked with laughter. "You absurd boy. As though I enjoy being bored to tears."

The earl feigned shock. "Am I to deduce your interest in poetry is on the wane?"

"Yes, and I only hope Alexa's is on the rise."

He looked up in surprise. "Alexa's?" He noticed for the first time that his mother was carrying a book in her hand. "What the devil is that?" he asked with sudden suspicion.

"A volume of Mr. Hormfeld's collected verse," Lady Winslow replied. "That is what brought him to me on the run. They are fresh from the printer. Smell the ink if you like."

"I shouldn't wish to do any such thing," her son announced in accents of loathing.

"I don't blame you," the countess said complacently, "for I know you dislike verse of any sort, particularly romantic verse. But the poems are quite pretty, if one isn't obliged to hear them trumpeted into one's ear by their creator."

"The cover appears handsome enough," the earl said,

turning it over in his hand. "I suppose it is personally inscribed?"

"Mine is, but that one isn't. It's yours."

Winslow dropped the book as though it were a burning coal. "Good heavens, Mama. What do I need with such drivel?"

"You could always put it in your library at Winslow Park," she said airily with a wave of a lavender sleeve. "The binding is handsome, as you say. You needn't feel under any obligation to actually read it. Or"—a new inspiration struck—"you might give it to Alexa as another token of your esteem."

"And be thought a queer nab?" he asked. "No, thank you, Mama. And how comes it that your poet is so free with his precious volumes?"

"He isn't," she contradicted, picking up the book on the carpet. "I am. I had promised him weeks ago to buy a few volumes to help him, for he is having them printed himself and he is dreadfully poor."

"Poverty is a state not unfamiliar to most poets," the earl observed, his eyes on his mother's face. "Just how few did you see fit to buy?"

"Two dozen," she answered in a small voice.

"Mama, you didn't!" His protest was immediate.

"Well, of course I did, Sebby," Lady Winslow said, "for I felt obliged to. After all, I am his inspiration at the moment, though I daresay that shan't last long. And I really don't begrudge the sum."

"How much did your generosity cost you?"

"The volumes would have cost a hundred pounds," she replied, so earnestly that he could not help smiling a little. "No more than what I would squander on one of my day dresses. But Mr. Hormfeld insisted on charging me only a mere fifty pounds and in fact foisted a fifty-pound note on me when I gave him the hundred. So I am quite satisfied that I got the better deal."

Her son shook his head. "Hormfeld got the better deal, but I shan't ring a peal over it."

"Thank you," his mother said sweetly. "You are always so understanding and sensible, just like your papa."

"There is, however, a limit to my sensibility, Mama," he informed her. "I must insist that you contrive to be rather less captivating to your poet, so you shan't feel under any further obligation to buy his wretched verse."

"I shall do my very best, Sebby," she said with a chuckle.

And there the matter of Mr. Hormfeld's verse rested.

Eleven

"I do wish you would make up your mind, Aunt Alexa," Penny complained when Alexa returned to Milsom Street and informed her niece that she was once again engaged to Winslow. "First you will have him and then you will not. I vow I've never known you to be so volatile and on such an important issue as marriage!"

Well aware that she was setting a poor example for her charge on how a lady of quality ought to conduct a betrothal and subsequent marriage, Alexa felt a momentary pang of conscience.

"It is because marriage is so important," she offered lamely, "that I have been a trifle undecided."

"But you are decided now, aren't you?" Penny asked, studying her closely.

"For the time being, yes," Alexa responded, and Penny, taking this as a sign that she would shortly realize her dream of being a bridesmaid at her beloved aunt's wedding, dealt her a fond peck on the cheek and then swooped off to tell Courtney the good news.

"And I do hope," said Courtney's sister two days later when Alexa climbed into the tilbury bound for a shopping expedition, "that I too can be one of your bridesmaids, along with little Penny."

"Bronwyn, don't you *dare* jest about this engagement!" Alexa implored.

Bronwyn's dark eyes twinkled at her friend. "Very well, my dear," she said, obviously not trying very hard to comply with this order. "But even you must own that the situation has its humorous side. You are perhaps the most feted lady I know. And there's Winslow, who has had more caps set at him than even a royal duke, besides being much handsomer than any of the dukes. And the two of you allied in such a ramshackle fashion."

"You may find yourself in as great a fix someday," Alexa warned.

"Not I!" Bronwyn said airily, taking a corner of the road expertly. "I am more than contented with my widowhood."

She then took pity on her friend and said no more about the engagement, but privately she was convinced that such a match—however oddly arranged—might be the making of both parties. Out of the corner of her eye, she watched Alexa's brooding face. The match had at first surprised Bronwyn, but further reflection had brought her close to Lady Winslow's point of view. The two were admirably matched, and Bronwyn felt that Alexa would be happy with Winslow and he with her. She knew better, however, than to point out such an obvious fact to so intractable a pair.

Now she pulled the tilbury up short in front of a millinery, and the two ladies descended to pass a full hour arguing over the merits of all the latest hats and bonnets. They rejected with much derision the current craze for the Oldenburg hat, a perfectly hideous fashion in Alexa's own opinion, and settled on two charming straw bonnets, perfect for the sultry summer weather.

As Alexa paid for her purchase, Bronwyn wandered toward the window, her eyes drawn by a tall, rather familiar figure entering a doorway down the street.

"Shall we try the hot buttered cakes at Sally Lunn's?" Alexa asked as they left the shop, carrying their parcels.

"If you wish it," Bronwyn said, so distractedly that Alexa dealt her a look of inquiry.

"Should you rather return home?"

"Oh, no . . . it's just that I could have sworn I saw Major Jayneway going into a dressmaker's shop. But what would Archie be doing in such a place?"

"Why don't we go and ask him," Alexa suggested, and after depositing the parcels in the carriage, they walked farther on toward the shop in question. Once inside, they found a veritable bevy of matrons with daughters in tow but not a sign of the major.

Bronwyn frowned. "Now, that's peculiar, because he came in here. I know it."

"It can't be that important, can it?" Alexa asked, her attention drawn away from Major Jayneway's whereabouts to some lace displayed on a table.

"I suppose not," Bronwyn replied, following her over to the lace, "but it is odd not to find him here."

"Is madame interested in the Brussels lace?" The owner of the shop came forward wearing an ingratiating smile.

Alexa allowed herself to be persuaded to buy a foot of the lace, and while the purchase was being wrapped, Bronwyn conducted a swift search for the major in the shop, a search that soon had Alexa in giggles.

"Bronwyn," she hissed. "I hardly think you will find Archie hiding under that table! You must be mistaken!"

"Impossible!" Bronwyn's tone was so insistent that Alexa was taken aback.

"That hair of his is quite distinctive," Bronwyn started to explain, then broke off as the shopkeeper handed the parcel of lace to Alexa. Impulsively, Bronwyn addressed the shopkeeper.

"By any chance did you happen to notice a gentleman in here within the last ten minutes? A very tall man. Sandy-colored hair."

A flicker of unease flitted across the shopkeeper's face.

"I cannot say, madame," she replied, pursing her lips and turning away at once.

"She is keeping something from us," Bronwyn complained as they left the shop and walked back toward the tilbury. "I'm sure it was Archie I saw. And I know why he was there."

"Do you, by Jove?" Alexa said, her eyes widening in anticipation.

"He was in there commissioning something for one of his *chère amies*!"

Alexa took another incredulous look at her companion, who appeared to be perfectly earnest.

"Bronwyn, that's ridiculous! Archie has never so much as dabbled in the muslin company."

"There is always a first time," Bronwyn said, setting her jaw. "And why else would the shopkeeper fight shy of telling us about his presence in her shop unless she thought that I was his wife."

Alexa was hard put to express an opinion of this rather besotted notion of her friend's. She climbed into the tilbury and waited while Bronwyn flicked the reins lightly on the horses' backs.

"That would serve as an answer to what he was doing in her shop, and why he didn't wish to be seen by us!"

"It could be otherwise," Alexa protested. "Perhaps he meant to pick up something for a female relation and fought shy of being seen there."

Bronwyn paused a moment to mull over this opinion before rejecting it.

"His mother is dead," she pointed out, "so he can't be commissioning anything for her. And he has few female relations other than a sister he can't abide who lives in Bristol."

Alexa raised her eyebrows in astonishment at such an extensive knowledge of the Jayneway family tree.

"How is it you know so much about Archie's family?" she inquired.

Bronwyn shifted the reins lightly in her hands. "Because of Courtney. We've seen him now and then in Bath, and he has taken a great interest in her, coming to call at least twice a week at Queen Square. And while I saw nothing against such a match if it ever came to fruition, if he is commissioning dresses for a *chère amie* at the same time he is courting my sister, he shall have a rude awakening coming.''

''I can't believe such a thing of him,'' Alexa protested, alarmed by the vehemence in Bronwyn's voice. ''Living in London, I'm sure any number of acquaintances would have delighted in passing on such an *on-dit* if he were dabbling in the petticoat line. But Archie has never shown predilection for any barque of frailty!''

''Perhaps not before now,'' Bronwyn replied, looking far from convinced. ''But all the same, he might have been under the spell of some bird of paradise, and I shall have to keep a sharper eye on him when he next comes to visit Courtney!''

Lady Hackett-Jones was known behind her back as the grand old lady of Bath, an epithet that even she might have accepted with equanimity since she was old, a lady and grand.

Lady Winslow had known her ever since they were girls squabbling over hair ribbons, and as such the earl had anticipated his mother's attendance at the ball the Hackett-Joneses were throwing in honor of Mr. Gideon Ramsey. He was, however, unprepared at being ordered to accompany her there.

''You have escorts aplenty, Mama,'' he said, trying his best to thwart such a plan over a lunch of steamed turbot and cold melon.

''None of them can hold a candle to my son,'' the countess answered, pointing a silver fork at him. ''Or have you suddenly grown ashamed of your decrepit mama?''

Winslow's shoulders quaked with laughter. ''Don't try and gammon me! Decrepit, indeed. You shall be the most radiant female within miles.''

''Next to Alexa,'' Lady Winslow amended, chewing thoughtfully on some melon. ''That is the other reason you should come along with me. You can't have forgotten that you promised faithfully to see her the night of the ball.''

Winslow frowned, recollecting nothing of the sort.

''I recall that you promised to see her there, Mama. I said nothing.''

''And that strikes me as something you do with uncommon frequency whenever Alexa is concerned,'' his mother chided. ''Confess, Sebby. You haven't see her since the day she came to tea, have you?''

''Well, no,'' he acknowledged, trying his best to avoid her quizzing stare. ''But I've been dashed busy. Had an appointment with my tailor and then had to ride out with Lamb, whom I met one day in town.''

''Which, no doubt, leaves Alexa with the continued belief that you are bent on slighting her,'' his mother complained. She laid down her fork and poked him with a forefinger. ''Upon my word, Sebby, I don't believe you young men have the first notion of how a courtship ought to be conducted. I wager you didn't even send her that volume of Mr. Hormfeld's verse, did you?''

''No,'' he answered thickly, ''but Alexa isn't interested in Hormfeld's poetry.''

''Probably not,'' Lady Winslow admitted, ''but she might be interested in yours. You might think about writing her a poem yourself.''

A look of mild revulsion crossed the earl's face. ''A poem, Mama? Who, me?''

''Yes, of course you!'' came the impatient reply. ''Who else am I talking to in this room? I daresay you must have composed a poem for some other chit during your mad larks in the past.''

He shook his head meekly. His mother was thunderstruck.

''Good heavens, what is the world coming to? All the same, writing verse can't be so very difficult, for Mr. Hormfeld does it with scarcely any thought at all, and you are ever so much cleverer than he is.''

''You are too kind, Mama,'' he drawled.

She studied him for a moment. ''I suppose I am partial,

but I should have to be a goose not to see how vastly you outshine him. Would you like me to help you with your poem, Sebby? I daresay nothing could be easier. I have heard any number of them from Mr. Hormfeld and consider myself practically an expert!''

Winslow laughed. ''Thank you for the offer, Mama, but I shouldn't even attempt such a herculean effort as to compose an ode to Alexa, however worthy she is of such tributes, nor,'' he said, anticipating her next words on the subject, ''even a simple sonnet. But to make amends for this failing, I shall accompany you to Lady Hackett-Jones's affair.''

The countess accepted his capitulation with becoming modesty and chewed meditatively on her melon. ''Sebby, I daresay you shall think me as curious as a cat, but I can't help wondering if you love Alexa.''

A piece of turbot appeared to have lodged itself in Winslow's throat as he choked. Coughing and swallowing hard, he glanced up at his mother's innocent face.

''My word, Mama, what questions you do ask over a simple luncheon. And what, may I ask, prompts such a question?''

''Your preference for a tailor's company over Alexa's, for one thing,'' the countess countered tartly.

A rueful smile crossed the earl's lips. ''Have I really been acting in such a *gudgeonish* fashion, Mama? No, you needn't answer that, for I see plainly from your face that I have. Will you forgive me if I promise to mend my ways at once and be as charmingly devoted to Alexa as I ought to be?'' he asked.

He said it all so winningly that Lady Winslow could do naught but bestow her blessing on him. It wasn't until later, as she sat idly sketching in her sitting room, that she realized her son had not really answered her question at all.

Promptly at eight o'clock, the countess of Winslow entered Lord and Lady Hackett-Jones's residence on Milsom Street, accompanied by her handsome son. Resplendent this evening in a glittering emerald green ball gown, she was led up the portals and the shimmering staircase to their host and hostess.

After chatting comfortably and shaking hands with his mother's old friends, Winslow passed with her into the ballroom, already teeming with music and the lights from a thousand candles. Automatically, he put up his quizzing glass. The sea of dew-laden cheeks caught his eye and drew a sigh, one which his mother overheard.

"Troubled, Sebby?" she inquired solicitously.

He put down the glass and gave her a small smile. "No, Mama, not troubled. But I shall undoubtedly be bored to tears before this night is at an end."

"They do look green, don't they," Lady Winslow admitted.

"If they were any greener, they wouldn't have hatched yet!" the earl opined.

"I daresay I shall have to adjourn to the card room after a bit," his mother went on. "But you must dance. You waltz divinely."

There was, however, no love of dancing apparent on Winslow's face at his mother's suggestion.

"You can't expect me to dance with nursery brats," he expostulated. "I promised to accompany you here. But no one, not even Wellington himself, can induce me to dance with such schoolroom misses as these!"

"Don't be idiotish," his mother commanded. "Alexa is far from being a schoolroom miss, and I certainly expect you to dance with her. There she is, with that pretty friend of hers, Mrs. Finch. Come along," she ordered briskly. "I wish to speak to her."

Under this prodding, Winslow had no alternative but to follow his mother across the crowded ballroom to Alexa and Bronwyn.

"Good evening, my dear Alexa," Lady Winslow said, greeting Alexa, who looked quite elegant in saffron-colored muslin opening over silver satin. The Ionic sleeves added a charming counterpoint to her hair, which was done up in a Grecian knot.

"Good evening, Lady Winslow," Alexa returned, emerging uncrushed from Lady Winslow's embrace. "Sebby."

"Alexa." He bowed formally.

The countess turned despairing eyes to Bronwyn, an avid witness to this encounter.

"Mrs. Finch, have you ever in your life seen such an odiously *civil* greeting, particularly between two who are betrothed?"

"Never, ma'am," Bronwyn replied, a devilish sparkle in her own eyes. "But perhaps Sebby is *restraining* himself and his ardor for our sake, ma'am."

"Bronwyn," the earl informed her, "you are almost as incorrigible as my mother." He held out his slim hand to Alexa. "You look radiant, my dear. And now I beg you to accept my invitation to waltz with all possible restraint, of course."

Laughing, she put her hand in his and followed him out onto the floor. "They mean well, you must realize," she murmured, darting a quick look at the speculative gazes following them.

"I should have been an orphan," her partner announced.

"You don't mean that!"

His eyes met hers and softened immediately. "No," he apologized. "I don't. But was there ever such a mother! We are passing under her nose, so do I beg you, look suitably enchanted by me!"

Giggling a little, she complied with his request, looking up at him in such a besotted way that he very nearly trounced on her foot.

"Will that convince her, Winslow?" she asked demurely when the countess was out of view.

"It should," he replied dryly. "It very nearly convinced me!"

She laughed again, enjoying the delicious feel of the music and the couples swirling all about them. She was also beginning to enjoy the ball, which only minutes before she had deplored to Bronwyn as being sadly wanting.

"What are you doing here, anyway, Sebby?" she asked. "Hardly your run of things."

He smiled down at her. "Try telling that to my mother. She's convinced that this is the only way to make amends with you."

Her hazel eyes danced. "Amends, is it? Don't tell me we have flown into another pet with each other, Winslow. And I do wish you would give me fair warning."

"We haven't quarreled," he said dampeningly. "But according to Mama, I have been slighting you by not dangling after you."

"How uncivil of you!" she exclaimed with another laugh.

"Don't be missish," he retorted. "Only this afternoon Mama informed me that a gentleman like me ought to be able to compose a decent ode to his lady love."

Her laughter broke out without restraint, making it all but impossible for her to dance. "I hope you shan't feel obliged to pen that ode," she said at last. "For I vow I have been up to my ears in poems already from Mr. Hormfeld."

The earl looked up with keen interest at this news. "What, Mama's poet? Have you stolen him from her?"

"Your mama is more than welcome to Mr. Hormfeld and any other poet I may unwittingly steal," Alexa said strictly. "And while you may laugh and think it a great joke, I assure you there is nothing in the least funny about being obliged to listen to the most dreary selection of verse and the most inept rhymes about my beauty!"

This drew a smile from him. "Come, come, Alexa!" he scolded. "You're as bad as Mama. I daresay half the females in Bath would give their wisdoms to have such odes written to them."

"They shall probably have their turn with Mr. Hormfeld if they are patient enough," Alexa said.

He whirled her around, and she caught sight of Major Jayneway in his regimentals. This brought a quick end to her views on poets.

"There's Archie," she said in an altered tone.

"So it is," Winslow said, following her gaze. "Thank God! I had begun to fear that mine was the only face that knew of whiskers!"

"Does it make you repine for your youth, Winslow?" she teased.

He blenched. "I'm not in my dotage yet, my girl!" he protested. "And I'd hardly repine for my youth. Didn't even know the first thing about tying a decent cravat back then!"

"Yes, I know," she said with a smile. "Your first attempt at the Mathematical still puts me into whoops whenever I think of it."

He stared across at her. "How comes it that you remember my first attempt?" he demanded.

"I could hardly forget it," she retorted. "Particularly when you came to dinner with this huge cloth swathed about your neck and midway it fell into the turtle soup!"

He laughed along with her. "I was a bit of an April squire, wasn't I? I had half forgotten you were visiting us that day."

"That comes as no surprise to me. You rarely took much heed of me."

"An April squire and a dolt," Winslow said in self-reproach. "But I hope that I am making up for such lapses now."

She felt a faint color stain her cheeks at his words, which she tried to dismiss as mere gallantry. Nevertheless, she was relieved when the waltz ended and he escorted her back to her chair, then went off to have a word with Major Jayneway, a circumstance that his mother viewed with acute disfavor from across the room.

"I would only admit it to you, Constance," she complained to Lady Hackett-Jones, who had finally finished her duties as a hostess and was enjoying a moment with her, "but Sebby can be such a nodcock. Just see how he leaves Alexa all to herself!"

Lady Hackett-Jones willingly squinted myopically into the distance. "Not alone, it appears to me, Elizabeth," she said in a booming alto. "She has someone with her."

"That little niece of hers is no protection from any would-be Brummell," Lady Winslow said darkly.

"Thought the announcement was in the *Gazette*," Lady

Hackett-Jones said gruffly. "Practically makes the marriage a *fait accompli*!"

"There's many a slip 'twixt the cup and the lip." Lady Winslow trotted out this old chestnut grimly. "And you needn't point out that we're talking about a wedding and not claret, for I know that. There!" She nodded in grim self-satisfaction. "Just so! The minute Sebby moves off, Colonel Montcalm comes in like a wolf!"

On the other side of the ballroom, Alexa was greeting Colonel Montcalm with every sign of pleasure. It was certainly enjoyable to see a familiar face among the downy sea surrounding her.

"What draws you to Bath?" she asked as Penny succumbed to the entreaty of a young gentleman down from Oxford and went off with him to dance the quadrille.

"You draw me, dear Miss Eiseley," the colonel said, promptly taking the chair Penny had just vacated. His eyes were very bright as he drew his head closer to hers. "I rode over to Ferring the other day, only to be informed by your brother that you had developed a sudden passion for the waters here."

He dealt her such a curious look that she wondered just how much George—whose tongue was prone to run on wheels—had told him.

"Shall you be here long?" she asked, changing the topic quickly.

"As long as you are here," he replied immediately and lifted her hand to his lips in a salute which startled her and alarmed Lady Winslow, who had been eyeing the exchange with some misgivings.

"Did you see that?" she hissed to Lady Hackett-Jones, who was obliged to inform her friend that she wasn't quite so eagle-eyed as she used to be in her youth.

"If Sebby isn't more attentive," the countess continued, undaunted by this revelation, "Colonel Montcalm shall steal a march on him with Alexa. Where is that dratted boy?"

"Montcalm, is it?" Lady Hackett-Jones swiveled her turbaned head sharply and clucked her tongue.

"What is it, Constance?" Lady Winslow asked at once.

Lady Hackett-Jones waved a bejeweled arm. "Nothing, Eliza. Merely that I had heard some prattle about him. You wouldn't be interested."

"Of course I would be interested!" Lady Winslow said trenchantly. "Tell me all."

Lady Hackett-Jones, after assuring herself that no one could overhear, bent her head closer to her friend's.

"Rumor has it he's in the suds. Hasn't a feather left to fly with anymore."

"But his inheritance . . . I recollect an uncle left him very well off."

"Squandered it." Lady Hackett-Jones sniffed. "Playing the Exchange, and his estates are impoverished. He's trying to hush the matter up, of course, or so they say. And Alexa Eiseley would have to be a silly chit to throw over your Sebby for the colonel. I daresay if she didn't have a fortune herself he wouldn't give her a passing glance."

"And that makes him twice as dangerous!" Lady Winslow said, putting two and two together and coming up with a fortune hunter. "Fortune hunters always go to such pains to make themselves pleasant."

Much as she wished to throw a spanner in the works between the colonel and Alexa, she deemed it improbable that Montcalm would attempt to seduce Alexa in full view of the guests in the ballroom. So she at last succumbed to the temptation of whist and made for the card room.

She was joined at the table after half an hour by Major Jayneway, who had had his attempts to dance with Courtney and Bronwyn rudely rebuffed and who gave proof that those unlucky in love did hold some advantage in cards, for at the end of play he was declared the winner.

"And I do think that unjust," Lady Winslow was complaining later to her son when he escorted her to the supper room. "For why should someone as handsome as Archie have a run of good luck at the gaming tables?"

"Are your losses so dear, Mama?" Winslow asked. "Shall I be obliged to pawn some heirlooms to redeem your losses?"

Her quick laughter rang out. "No! As though I don't know any better than to stake jewelry, which I have never done even when I was sorely tempted. I recollect once Lady Partridge did such a besotted thing—stake her jewelry, I mean—and a rather pretty little bauble it was! But then she lost it and was obliged to tell Partridge about it, and he cut the ugly over it, practically forbidding her to gamble anymore, which made her so testy that she moped herself into a decline and eventually ran off to the Continent with one of her cicisbeos."

"What a fetching story, Mama," the earl drawled, his laughter very bright in his eyes. "Are you giving me fair warning of following in Lady Partridge's footsteps and running off with your poet?"

"Good God, no!" Lady Winslow ejaculated in real horror. She halted at the door of the supper room. "My word, Sebastian, where are your manners? Alexa!"

"Alexa has already gone into supper with Penny, Bronwyn and Colonel Montcalm."

This offhand mention of Colonel Montcalm startled the countess. "Sebby, you and I must have a little talk. It's urgent."

"Yes, whenever you like, Mama," he agreed indulgently as he led her gently into the supper room. "Only I see Alexa in the corner signaling to us, so I suppose we must postpone our little talk for the time being." He led her toward the table with the others.

"You shall join us, Lady Winslow, won't you?" Alexa invited.

"My dear, we shall be delighted to," the countess replied, sitting down next to the colonel, who was preparing to enjoy the repast, which included not only lobster patties but a goodly selection of other dishes, including succulent duckling and hot buttered cakes from Sally Lunn's. As she ate, the countess prattled on happily about the ball, her losses in the card room and her profound relief that no cits or mushrooms had found their way into the party.

"For so many of them are naught but fortune hunters,"

she said, forking another lobster patty into her mouth and directing a circumspect look at the colonel.

"How do you know so much about mushrooms and cits?" Winslow inquired, helping himself to another portion of cake. "You're hardly the type to be acquainted with them."

"Nevertheless, one hears the most alarming stories," his mother informed them. "Not, of course, that every fortune hunter *must* be a cit, for I daresay more than a few are of respectable birth. Wouldn't you say, Colonel Montcalm?"

The colonel, a bit surprised at the entire topic, glanced up momentarily to meet her steely blue eyes.

"What would I know of fortune hunters, ma'am?" he asked with aplomb.

"Why, nothing at all, I'm sure," she said innocently but with a look that spoke volumes.

The evening passed without further incident, but the countess's conviction that the colonel was hankering after Alexa's fortune led her the next morning to pay an unexpected call on her prospective daughter-in-law to warn her.

Her worst fears were realized when she stepped into the drawing room to find Alexa, looking lovely as always in a gauzy summer frock, entertaining with every sign of enjoyment the fortune hunter himself!

The countess's response was immediate and aimed at ending the tête-à-tête in progress. Inserting herself bodily between the two of them on the couch, she turned the conversation, not without difficulty, toward weddings and betrothal plans in general, and those of her son and Alexa in particular.

Colonel Montcalm, recognizing a master strategist at work, had no choice but to withdraw, only pausing momentarily to remind Alexa of her promise to accompany him on a ride to the Saxon fortification at the Lansdown some time in the future.

"Is Colonel Montcalm a very old friend of yours, my dear?" Lady Winslow asked after he had been dispatched.

Alexa looked up in some surprise. "I've known him ever since my come-out. And although he is not among my intimates, he is the drollest person and really quite pleasant, don't you think, ma'am?''

The countess, who had a rather different image of the colonel, confessed to a lack of acquaintanceship with the colonel. She also debated inwardly how to warn the other woman about Montcalm's intentions. It might, under the circumstances, be considered somewhat *de trop*.

Finally, she decided that for the moment the less said about the colonel the better and pressed on to have Alexa set a date for the wedding. Alexa, however, feeling as though she were drowning in the tide of all the wedding talk emanating from the countess, felt unable to make any such decision. Her unexpected display of missishness brought a frown to the countess's brow.

''My dear, are you afraid of the wedding?''

''No, heavens.''

Lady Winslow reached across to clasp her hand. ''Really, if you are, you have no need to be embarrassed. Such bouts of nerves are quite common, I assure you. Even I on my wedding day felt the strongest misgivings, but once I had married Winslow I was most content. And I know that you and Sebby, having known one another practically all your lives and being such good friends, shall be equally suited for marriage.''

''Yes, I'm sure we shall,'' Alexa said, feeling nothing of the sort. ''But must we set the date today?''

''No, my dear, but soon, very soon,'' Lady Winslow said, her words falling on Alexa's ears like a gaol sentence from a judge.

Twelve

In the week that followed, Alexa encountered the colonel with increasing frequency during her daily rounds of Bath. At first she thought it the sheerest coincidence that he should be walking down Russell Street to the Pump Room when she arrived to take the waters. But she soon realized that if she ventured out with Penny, perhaps to Sydney Gardens, inevitably before the outing ended they would cross the colonel's path.

Although gratified to receive such assiduous attention from any gentleman, she was uncertain that she wished to encourage him lest Winslow, in another fit of pique, accuse her once again of being a hurly-burly female.

Lady Winslow, for her part, did not consider Alexa a hurly-burly female. Her lively imagination had sketched quite a different role for Miss Eiseley, that of an innocent pursued by the colonel for his own nefarious ends. Such imaginings caused her great alarm but left her son singularly unmoved.

Not even the countess's coy hint one morning as they sat

together in her sitting room that Colonel Montcalm appeared to be running tame in Alexa's establishment, a minor lapse into exaggeration, bestirred the slightest spark of interest in the earl, which led his mother to remark acidly that one would almost think he wished Alexa to marry some other man.

Her words were so near the mark that the earl glanced up guiltily.

"How can you think such a thing of me, Mama?" he protested.

"I don't know," she retorted, pushing away her stitchery in distraction. "But I do know that you and Alexa have been acting peculiar for two about to embark on matrimony. Had your papa ever witnessed the slightest sign of partiality in me for any other gentleman he would have combed my hair for it!"

"Now, that is nothing but a hum," Winslow said with a resounding laugh. "Papa doted on you, and if a hundred cicisbeos would have pleased you, I think he would have selected the hundred himself!"

"He would have done no such thing!" she contradicted. "And how can you sit there talking of cicisbeos in such an outrageous fashion! Unless you believe Alexa is selecting hers, and I for one don't think such a vulgar thing of her! Why have you done nothing to stop this ruinous flirtation between her and Colonel Montcalm?"

Winslow's shoulders moved in a careless shrug under his coat of blue superfine. "What would you have me do, Mama? The colonel is one of Alexa's friends. I can scarcely forbid her to see him."

"You might not give her so much opportunity to see the colonel!"

For the first time the earl was nettled. "What does that mean, Mama?"

"It means, you bobbing block, that you might take a greater interest in Alexa's activities," she said acidly.

He smiled at her. "Are more roses in order?"

She sniffed. "That, among other things!"

"I see what you have in mind. I should try and outdo

him." He grimaced sharply. "Mama, do try and understand. I've never competed for any female in my life."

His mother, who had picked up her embroidery and succeeded in making two stitches, now threw the tambour frame down again at this prime example of male stupidity.

"This isn't just any female," she said, goaded and out of patience. "It's Alexa. The woman you have chosen to marry."

"Yes, yes, I know," he said, trying to calm her, but the countess was in no mood to be placated.

"Do you wish to be jilted, Sebby?"

"No, by God, then I wouldn't have any standing left me at all, would I?" he teased.

His mother, however, was not diverted by this attempt at levity. "Sebby, I'm convinced that if you would only apply yourself you could win Alexa back."

"What? Have I lost her already?" he inquired but instantly regretted the jest when he saw his mother's face. "Mama, I'm sorry! It was a poor jest, for I know well the affection you bear Alexa. And I am devilishly fond of her myself! However, if she has thought better of her alliance to me and actually prefers the colonel, I think we must grin and bear it."

"I shall do no such thing!" Lady Winslow declared in her most autocratic manner. "I see nothing funny about Alexa being hitched to a fortune hunter!"

Winslow sat back, mildly shocked. However agitated his mother became, she rarely cast such aspersions willy-nilly.

"Now, Mama, that is coming it too strong!"

"No, it is not," Lady Winslow said, so violently that her son put up his brow.

"I presume you have some substance to your charge?" he asked cautiously.

She gestured impatiently. "Of course I do. I am no prattle box! I pried the information out of Lady Hackett-Jones. The colonel by all accounts is up the River Tick because of his gaming and consequently is hanging out for a rich wife, who will resolve all his tiresome debts. That is why he is applying himself to Alexa. She has those fortunes both her father and mother left her!''

The earl digested this news but found nothing out of the way about it.

"Many gentlemen wish to marry an heiress," Winslow pointed out. "Even if there is some modicum of truth in what you say, Montcalm must have other charms to endear him to Alexa."

"Don't be so stupid, Sebastian!" his mother implored. "Really, I have never known you to be such a slowtop before! How can the colonel be endearing to Alexa when he is a sham? You can't wish her to marry so disastrously, can you?"

"No, I suppose not," Winslow agreed, his brow creased in thought. He left the sitting room to mull over the situation his mother had set before him. Winslow's opinion of Montcalm was not high, but hitherto he had never considered the colonel in the light of a fortune hunter. If his mother were correct, something must be done to alert Alexa.

Had it been some other gentleman dangling after her, Winslow would have done his best to nurse the tendre along until he could stage a graceful retreat from his own bogus betrothal to her. But he could not stand aside for one of the colonel's ilk. With that thought firmly fixed, he gave the reluctant order for a carriage to be brought around.

A half hour later, firmly ensconced on an Egyptian couch in Alexa's drawing room, he finished the sorry tale of the colonel's dubious financial matters. Throughout the recital Alexa had sat still, the pallor of her face more than matching her white French muslin. Now she arose abruptly.

"It's not possible."

A strand of hair had fallen free across her cheek, and Winslow resisted the urge to tuck it back over her ear.

"I'm afraid it's much too possible, my dear," he said gently. "The colonel's estates are badly bankrupt, and he has been amassing gaming debts for years!"

"So have many gentlemen known to the two of us," she reminded him swiftly. "And I shan't believe such a thing of the colonel. How came you by your information?"

He fell silent a moment, not wishing to involve either his mother or Lady Hackett-Jones. "That I cannot divulge," he said finally.

"You aren't perchance playing dog in the manger and making all this up, Sebby?" she asked.

His blue eyes focused on her, and she felt a moment of acute discomfort.

"Is that what you think of me, Alexa?" he asked coldly.

"Oh, pray don't get on your high ropes," she protested. "Of course I don't really believe you would invent such a tale. But you did cut up so stiff once before when I did naught but dance with Colonel Montcalm."

"I assure you, such jealous rages are behind me now," he said blandly. "Indeed, if some more worthy applicant for your hand had caught your fancy, I would be earnestly wishing you happy!"

"Very noble of you," she scoffed, pacing the length of the room.

He stretched his Hessians out toward the fire and watched her lithe figure sweeping back and forth.

"Permit me the liberty of asking just how serious are your feelings for Colonel Montcalm."

"He is a friend," she said, raising her chin challengingly. "And I saw nothing amiss in seeing him while he was in Bath."

"Now who is cutting up stiff?" he quizzed, wagging a finger at her. "You don't have to explain your actions to me, my dear."

She flushed indignantly. "I know that! All the same, I feel strangely compelled to do so. Being engaged to you, Winslow, even bogusly, has made my life suddenly fraught with difficulty."

A smile curved the corner of his lips. "Yes, I realize that. But at least you are not obliged to live with a mother who has marriage and my wedding on her brain!"

She sank into a chair, chuckling, then sobered. "I still find it difficult to believe that the colonel could be a fortune hunter."

His gaze was steady. "Are you calling me a liar?"

"No, of course not. But perhaps those sources whom you cannot divulge misunderstood the colonel's situation . . ." She broke off her words as the whirlwind that was Mrs. Finch suddenly burst into the drawing room, depositing apologies, sunshade, reticule, gloves and finally herself on a Trafalgar chair.

"Alexa," she wailed, "you must hide me for an hour or two."

"Are the Runners after you, Bronwyn?" the earl inquired, meticulously picking up the sunshade, reticule and gloves, which had fallen along the wayside.

A shudder shook Bronwyn. "If it were *only* the Runners," she said with some emotion. "It's Mr. Hormfeld. And how can you be so unfeeling as to sit there laughing at me, Alexa, particularly when it is all your fault?"

"My fault?" Alexa asked, her eyes brimming with laughter. "Pray, what did I ever do?"

"You foisted him on me," Bronwyn accused as she shuddered again. "Don't bother to deny it. And now he does naught but sigh whenever he claps eyes on me, sends me the most dreary verse to read and camps at my doorstep whenever I venture out."

"Of course he does all these things," Winslow said, hugely enjoying this recital. "He is a poet. You are his muse."

"Then I wish he would find another posthaste," Bronwyn wailed. Oh, heavens"—contrition spread over her face—"have I interrupted while Sebby was making love to you, Alexa?"

"No, of course you didn't," Alexa replied dampeningly.

"There is no 'of course' about it," her friend retorted. "And that smacks to me of incivility on his part." She gazed contemplatively at Winslow, who was struggling with a twitching lip. "You ought not to be so complacent, Sebby. I vow several gentlemen I know would be only too willing to apply for Alexa's hand, and if I encourage her, she might jilt you yet!"

"How uncivil of you!"

She dealt him a speculative look. "Colonel Montcalm has been growing quite particular in his attentions to Alexa."

"So I have heard," Winslow replied, polishing his quizzing glass. "But I do think Alexa deserves better than a life in the military!"

"Bronwyn," Alexa interrupted this discussion of her future to interpose a query of her own, "have you ever heard anything about Colonel Montcalm's estates?"

"They're in Kent," came Bronwyn's prompt rejoinder. "Why do you ask?"

"Because"—Winslow spoke for Alexa—"she doesn't believe me when I say that he's a fortune hunter."

Bronwyn clutched a hand to her bosom. "You must be mad with jealousy, Sebby. But even so, there is no reason for such slander!"

"I am not mad with jealousy," he replied testily.

"Have you heard anything, Bronwyn?" Alexa asked, paying little heed to the earl's mutterings. "About the colonel's estates, I mean?"

Bronwyn, her brow wrinkling in thought, paused a moment before acknowledging that an *on-dit* or two about the colonel's precarious financial situation had reached her ears.

"But I had dismissed that as mere prattle," she said, looking from the earl to Alexa. "Do you mean that it is true?"

"If only we had some way of determining it for certain," Alexa murmured half aloud, half to herself.

The earl glanced up. "You might ask him," he suggested.

"Don't be daft!" Bronwyn replied with the ease of old friendship. "If the colonel is a fortune hunter as you suspect, confession would be the very last thing on his mind."

"You are right," the earl said with a grim nod. "I suppose I could confront him."

But no sooner was this suggestion out of his mouth than it was hooted down by his two companions in the room.

"Don't be foolhardy, Winslow," Alexa implored. "Any time a gentleman I've ever known confronted another, it ended at dawn with pistols drawn at twenty paces. And we can't have you doing that. Only think of the reaction of your poor mama.''

"I would rather think of the colonel's mama," Winslow retorted, rather stung by this reaction. "I am rumored to be an excellent shot."

"The colonel's mother is dead," Bronwyn said, literal-mindedly. "And there is no need to boast about how excellent a shot you are. Neither Alexa nor I shall be impressed."

"Then I suggest the two of you come up with a likelier scheme," the earl suggested acidly.

A momentary silence fell over the room as the two ladies endeavored to follow his command. It was Bronwyn who emerged first from her reverie.

"Sebby," she asked, "if the colonel is a fortune hunter, it stands to reason he'd liefer have the largest fortune he could lay his hands on, wouldn't he?"

Winslow shrugged. "I suppose so, but—"

Bronwyn hushed him with an excited hand. "All we need do is tell him of someone with a much larger fortune than Alexa and observe his actions. If he continues to pay Alexa court, then we know that in all probability he was sincere in his attachment. However, if he throws her over for that other heiress, we shall know he is naught but a basket scrambler!"

The earl eyed her with mounting respect. "Bronwyn, have I never told you hitherto how brilliant you are? Such imagination and logic! I wouldn't put it past you to pen one of those circulating romances!"

"Oh, I'm sure I could," Bronwyn agreed. "Anything but poems!"

She turned to Alexa, who sat with a frown on her face. "Don't you think me brilliant, too, Alexa?"

"Of course," Alexa said, rousing herself. "But I've been trying to think just who in Bath has a much larger fortune than me. You both admit that Bath is rather thin of company now."

"Oh, it needn't be anyone blessed with a real fortune," Bronwyn exclaimed at once. "In fact I'd rather it weren't, for I should hate to foist the colonel onto some innocent who just might be captivated by him."

"He is rather dashing in his regimentals," Alexa agreed almost wistfully.

"What we need," Winslow said autocratically, "is a lady of sense and quality who will send the colonel packing forthwith and shan't be in any danger of losing her heart."

Bronwyn beamed at him. "My sentiments exactly, Sebby."

"But where are we to find such a paragon?" Alexa asked skeptically. "And how are we to induce her to assist us?"

The earl smiled broadly. "I think we need look no further than this very room. Bronwyn!"

Bronwyn gave a start of surprise at being thus singled out. "Me? Sebby, you have gone queer in the old attic."

"You are the only one who could pull it off, Bronwyn," he coaxed. "Only think of your great skill at amateur theatricals! Your reputation in those circles has preceded you. My mama was telling me only the other day about your prowess. And I promise you that I shall be at hand, so the colonel shan't seduce you."

Bronwyn choked. "How flattering you are, Sebby!"

His eyes smiled back at her. "You'll do it?"

"Why not? At the very least it shall get my mind off Mr. Hormfeld. But how shall I capture the colonel's attention? We are no more than bowing acquaintances!"

"I shall tell him how rich you are," Alexa suggested, but Winslow immediately vetoed such an idea.

"He'll suspect you are trying to test him."

"Then you do it," she retorted.

"That won't wash either," Bronwyn pointed out. "For he might suspect Sebby of acting dog in the manger over you. What we need is the services of a disinterested third party."

"Such as?" Alexa asked skeptically.

"Such as Archie," Winslow pronounced, snapping his fingers. "I'll speak to him tonight, and he'll find a way of planting the seed in the colonel's ear. They're both military men, and he's bound to swallow Archie's story."

"Do you consider Archie so trustworthy yourself, Sebby?" Bronwyn asked.

The earl appeared shocked at such a question. "Of course I do. Archie's true blue and shall never stain!" He turned to Alexa, sitting on the couch. "Now then, when do you see Montcalm next?"

"I have an engagement with him tomorrow afternoon to ride to the Saxon fortifications."

Winslow rubbed his hands together. "Splendid. I shall contrive to be there as well, exercising my bay. Mrs. Finch, would you oblige me with your company?"

"My lord," said the new heiress, "I shall be delighted!"

Thirteen

The sight of Bronwyn and Winslow exiting arm in arm remained with Alexa long after her friends had vanished from sight. Indeed, the lingering image had sparked an unfamiliar emotion within her breast, which she identified later in the day as jealousy.

"But that's absurd," she told herself aloud, feeling as cross as crabs—her disposition not aided in the least by what appeared to be a mounting pile of shopkeepers' bills in front of her. "Bronwyn is my dearest friend, and she has not the slightest interest in Winslow. She would have told me if she had!"

So saying, she made another attempt at discerning the exact figure owed to the glover, but her mind was not on matters of business, and she found herself dwelling more and more on Bronwyn and Winslow.

Although she was certain of Bronwyn's lack of feelings for the earl, she was less sure of his for her friend. If Winslow had decided to find a wife of his own—a course she herself had urged upon him only days ago—Bronwyn, charming, beautiful and lighthearted, would be an excellent partner.

"But even should he marry Bronwyn or some other female, what matter is it to me?" she demanded of herself petulantly, and she was jolted by a tiny voice piping up from within: "Perhaps more than you may think."

Before she had a chance to refute such heresy within the ranks of her own heart, James the footman entered with the day's mail, and she plunged gratefully into the task of sorting through the many cards and invitations for the week ahead. Judging by the large number of cards on the tray, Penny was making quite a debut in Bath society, and Alexa went to find her and discover just which invitations she wished to accept or decline.

"Oh, not the Hackett-Joneses *again*, Aunt Alexa," Penny pleaded when she was finally located in the small parlor at the back of the residence, dutifully practicing the pianoforte. "I shan't be able to bear it. I know it is uncivil of me to say such a thing, but Lady Hackett-Jones is a tartar, and she glares at me if I so much as say a syllable to her precious grandson!"

Alexa laughed as she sat down on the bench next to Penny. "Lady Hackett-Jones is very fond of young Gideon. I daresay that makes her a trifle brusque. He boasts a rather tidy little fortune, you must realize, and she wouldn't wish him to become embroiled with someone on the scramble for it."

"I don't care a fig about his tidy little fortune," Penny said with a lack of foresight that George Eiseley would have deplored. "And I'm not trying to ensnare him."

"Well, then," Alexa asked mildly, "I don't suppose we need care a rush about what Lady Hackett-Jones may think, do we? And it's merely a picnic, my dear. I'm certain that Lady Hackett-Jones shall not feel obliged to jaunter about the countryside with you and young Gideon's set."

Penny chuckled aloud at the image of Lady Hackett-Jones fighting off the ants sure to congregate at any picnic.

"Oh, then it's quite all right, Aunt Alexa. For I quite like

Gideon. It's just his grandmother who puts me into a quake.''

Alexa put the Hackett-Jones invitation into the pile to accept, remarking as she did so that by the time Penny had finished her come-out in London, she would be well versed in the foibles of such grandmothers as Lady Hackett-Jones.

"I'm beginning to think I might not do a season next year," Penny said, fingering the keys of the pianoforte idly.

"Not do a season?" Alexa was incredulous. "My child, what nonsense is this? You have prattled of nothing but a season to me for years. Pray, what maggot has flown into your pretty little head?"

"It shall be frightfully expensive," Penny said in a voice as plaintive as the tune she was playing.

"Your father is not such a purse squeeze as to begrudge you, whatever it costs!" Alexa pointed out. "And I consider it high time that he remembered he has a daughter almost of age. So what is amiss, Penny?"

Penny hung her head. "It's just that . . . perhaps you wouldn't wish to sponsor my come-out," she divulged in a voice so low that Alexa had to strain to hear.

"Why, in heaven, not?"

Penny shrugged. "You shall be busy. After all, you and the earl shall be getting married."

"Penny." Alexa laughed and turned her niece's face toward her. "I'm not about to abandon you or our plans just on that account. Now, don't be goosish. When or if I do marry the earl, I still fully intend to sponsor you in the ton. So let's have no second thoughts now, is that understood?"

"Perfectly," Penny said, lifting shining eyes up to Alexa. "But I thought it might be greedy of me to yearn for a London season, particularly when you have already done so much, introducing me to everyone here in Bath."

Alexa patted her hand. "Bath society is all well and good, but it is nothing when compared with London. And as for the young gentlemen you have met, they are charming, I'm sure, but they pale to nothing when compared with the men of mode in London."

"Men such as Lord Winslow, I suppose?" Penny asked, lifting curious eyes to her aunt.

"Well, yes." Alexa agreed reluctantly, since the earl undoubtedly deserved his reputation as a nonpareil. Nevertheless she wondered why Penny should be so preoccupied with Winslow. "Penny," she asked, frowning, "you don't have a tendre for Winslow, do you?"

Any suspicion that Alexa might have had dissolved as Penny erupted into whoops. "A tendre for Winslow? How can you even think such a thing, Aunt Alexa. He is much too old. I vow he must be every part of thirty!"

Alexa's lips twitched as she thought of the earl sustaining such a blow to his consequence.

"Yes, every part of thirty. But you must not remind him of that, for as a gentleman nears his dotage he is bound to take umbrage at such trifles!"

"Anyway," Penny pressed on, "that is past speaking of—the earl, I mean. He is in love with you, and you with him."

"Yes, very true," Alexa said, feeling the awkwardness of her situation multiplying by the intent gaze on the girl's face.

"Aunt Alexa, what does it feel like?"

"What does what feel like?" Alexa asked distractedly.

"Love!" Penny said breathlessly.

Alexa nearly jumped at the word. "Love? Oh, I don't know. It's rather difficult to put into words."

Penny nodded sagely. "I suppose it's fireworks and parades and everything else they say?"

"That is probably as good a description as any," Alexa agreed, and before Penny could continue the inquisition that was more discomfiting than she might have imagined, she beat a hasty retreat.

The following afternoon Alexa, garbed in her crimson riding habit, was ready for her outing with Colonel Montcalm. Originally planned as nothing more than an agreeable ride with a friend, it now loomed like a test of mettle. After listening to Winslow the day before, Alexa had fully expected horns to sprout from the colonel's head, but in feature and demeanor he was just as he had always been: tall, handsome and very gallant.

Mounting the bay he held quiet for her, she toyed with the possibility that they might have misjudged the colonel. This thought recurred with alarming frequency during the first half hour of their ride toward Lansdown.

"You are very quiet this afternoon, Alexa," he said, cocking his head at her.

She smiled, her riding hat set at a jaunty angle on her head. "Am I, sir? It was quite unintentional, I promise you. I rather thought I was enjoying the scenery as any traveler must!"

"Travel is an enlightening experience," the colonel agreed.

The horses cantered along happily. "How much longer do you plan to remain here in Bath?" he asked.

She shrugged. "That depends on Penny. As soon as she tires of routs, breakfasts, balls . . ."

He smiled. "If you leave the matter to your charming niece, I predict you shall be here for at least another month. You might then become a year-round resident, like your friend, Mrs. Finch."

Alexa, coming instantly alert by the intrusion of Bronwyn's name, smiled across at him. "That would be impossible. I am too addicted to the pleasures of London!"

"Is Mrs. Finch a very old friend of yours?" Montcalm inquired in an offhand way.

"Oh, yes," Alexa replied, adopting a similiar tone. They might have been discussing the weather! "Quite a bosom bow!"

She glanced up, catching a frown on his face, and wondered if she had erred by laying such stress to her friendship with Bronwyn.

"I don't believe I am acquainted with her family," the colonel said after a pause. "Her father . . ."

"Was Lord Henry Brinkley." Alexa furnished the information with aplomb. "Cousin to Lord Smithers. You may have heard of him."

"Indeed, yes." The colonel nodded enthusiastically. "I have not had the pleasure of his acquaintance, but he is well known in these parts as being the first to try and breed Arabian horses."

"I believe Bronwyn mentioned something to me about her cousin being horse mad," Alexa admitted.

A brief silence fell as they rode on.

"Mrs. Finch is a widow, I believe?" the colonel inquired next.

"Yes," Alexa answered carefully, witnessing the intent look on her companion's face. "Her husband, Captain Harry Finch, fell at Salamanca. A great tragedy, for he was quite the best of young men and loved nothing more than a good jest, forever wagering huge sums of money on this or that race. At one time, I believe, his father feared Harry would squander the family fortune when he came into it, but in actuality he increased it threefold."

The look of interest on the colonel's face seemed to increase by an equal portion.

"Of course," Alexa continued, "Harry's luck ran out at Salamanca. And all his friends grieved, particularly Bronwyn, who had only married him six months previous."

She paused, enabling her companion to collect his wits and utter a sympathetic sound.

"Does she still wear the willow for him?" he asked as their horses passed through one of the knolls of Lansdown.

"Not to my knowledge," Alexa replied. "Why do you ask?"

Her blunt query caught him by surprise, and she was gratified to see from the sudden flush that he was put out of countenance, at least momentarily.

"No reason at all, Miss Eiseley," he said smoothly as he composed himself swiftly. "Except that it would be a great pity if someone as young as your friend, who is blessed with such gifts of charm and so excellent a character, were to pine herself into a decline."

This rather melancholy view of Bronwyn was almost enough to overset Alexa, but she managed to reply with only the faintest tremor that Mrs. Finch appeared in no difficulty of such a decline.

"Especially now that she has Courtney, whom she escorts about in company. I believe that for the Season next year she may even go on to London, where I am sure she will find herself besieged by a horde of suitors."

At the mention of such unfavorable competition, the frown returned to the colonel's brow.

"Is there any gentleman in Bath of whom Mrs. Finch is particularly fond?" he asked.

"None that I am aware of," Alexa replied, touching the heel of her riding boots to the bay's flanks. "Of course," she said when the colonel had caught up to her, "that situation might change tomorrow. A gentleman may arrive who will sweep her off her feet, especially if he takes care to cater to her every whim."

"What sort of whims?" the colonel demanded.

A look of pure mischief danced in Alexa's hazel eyes. "Well, poetry, for instance," she said.

At her words, the colonel turned around in his saddle and blinked. "Poetry! Oh, you mean fellows like that Byron. Rather havey-cavey outfit if I do say so. Never saw much point to it."

"Actually," Alexa asserted, "I was thinking of Bronwyn. She has a great liking of verse, not Byron's, mind you, but those of her suitors."

The colonel stared at her. "Her suitors' verses?"

Alexa nodded and swallowed a giggle. "Harry used to write her a sonnet a day. That was when he was courting her, of course. And I believe it was his prowess with a couplet that made her look favorably on his offer. And there are her other preferences, such as the color puce."

"Puce?" The colonel's force in uttering this ejaculation nearly caused his horse to bolt, but he kept a rigid hand on the reins.

"Yes," Alexa replied again, throwing herself wholeheartedly into the tale she was spinning. "Bronwyn quite dotes on the color."

The colonel paled visibly. "She dotes on puce?"

"Yes, it is her favorite color on a gentleman. I recollect that Harry once commissioned a puce waistcoat from Weston especially to please her. Bronwyn said it brought out the beautiful pallor of his face!"

Wondering if she had overdone the thing, she darted a quick look across at the colonel, who could be seen pursing his lips and murmuring "how intriguing" to himself.

"And," Alexa continued, undaunted, "her second favorite color for gentlemen is orange."

"Orange!" Montcalm lifted his head. "My word, first puce and then orange. A lady of considerable imagination."

"Oh, yes," Alexa agreed. "Bronwyn is nothing if not imaginative."

Much to her disappointment, for she was bent on enlarging this portrait of her friend, they were fast approaching the fork in the road where, according to the plan Winslow had laid in front of her the previous day, he would be riding with Bronwyn, Courtney and young Mr. Kitteridge.

Whatever doubts Alexa might have entertained about the colonel's duplicity soon vanished. His persistent questions about Bronwyn had proved his interest in Mrs. Finch, a truth which hit home even more forcibly when they encountered Winslow's party.

To no one's real surprise, except perhaps young Courtney and Mr. Kitteridge, the colonel adroitly maneuvered himself to Bronwyn's side and remained there, speaking to her rather passionately on matters poetical.

Bronwyn, knowing the role expected of her, smiled encouragingly at him, and in short order they were deep in conversation, witnessed by Winslow with some satisfaction. Turning his head, he spotted Alexa with a look of rather different emotion on her face. He dropped back for a word with her.

"The fish seems to be rising to the bait," he murmured.

"Rising to it?" she scoffed. "He is gobbling it down whole."

Seeing her scorn, he said, "It must be odious for you to witness. I know how much you doted on him."

"Don't be daft, Winslow," she said tartly. "I didn't dote

on him. He was merely a friend. But of course," she acknowledged, "it is not particularly pleasant to learn that all he wanted from me was my fortune!"

The earl nodded sympathetically. "Will it ease your shattered pride any to know that Mrs. Finch has the added attraction of a fortune approaching fifty thousand pounds?"

Alexa looked up in shock. "Winslow, you're hoaxing me. You actually told him that?"

"I told him nothing at all. It was Archie who told him. The exact figure we hit upon was fifty thousand, two hundred and forty-two pounds."

Alexa grinned. "I shouldn't wonder, then, that he threw me over for Bronwyn. I just hope he doesn't make life too difficult for her."

Bronwyn, however, was equal to the task of flirting with a fortune hunter like the colonel, which she did with so much skill during the afternoon at the Saxon fortifications that he was encouraged to hope that her fortune—all fifty thousand, two hundred and forty-two pounds of it—would soon be in his debt-ridden hands.

"He has been attentive," Bronwyn confided gaily to Alexa later in the week. "And so many references to my widowed state!" She smoothed her lime walking dress worn under a Paris green spencer. "And how he hoped my poor heart had mended after the sad tragedy of poor Harry." Her laugh rang out. "I don't think I have been called poor quite so many times by any gentleman!"

"And, of course, he thinks you no such thing," Alexa exclaimed. "Did Winslow tell you that you have a fortune approaching fifty thousand pounds?"

"Oh, yes! And I do think it deuced inconvenient that I never knew of it beforehand."

She laughed again. Alexa wrinkled up her nose slightly. "Bronwyn, you don't find this whole scheme slightly odious?"

"Odious?" her friend retorted. "Not in the least. That wretched man was trying to wrangle your fortune from you. And I have not a jot of sympathy to waste on him." She paused, a reflective look on her face. "And while he may be good-looking, he has some dashed peculiar tastes."

"What do you mean?" Alexa asked innocently.

"He brings me poems to read!" Bronwyn informed her. "Can you think of anything more stupid to do, particularly when Mr. Hormfeld brings them to me by the bushel, or at least he did. I am beginning to hope the poet has finally been discouraged!"

"Congratulations," Alexa said. "But do you mean to say that the colonel's versifying is not up to snuff?"

Bronwyn shrugged daintily. "Heavens, Alexa, I know better than to read the stuff! I threw them straight into the fire. After he had gone, of course! Even Harry when he was alive swore that however much he loved me, he'd be touched in the cockloft if he'd try and compose a sonnet. And that pleased me, for there is nothing so odious as verse when one doesn't dote on it. But versifying is the least of Colonel Montcalm's foibles. Would you believe he came calling on me yesterday wearing the horridest waistcoat imaginable?"

"Was it puce?" Alexa inquired, controlling herself with the greatest effort.

Bronwyn's eyes narrowed in sudden suspicion as she swiveled her head toward her friend. "No, orange! Which, you shall agree, is nearly as bad as puce. Do I detect your hand at work here, my girl?"

Alexa feigned innocence. "I merely mentioned that you were fond of those two colors on your gentlemen callers."

"What a wretch you are! Orange and puce? Oh, Alexa" —Bronwyn's voice started to crack—"what if he should try and wear them together?"

The vision these words conjured up was enough to cause an immediate cessation of the conversation for several minutes. After they had exhausted themselves laughing, Alexa wiped her streaming eyes.

"I vow, no more! It positively hurts. And to think I might have married him."

"Married who? The colonel? Don't be silly!" Bronwyn said dismissively.

Alex stared at her. "What makes you so certain I wouldn't have accepted his offer? I'm quite sure he would have made one."

"Oh, I haven't a doubt about that," Bronwyn replied complacently, the curve of her mouth lifting in a smile. "But I don't think you so skittle-brained as to have said yes to him."

"Skittle-brained . . ."

"Particularly," Bronwyn went on, "when there is Sebby to consider."

Alexa flushed scarlet. "I told you before that my business with Sebby is nothing but a hum. . . ."

"Yes, I know," Bronwyn replied, shooting another quizzing look at her friend, "but why don't you try and tell me again. That way you might yet convince me as well as yourself!"

While Bronwyn was engaged in testing the limits of Alexa's good humor by such remarks, the earl was doing his level best to extricate them both from the attentions of the colonel. He had risen early enough to pay a visit to Colonel Montcalm's quarters, catching him on the verge of setting out for Mrs. Finch's in what appeared to be an eye-blinding cravat of puce.

"Off to pay homage to the lovely Mrs. Finch, Montcalm?" Winslow inquired, wrenching his eyes away from the neckcloth with some difficulty.

The colonel smiled indulgently from his doorstep. "I believe I have that pleasure, Winslow. You shan't begrudge me that, I hope, since you are all but betrothed to Miss Eiseley."

The earl snorted. "Fancy your remembering that. There was a time when my betrothal didn't stop you from paying Alexa court," he said affably, but his eyes had darkened at the mention of Alexa's name.

The colonel, inhaling a judicious pinch of snuff, did not notice the change in the earl's countenance.

"Happily, a more suitable arrangement is forthcoming in my future," he said, preening ever so slightly.

"With a fortune twice Miss Eiseley's?"

Montcalm drew back his shoulders and scowled. "Are you hinting at something, Winslow?"

"Hinting? My dear fellow, I never hint. But I have often wondered to what lengths a fortune hunter will go in order to capture a fortune. I suppose that depends on how pressing his needs are." He flicked a negligent smile at the colonel's infuriated face. "And your needs are devilishly pressing, aren't they?"

The colonel smiled unpleasantly. "Get out of my way, Winslow, before—"

"Before what?" The earl made a challenge of the words. "Before you call me out? I should think twice if that is on your mind. I am alleged quite a good shot."

"Good shot or not, I find your comments about me and Mrs. Finch insufferable!"

"Quite understandable," Winslow said, adopting a friendlier manner. "I daresay if I were a fortune hunter, too, I would feel the same outrage as you."

The color in the colonel's cheeks drained away. "I will not be talked to in such a fashion," he hissed, attempting to move past Winslow on the stairs. A lanky arm shot out as the earl pulled the other man back.

"You may not be in such a pelter to get to Bronwyn's if you spare me a minute."

"I have already spared you several minutes," the colonel said caustically as he brushed the earl's hand from the sleeve of his coat. "Are you trying to fix your interest in Mrs. Finch as well as Miss Eiseley? Never thought you prone to dabble in the petticoat line myself. And while you may have some justification in taxing me about Miss Eiseley—although, I assure you, my actions were the merest form of friendship—you have no such justification concerning Mrs. Finch."

"Probably not," Winslow agreed, squaring his jaw. "But Bronwyn is a good friend of Alexa's."

The muscle in the colonel's cheek tightened. "I see, and you mean to besmirch my reputation to her?"

"No."

The colonel's surprise was obvious. "No?"

"That's what I said," Winslow responded cordially as he reached out a meticulous hand and flicked a piece of lint from the colonel's coat. "I don't mean to tell Bronwyn a thing about you. I shan't need to. I had rather meant to tell you a few things about her."

The colonel's frown reappeared. "What sort of things?"

"That fortune of hers to start with. It doesn't exist!"

The colonel laughed harshly. "You're foxed, Winslow. It exists, all right. I don't know what game you're running, but you've chosen the wrong fellow. Jayneway himself told me all." He made to move down the stairs once again.

This time Winslow made no effort to detain him. "Yes, good old Archie," he said as the colonel passed. "The best of good fellows, don't you agree? I suppose he divulged that Bronwyn's fortune came to exactly fifty thousand, two hundred and forty-two pounds?"

The colonel turned around. "What the devil?"

"In a word, it's a hoax, man! Bronwyn doesn't have such a fortune. Oh, she has something, I suppose, bound to since Harry weren't a pauper. But as for having a fortune twice as grand as Alexa's . . ." He allowed the sentence to remain unfinished.

The colonel began to stammer. "Y-you tricked me. A deliberate hoax. You and Jayneway between you!"

"Actually," Winslow drawled, "if you must know the particulars, all four of us were in it together."

"You mean Mrs. Finch and . . ." A stricken look came into the colonel's eyes.

"Yes," the earl said with infinite relish. "Alexa! So if you are thinking of trying to return to her good favor, I advise you to put that out of your head. You showed your true colors for once."

"Blast you, Winslow. Meddlesome cur. I've half a mind . . ."

"I have always found dueling rather tiresome," the earl observed, "particularly since one is obliged to rise at such shockingly early hours, but if you wish to call me out, Montcalm, I am at your disposal."

Quite obviously the colonel would have liked nothing better. Angry he certainly was. But he was no fool, and another look at the dangerous tilt of Winslow's brows and reason intervened.

"A duel solves nothing," Montcalm observed thickly.

"Quite true," the earl said, much struck by this truth, "and more often than not it leaves one of its protagonists dead or at least suffering from a prodigious loss of blood. You are quite right to take the more reasonable avenue, Colonel. And if you would take some additional advice from me, I should leave Bath if I were you. For once word of this escapade gets about, I don't think anyone here shall wish to receive you!"

With that parting shot he bowed ironically and moved off, whistling happily to himself.

Fourteen

Later that same afternoon, Winslow peered into the open doorway of the general's sitting room and spied his mother garbed in a colorful half dress of Indian mull muslin, her head bent over a letter in her lap.

"Am I interrupting, Mama?" he asked.

The countess jumped a little at the sound of his unexpected voice but waved him in at once, hastily laying aside the letter.

"A love letter from your poet?" he asked and won a quick disclaiming laugh from her.

"It is a note from Leigh. At least," she chuckled, "I think it is from him, for I vow he has the muddiest hand in Christendom."

"Then he must take after me," Winslow confessed ruefully as she drew him down on the settee next to her.

"What brings you in so early, my dear?"

"I thought you might like to know that you needn't worry your pretty little head any longer about a certain colonel we both know."

His mother sighed with audible relief. "I might have known you would send him packing, Sebby!"

Her confidence brought a smile to his lips, and he swiftly put her in mind of all that had transpired. At his mention of the colonel's puce neckcloth, a touch which he rightly credited to Alexa's imaginative powers, the countess was nearly undone.

"Oh, heavens," she gurgled with helpless laughte , "I should have given a monkey to see that. Puce, you say?"

"Yes, Mama," Winslow said, barely repressing a shudder at the memory, "definitely puce."

"And definitely *de trop*." Her eyes danced saucily. "Even in my day when the gentlemen did favor bright colors, no one would dare assault passersby with such a vile hue. I'm very proud of you, Sebastian. Such strategy. Imagine foiling the colonel so easily. You see what you can do when you have a mind to it. Of course, I have always maintained as much and am gratified to have you bear me out."

He smiled at the compliments she was doling out with such a lavish hand, insisting that his role was a minor one when compared to Bronwyn's, Archie's and Alexa's.

"There is plenty of credit for all," Lady Winslow said large-mindedly. "Do you know I have half a notion of putting the four of you in one of my amateur theatricals later this summer. What fun it shall be!"

Fun it might be to Lady Winslow, but her son had another view of it.

"I don't know what Alexa or Bronwyn might say to such a scheme, Mama," he said promptly, "but for myself and Archie, I decline."

"How vexatious of you," she said, parting reluctantly with the stirring image of her son in the role of the brooding Dane. "Tell me, how is Alexa taking this foiling of her colonel?"

The earl sobered a little. "She appears to be sustaining the loss admirably."

Lady Winslow exhaled the breath she had been holding. "Good. Alexa always was a sensible sort of girl. And you might show some sense yourself and set the date for your wedding to her. That shall help to take her mind off things. In fact,'' the countess pressed her attack, ''if you are free tonight, we can sit down and thrash out all the details for the ceremony and the betrothal party. I did tell you that I plan to give a party for you, didn't I? And if not, I am.''

At her mention of his wedding, Winslow had uttered a strangled sound. ''I apologize, Mama,'' he said as she cast a curious eye toward him, ''but I must once again desert you and your plans, for I am promised to Major Jayneway for dinner.''

His mother flung her hands up to the ceiling. ''Sebastian, however shall we plan your wedding?''

''Well, perhaps we shouldn't,'' he said nervously.

The countess stopped, her mouth rounded in an O. ''What did you say?'' she demanded.

''I mean perhaps we shouldn't plan it too much. Things always go best if there's some surprise left.''

''Don't be doltish!'' His mother sighed. ''A wedding surprise, indeed. I've never heard anything so idiotish in my whole life. If you don't mean to take a hand in things, I certainly shall. We shall have your betrothal party here on the seventh,'' she said decisively. ''I trust you will be able to attend?''

Completely ignoring her sarcasm, Winslow quickly computed the days remaining in the month. ''But that would be in a fortnight!'' he exclaimed.

''I am pleased to see that you can still count,'' the countess commented with some acerbity. ''And pray don't offer me yet another of your addled excuses. I shan't listen to them. We are having the party, and that is that. Now, why don't you run along to that dinner with Major Jayneway and leave all the details to me. It shall be the grandest party Bath has ever seen.''

Winslow obediently bowed out of the room, leaving his mother free to pick up the letter from Leigh and to peruse the lines again with an enigmatic smile on her lips.

Some hours later, Winslow sat back in the book-lined library of the Jayneway family home, holding a glass of brandy. Sampling it, he gave a sigh of real pleasure and smiled across at his host, who was holding the decanter with an inquiring eye.

"I always did say you were an excellent judge of brandy, Archie. I'm tempted to steal all the bottles from your cellar."

"Steal away," the major invited, laughing as he poured a generous amount into his own glass and settled into one of the matching wing chairs in front of the mahogany cabinet. "It's my uncle's cellar, not mine. His house too, if it comes to that!"

The earl swirled the brandy lightly in his glass. The aroma was sweet and inviting. "You'll be pleased to learn that our campaign was a success."

The major looked up, puzzled. "What campaign?"

"Montcalm."

"Ah, yes," the major said, almost absentmindedly. "Good. Good."

He rose to kick a log in the fireplace and stood a moment lost in thought.

Was it his imagination, Winslow wondered curiously, or had Archie been somewhat distracted all evening? His company at dinner had been as congenial as always, but the earl suspected that something was lurking just under the surface.

He took another sip of the brandy and patiently bided his time. Whatever the problem, Archie would come to it in his own way. Meanwhile, there was the brandy and some cigars, and he meant to enjoy both.

By the time Winslow's cigar was half smoked, the major broke the silence that had fallen in the room.

"I've a problem, Sebby," he announced, stubbing out his cigar.

"Gaming debts?" The earl hazarded a guess.

The major recoiled. "Nothing of the sort! What type of bag pudding do you take me for?"

The earl lifted a puzzled brow. "I beg pardon, Archie. It's just that you've been frequenting the card rooms so often during your brief stay in Bath. I consider myself an avid card player, but you cast me in the shade."

The major was in no mood to listen to his friend's jesting.

He reached a hand into his coat pocket and drew out a fifty-pound note, which he handed across.

Winslow's puzzlement mounted. "Forgive me, Archie, but I had rather thought you were the one in need, not I!"

"Look at it," Jayneway muttered as he drained his brandy.

Obligingly, Winslow picked up the fifty-pound note and turned it over idly in his hands. It looked to be a perfectly ordinary fifty-pound note. Nothing to attract the major's fascinated attention.

"Archie," he said in a tone of mild protest, "I fail to see the point—"

"Now look at this one," Jayneway commanded, producing another fifty-pound note. "Are they the same?"

"Of course they are," Winslow started to say, but as his fingers touched the second bill his opinion changed. Something was different about it. He darted a quick, questioning look at his friend.

"That one"—Jayneway tapped the first of the notes—"is counterfeit."

The earl whistled sharply through his teeth. "And what the devil are you doing with it?"

"Trying to deduce who made it and the others that have been floating in and about the kingdom for the last six months!"

The earl stared absently at the two bills in front of him. "Rather out of your league, isn't it?"

Archie nodded. "You remember my Uncle Geoffrey?"

"The one who works for the Lord Chancellor?" Winslow asked, rubbing the two bills between his fingers with keen interest. "Never was quite sure what your uncle does for him."

"He came to me about six months ago asking if I would help him with this. I can circulate more freely now that the gout has laid him up. I was glad to help, especially since I've been thinking to sell out my commission in a few months."

Noticing that his cigar had gone out, the earl stooped to

relight it in the fire. "And what have you discovered so far?"

The major raked his fingers through his tousled hair. "To begin with, the bills are always fifty-pound notes, and they have shown up with alarming frequency at gaming tables and shops frequented by the *haut ton*."

Winslow interrupted his cigar lighting. "Do you suspect someone of our station of the counterfeiting?" he demanded.

"It sounds preposterous, I know. But all the evidence points to it. So far I've discovered five of the bills myself, and Uncle has given me twenty others. God only knows how many others are floating about undetected. Don't need to tell you that counterfeiting on a large scale could ruin the kingdom."

"Yes, I know," the earl said, sucking on the cigar with a meditative look on his face. "What evidence have you amassed so far?"

The major launched into a quick history of his investigation. "The notes I encountered have turned up in London during the Season, in Brighton about six weeks ago and in Bath within the past two weeks."

"So you think the counterfeiter is here in Bath?" Winslow asked, seizing upon this point.

"I suspect so," Archie said carefully. "I have no real proof."

The earl's eyes locked with his friend's. "Then you do have a suspect!"

"Yes, but I need proof. My uncle shan't listen to wild suspicions, nor would I if the situation were reversed." His head shot up. "I don't need to tell you he is anxious to end this matter. It's his feeling and mine that the bills are coming from one source. There's a pattern here. London, Brighton and Bath on the approximate dates I mentioned."

Winslow scowled. "London is always filled during the Season," he observed. "And Brighton is quite the watering hole. Which leaves you Bath." He paused, his eyes darkening.

The major nodded. "That's how I see it, too. Bath is the

key. It's not half as popular as it used to be. That narrows it down to someone who is here now and in all likelihood has been to London and then Brighton within the past six weeks.''

The earl settled back into his chair, stretching his lanky frame out. ''It sounds more and more as though you have strong suspicions as to who the culprit might be.''

The major shook his head. ''Not a suspect in so many words. Merely someone who might be passing the fraudulent bills unwittingly.''

''You are too charitable!'' Winslow scoffed. ''If I were you, I wouldn't hesitate a jot in following my instincts and arresting this person. You have the power, I presume?''

Jayneway nodded almost absently. ''My uncle has given me the necessary authorization, and I mean to bring in a constable as well when it comes to an arrest. But I should hate to do so until I'm positive.''

''Then I suggest you confront this party and beat the truth out of him.''

This forthright suggestion found no favor with Major Jayneway. ''Can't do that, Sebby. And anyway it's not a he.''

Winslow was jolted. ''A female, Archie?'' he spluttered.

''Not just a female,'' Archie said delicately, ''a lady. One of quite high position.''

The earl took a pull on his cigar, not realizing that it had once again gone out.

''The devil you say! I never thought a female could be the counterfeiter. Rather a freakish occupation, all in all. But still within the realm of possibility, I suppose. Of high standing, you say?''

''Very high,'' the major said, an enigmatic look fixed on his face.

''It makes no matter,'' Winslow said with authority. ''You must do your duty by your uncle and your kingdom. Good heavens, if this scheme spreads any further, all our lives would be in jeopardy. Our money would be worthless. Napoleon tried something like this during the war, and it's dangerous even in peacetime.''

"It's not as simple as you make it out to be, Sebby," Jayneway said. "Point of the matter, I'm a friend of the lady."

Winslow paused, considering this news. "Devilish ticklish, that!"

Jayneway nodded his agreement.

"Here's what I propose you do," the earl said briskly. "Talk to someone in her family. Must be some male about looking after her affairs. Tell him what you suspect, but discreetly, lest he challenge you to a duel. If he's got any wit at all, he'll thank you and take the proper measures toward clearing her name."

"Something along those lines had crossed my mind," the major said, stroking his chin.

The earl beamed. "Good, and if I were you, I'd see to it straight off."

"I rather think I am seeing to it right now," Archie replied, bestowing a meaningful look at his friend in the wing chair.

For a moment Winslow sat frozen, then, crushing his cigar out, he rose with his eyes ablaze.

"You suspect my mother of being a party to this scheme, Archie?" he roared. "You are all about in your head!"

"I told you I'm convinced she is an innocent party."

The major's voice was calm, his manner quiet. Not so the earl, who continued to rant and rave for several minutes, giving full vent to his emotion by striding up and down the library floor.

"I hope you have some evidence for your suspicions," he said, standing in front of the major's chair. "For even though we have been friends for years—"

"Oh, do give that over," Jayneway said dampeningly. "I shan't meet you at dawn no matter how many gloves you fling in my face. And I've been having quite a bad enough time of it myself, so you needn't glower at me. I told you I had suspicions, nothing more. That note, for instance"—he jabbed a finger at the bogus bill—"I got that from your mama during one of our games of whist this week."

Winslow stared at the fraudulent bill. "Impossible!"

"I saw her myself, Sebby," the major said patiently. "She took it out of her reticule and handed it over to me along with some jest about how I would soon reduce her to penury. I spotted it immediately for a forgery."

"Did you suspect her before this?" Winslow asked.

Jayneway looked uncomfortable. "Not exactly. I told you the bills had been circulated in London and Brighton. Well, your mother was in both cities at the right times, and when she came to Bath, suddenly they appeared too. What else could I do but suspect her?"

Winslow looked black. "I hardly cherish the notion of my mother in the role of a counterfeiter, Archie."

"I didn't say she was that!" the major expostulated. "I rather think that someone she knows, perhaps one of her own set, has been slipping the bills through her. Your mother, bless her heart, wouldn't think to notice anything amiss. Even you saw nothing wrong with the bill until I prompted you to examine it more closely."

The earl grunted. "What do you wish me to do?"

"Help clear your mama's name, of course," Archie said bracingly. "I thought of first going to her and telling her my suspicions, but I rather feared she would treat it as a lark."

Winslow grimaced. Knowing his mother, that was probably what she would have done.

"That's why I told you the facts, Sebby. You must talk to her and ask her help in remembering just who was about her in London, Brighton and Bath."

The earl dropped into a chair. "Archie, what you ask is impossible. My mother knows scores of people. She won't be able to recall . . ."

"She must be able to remember those who were with her in all three cities. Start with her friends here. That Hackett-Jones group, for instance. I wonder if they were in London and Brighton with her."

"And what do I say if she demands to know why I am so curious about her friends?" Winslow asked.

"Tell her the truth! But gently, of course. We must have her cooperation. She's our only lead thus far. Without her the search is bleak. I'm sorry it's your mother, Sebby."

"Not half as sorry as I am," Winslow replied grimly.

An hour later, he returned to Pulteney Street and gained entrance to his mother's bedroom, but not before coming to cuffs with Wilhelmina, the female dragon who served as the countess's abigail and who counted it chief among her tasks to keep everyone—particularly the earl—from ever disturbing the countess in her bedchamber.

"Can't a son even wish his mother a good night?" he grumbled to the countess.

"Of course you may," she replied gaily as he pecked her cheek. "But whatever did you say to dear Wilhelmina, for she was positively blushing as she left? No, on second thought, don't tell me. I'm better off not knowing. I daresay she was just shocked to see that you had returned so early. Did the major frighten you away?"

"You might say that," he replied vaguely, noticing that her hair had been brushed and that she was ready for bed. "You are retiring early this evening, Mama."

"I have a touch of the grippe," she divulged. She added quickly at his quick exclamation, "Don't you baby me either, Sebby. I am convinced it is nothing to signify, but you know Wilhelmina and how she coddles and bullies me. And if I don't go to bed this evening with a hot brick, she shall show hackle, and if I then do succumb to an even *viler* ailment, she shall be hard pressed not to tell me she told me so, which, of course, I shall never be able to tolerate!"

This recital earned her an appreciative laugh from the earl and another peck on the forehead, which did feel a trifle feverish.

"I owe Wilhelmina an apology. She did not tell me you were ill. Loath though I am to admit this, I find myself allied with your abigail on this point. You'd best get into your bed with your hot brick!"

"I am not on my deathbed," the countess protested bitterly, "and what did you wish to see me about? Were you perhaps wondering if I had dispatched the invitations to your betrothal party?"

Since this was the furthest thought from Winslow's mind, he was taken aback but not for long.

"Actually, Mama, I just came to wish you a good night, but since you bring the matter of the invitations up, have you dispatched them?"

The countess gave a sad shake of her head. "Wilhelmina would hear me coughing and take it into her brain that I was all but languishing from consumption. I'll dispatch the invitations the first thing tomorrow morning."

"Perhaps we should delay sending them out," the earl said quickly. "You may think it merely the grippe, but I shouldn't like to have you burdened with the details of a party while ill."

"It is no burden at all!" Lady Winslow exclaimed. "And I am not ill. You and Wilhelmina will turn me into an invalid if you are not careful."

He smiled at the image of his energetic mama languishing on a daybed the way most invalids he knew did. "Promise me you shall delay the party preparations until you are feeling better."

"Well, of course, Sebby, if you insist!" she said, giving ground gracefully. "But I am beginning to wonder if I shall ever see you set foot into the parson's mousetrap!"

He smiled down at her. "Don't worry, Mama. If ever I set foot in it, you shall undoubtedly be at hand to witness the event!"

Fifteen

The next morning, Wilhelmina informed Winslow that his mother was much recovered from her bout with the grippe. Even so, he was reluctant to divulge the major's suspicions to her. Instead, he allowed her to prattle on about her plans for the betrothal party, ignoring his suggestion that she hold off on issuing the invitations.

"You sound exactly like Wilhelmina," she expostulated as she drew the folds of her cornflower blue dressing gown closer about her. "She wouldn't even let me get out of bed until I pulled myself out bodily and gave her a direct order. Sometimes I think she forgets just who is the servant and who is the mistress."

"A failing common to most faithful retainers," Winslow sympathized.

"Yes, and I vow between the two of you I shall shortly conclude that I am an invalid and begin to quack myself. Whatever the two of you may think, I am not going to drift away into a decline."

Winslow patted her hand. "No, of course you aren't," he

soothed at once. "But perhaps you have been overdoing, Mama."

"Overdoing? Fustian!" she exclaimed.

"Now, now, Mama. Not content with helping Rowena during the Season in London, what must you do but embark upon an excursion to Brighton with the general and his set, playing whist, if I know Cathcart, for all hours of the night."

At these reminiscences, Lady Winslow colored up guiltily. "But I am perfectly up to it!"

Winslow laughed as he shook his head. "Mama, even I wouldn't be up to the duke of York's whist playing, and I am some years your junior! And confess, all the time you've been in Bath, you have been worrying your pretty little head about me, and I hold myself to blame for finding you in such queer stirrups."

"I am not in queer stirrups," Lady Winslow said, looking mulish.

"No, of course not. But you shall contrive to spend a quiet day at home."

Since Winslow did not usually direct orders to his mother, he found her surprisingly complacent when he did so now.

"Oh, very well, Sebby," she surrendered good-naturedly. "But I shall be bored to tears."

He smiled. "I am on my way out on some errands. How will it sit if I bring back several of those circulating romances that you are so addicted to?"

It was evident from his mother's reaction that the circulating romances would help to alleviate the boredom, and he took his leave. Since his mother had no need of her carriage this morning, he took the liberty of driving it not toward the nearest lending library but instead toward Milsom Street and Alexa.

He found his betrothed listening to her niece practicing the pianoforte. With a look of sublime relief as she glimpsed his tall figure dressed in biscuit pantaloons and a coat of Bath blue superfine, she excused herself to Penny, confiding later to the earl that poor Penny boasted as little musical prowess on the instrument as she herself.

"I had always thought that you played superbly," he said gallantly.

Her ready laugh sprang out. "Indeed you do not! I distinctly recall you once saying that a cat or a dog could play as well as I."

"I never said anything that uncivil, Alexa!" he protested. "And if so, I must've been in a distempered freak."

She laughed. "You were all of eighteen at the time," she recalled, bestowing a forgiving smile on him. "And rather high in your instep."

"Odious creature!"

"And my fingering was very bad," she said, leading him into the Crimson Saloon and settling on the Hepplewhite couch. "You are up early, Sebby, even by Bath standards."

"I know," he said. "Alexa, I've been doing some thinking about our situation. I think you should cry off today. Immediately. We've both agreed that we shouldn't suit, so it can't be a great shock to you."

"Of course it's not a shock," Alexa said, conscious of her heart, grown suddenly heavy in her chest. "But is there some reason why I must cry off today? Immediately, as you put it?"

He nodded then grimaced. "But I can't tell you."

She stiffened. "I see."

"No, you don't," he retorted. "I'm only doing it to protect you and your reputation."

A lift of her hand quelled any further response from him.

"Such protests are unnecessary, Sebby. If you have found another female willing to marry you, as I presume you must from these peculiar statements, I have nothing but happiness to wish you. And I shall, of course, cry off from our engagement." She eyed him thoughtfully. "I'm not surprised that you were able to attach yourself so quickly in only a se'nnight, since you are alleged to be such a matrimonial prize, but I must own to some curiosity. An odious failing, I know, but just who is the lucky female?"

"Do spare my blushes, Alexa," the earl responded testily. "I don't wish to be saddled with a wife, period. It's just that for my mama's sake . . ."

"I see. Your mama has taken me in a sudden dislike."

Winslow sighed noisily. "Don't be a cocklebrain," he said thickly. "Mama loves you and shan't hear a syllable against you. Here I am trying to do something to benefit you, and see what is the result!"

Alexa interrupted this bitter complaint without a qualm.

"Sebby, I'm beginning to think that you are either foxed or mad. And while I don't feel any distinct pleasure speaking to a gentleman betraying symptoms of either state so early in the day, I should like an explanation!"

An explanation? Was there ever such a female? Winslow wondered to himself.

"Oh, very well," he said reluctantly, "but what I have to say is for your ears alone."

Her eyes flashed magnificently. "Are you accusing me of being a gabblemonger, Sebby?"

He heaved a sigh heavenward, implored her not to be a wet goose and quickly related what the major had revealed the previous night.

"Your mother—part of a counterfeiting scheme? Preposterous!" she exclaimed. "I hope you told Archie so."

"I didn't have to. He knows that plain enough. Thing is, he thinks one of Mama's friends may be using her as a dupe. Nasty business, that!"

Alexa's brow puckered in a sudden frown. "Does your mother know of this, Sebby?"

The earl shook his head. "I meant to acquaint her fully with it last night, but she was feeling out of curl. This morning all she would talk about was our wedding, which made me realize that next to clearing Mama's good name I must take steps to keep yours safe, which is why I wish you would stop being so missish and cry off."

She stared at him absently. "You seem inordinately interested in keeping my reputation spotless, Sebby."

"Don't be a ninnyhammer," he growled. "You see how imperative it is that you cry off today."

"No, I'm afraid I do not."

He scowled. "Weren't you attending to me? I've just finished telling you—"

''The most outrageous tale I've ever heard,'' she agreed. ''And I need no convincing that your mother is perfectly innocent of any wrongdoing and that it shall come to rights in the end.''

''I share that hope. But there is no telling what any of us close to her shall have to endure in the meantime. And I shan't be responsible for any scandal that may attach itself to you if you are my betrothed.''

''And what if I did cry off in the midst of such a bumble-broth? What of my good name then?'' she demanded.

He sat, looking confused. ''What do you mean?''

''Well, I shouldn't like it said of me that I abandoned a friend like Countess Winslow in the lurch.''

Winslow threw up his hands. ''Of all the absurdities,'' he railed. ''We aren't in the lurch, and you haven't abandoned us. You know we intended to end this hen-witted betrothal long ago and simply lacked the necessary courage.''

''Yes, we know that and so does Bronwyn. But who else? And how shall it look to the world? Precisely as though I believed the very worst of you and your mama. And I shan't have that! So let's not have any further prattle about crying off until we have solved your mama's sticky situation. And just how do you plan to resolve it?''

''I don't know,'' he admitted. ''And I do wish you would do as I ask.''

''Sebby,'' she said gently. ''I know you mean well, but my mind is set. And I think we should put our heads together toward finding out just which of your mama's friends is passing out these counterfeit bills. And I think the sooner your mama knows what is happening the better.''

Reluctantly, Winslow surrendered. ''I suppose I must return and tell her.''

''Shall I come with you? I know you might think it forward of me, but I should like to help.''

Far from spurning her suggestion, Winslow was gladdened by the idea of her support.

''Actually, I promised Mama to bring her some lending library romances,'' he told her as they walked toward his carriage, "but I'm sure she'd rather fancy a chat with you than any stuffy book."

The truth of this last statement was proved correct when Lady Winslow caught sight of her son and his companion coming through the door of her sitting room.

"Sebby!" she exclaimed. "I vow you must be a mind reader. How did you know I have been bursting to speak to Alexa! My dear"—she patted the sofa invitingly—"do come and let me have your opinion on lamb."

Alexa, while complying with the first of the countess's requests, was totally baffled by the second.

"Would that be Lady Caroline Lamb, ma'am?"

"No, no, no." The countess laughed heartily. "Although I daresay her antics would keep any conversation going in these parts. No, it was the four-legged variety of lamb that I was speaking of. For your betrothal party on the seventh." She dealt a severe look at her only son. "Do you mean that Sebby hasn't told you yet?"

"The opportunity didn't arise, Mama," Winslow protested lamely.

Her brows raised in amusement. "Indeed? One would almost think you were turning cat in the pan, my dear. But Alexa and I shall hold you to your promise, won't we, my dear?"

"By all means," Alexa said, enjoying the discomfiture on the earl's face.

"Now then." The countess's voice turned brisk. "Do you prefer lamb or pheasant for your betrothal dinner?"

"Whichever you think best, ma'am."

Lady Winslow shook her head. "My dear, you sound just like Sebastian, and he has not a jot of interest in the party. I suspect he'd much rather elope!"

"That would be romantic," Alexa agreed, chuckling at the sight of the irritated earl at her elbow. "However, Sebby has never struck me as the romantic sort. Not even when he was younger and subject to freakish whims."

"If the two of you are going to malign me, I'd much prefer to leave you alone," Winslow announced testily. "You will do a much better job of it if I weren't at hand."

"Now, now, Sebastian, don't fly into the boughs. Don't you know when you are being roasted? What's wrong with you? You have been acting most peculiarly of late."

"There is a reason for that, ma'am," he said grimly, recalling the purpose of his visit to her. "Do you recall my dining with Major Jayneway last night?"

"Certainly," the countess retorted. "I may have had a bout with the grippe, but I'm not senile, and I do wish you would sit instead of hovering over us."

Obediently, he sank into the chair opposite them. His mother beamed. "That is so much better. Now, what is all this talk of Archibald Jayneway?"

"Archie had a problem, Mama, one which he confided in me. It appears that someone is passing fraudulent bank notes in the kingdom."

One of the countess's hands froze in midair. "Fraudulent? How extraordinary!"

"There's more," Winslow continued, watching her carefully. "Archie said it has been happening with such frequency that his uncle, the one who works for the Lord Chancellor, asked him to look into it. Seems there's a pattern. The bogus bills first appeared in London, then in Brighton and now in Bath. He showed me one last night. He got it from you, Mama, during one of your games of whist this week."

If Winslow had any doubts about his mother's innocence they went by the board now.

"From me!" she exclaimed, rising imperiously from the couch much the way Athena was rumored to have sprung from the head of Zeus. "Are you saying that Major Jayneway accused me of having a hand in such an outrageous scheme?"

"No, of course not," Winslow said quickly. "Archie knows full well that you are innocent. Nevertheless, he did wonder where you might have gotten the bank note from."

"Who can remember such a thing?" she asked dismissively.

"Mama, you must try and recall. I'm afraid that at the moment you are Archie's only clue to unraveling this coil.

You were in London in April and May when the bills first began to appear, and also in Brighton in June, and now here you are in Bath.''

The countess stared at her son with stricken eyes. "Then I *am* a suspect!"

"You are no such thing," he enunciated slowly. "But you are his only lead at the moment. That's why he asked me to dinner last night, so he could lay this information before me. Do try and think, Mama. Was there someone in your group of friends and admirers who was also with you in London, Brighton and now Bath?"

"Possibly, but I'd hardly sit down and draw up a list for you," she retorted.

He caught her hands in his and looked deeply into her eyes. "I'm afraid that's very much what I wish you would do," he said.

At this her eyes flew wide with agitation. "But Sebby, I really cannot."

He frowned. "I know it must be difficult to remember."

"I am not in my dotage yet," she complained bitterly. "And my memory has always been alleged to be one of the best in the ton. I daresay if I put my mind to it I shall be able to recall the names, but I shan't hand Archibald Jayneway any list of suspects who also happen to be my friends. That would be infamous."

In the face of his mother's misplaced loyalty to her friends, Winslow felt momentarily stymied. Alexa, however, was not.

"Dear Lady Winslow," she said quietly. "You don't seem to realize that the counterfeiter, whoever he may be, has been trying to implicate you in this crime. I scarcely think you need have any scruples about protecting him."

"But Alexa, I don't know who he is," Lady Winslow protested. "So I should be casting doubt on the innocent as well as the guilty."

"Disagreeable though that may be." The earl leapt again into the fray. "You must try and apply yourself to the task. Do you know that enough of these bills could render our currency worthless, Mama? I assure you there is no greater way to cause the kingdom to collapse!''

"I'm sure you are right," his mother agreed readily. "And I don't wish to bring down an entire kingdom, or even a mere city, but I don't think I can point the finger of blame at any one of my friends and subject them to the major's interrogation!''

"Perhaps you can help without the finger pointing, ma'am," Alexa said, her face gleaming with sudden inspiration.

"What do you mean?" Winslow demanded, his face as curious as his mother's.

"It appears to me that all Major Jayneway wants to know is just which of your mama's friends happened to be in Bath, Brighton and London at the same time as these bills appeared. Is that not so?''

The earl nodded.

"I propose to give a party. We'll invite those that you name, Lady Winslow, along with Major Jayneway, of course. There shan't be any need for interrogation. And perhaps at a whist table another of those bogus bills might be passed. To allay any suspicion, I shall invite some of Penny's little friends.''

"That may do the trick," Winslow said softly. "Are there many of your friends to invite, Mama?''

"About a dozen," the countess divulged. "But Sebby, I don't think any of them could be responsible—''

"We must let Archie judge that for himself," he told her gently, clasping her hand. "Alexa is right that your friends shan't suspect a thing. So why don't we retire to the library and leave you to draw up your guest list!''

Sixteen

Some twenty-four hours later, Alexa Eiseley was up to her pretty little neck in preparations for the ball she had so impulsively suggested. Recalling the marquesses, earls and mere viscounts which had dotted Lady Winslow's guest list—the sight of which had rendered her a trifle giddy and had caused even Winslow's brows to knit involuntarily—she deemed this the grandest party she was ever likely to give in Bath and threw herself into the arduous tasks of supervising the housecleaning, ordering the flowers, deciding on the menu and hiring the musicians for the Friday night affair.

There was also Penny to placate.

The younger Miss Eiseley had been in raptures at the idea of a ball, but her glee had turned to gloom when she discovered just whom her aunt wished to entertain.

"I don't see why we need to invite so many elderly dragons," she protested on Wednesday morning as they sat together pondering the menu. "Lady Hackett-Jones is quite bad enough, but I have heard that the Marchioness of Auberville is even worse."

Frowning, Alexa laid down the menu. "You must not listen to *on-dits*," she chided gently. "And you must get accustomed to such dragons, as you call them. After all, you shall be meeting quite a few dragons in London during your come-out. And the marchioness, while rather starched up, cannot hold a candle to the odious Mrs. Drummond-Burrell, who is also a patroness of Almack's."

"Good heavens, is she on our guest list, too?" Penny asked with a visible shudder.

Alexa chuckled. "No, and pray don't worry over them. All you need do on Friday is smile and steer clear of them. I shall see to them. You will have quite enough to do with the younger set. Now, is there anything else you wish on the menu before I turn it over to Alphonse?"

Friday morning dawned bright and clear, the sort of weather that hostesses back in London prayed for and seldom received as their due. For most of the day, Alexa tended to one domestic crisis after another. By the time evening fell she had faced down a mutiny in the kitchen and fired a tipsy footman. By all rights she should have been hagged to death, but when the eight o'clock hour sounded, she took her place on the gleaming stairs dressed in a beguilingly simple azure ball gown cut along Grecian lines, looking, as Penny informed her, bang up to the nines, an opinion Winslow echoed some minutes later when he arrived with his mother.

"I don't know how you contrive to do it, Alexa," he said, "but you are looking even more radiant than usual."

The unusual warmth in his voice caused the color to rise in her cheeks. "Thank you, Sebby," she said, making a quick recovery. "You are looking quite the thing yourself."

"I must own I was tormented by indecision," he confessed, winning a quizzing look from her. "Whether to wear this neckcloth or a puce one *à la Montcalm*. I trust I made the wiser choice?"

Swallowing a laugh, Alexa watched his tall figure glide off with the countess. No further time could be wasted speculating on neckcloths, even the handsome one Winslow was sporting, for more guests were ascending the stairs.

A sea of faces soon engulfed her, and she spent the next half hour shaking hands, dropping curtseys and accepting the flirtatious gallantries of the younger gentlemen. When at last the final guest had been greeted, she breathed a sigh of relief and swept off into the ballroom, where the musicians were dutifully plying their instruments. A few of the more courageous of the younger couples were dancing, watched over by their elders.

Surely none of the illustrious personages gathered here could have a hand in such a heinous crime as counterfeiting!

"This is the most peculiar ball I've known you to give!" Bronwyn's comment summoned Alexa from her reverie.

She found her friend standing beside her in a yellow gown with matching roses twined about her hair and a questioning look in her dark eyes.

"My dear Bronwyn, how exquisite you look!"

Mrs. Finch, however, was not about to be distracted by idle compliments. "What is going on, Alexa?" she inquired bluntly.

Her question put Alexa at point non plus. However much she trusted Bronwyn, she was certain neither the earl nor the major would wish her to inform any more people about the counterfeiting scheme. And yet, gazing into Bronwyn's waiting eyes, she did not have the courage to lie.

"I can't tell you," she said, feeling the statement an indifferent compromise at best. "I'd like to but I can't."

Bronwyn did not appear at all offended. "Well, good. At least I know that this isn't an air dream and you haven't gone suddenly queer in the old attic. Wouldn't have missed this anyway, especially since Mr. Hormfeld hinted he might call on me this evening."

Alexa chuckled. "Don't tell me he is still dangling after you!"

"Oh, his interest is on the wane," Bronwyn said cheerfully. "He's taken to borrowing money from me. He pays me back, of course, but that is a sure sign that a suitor has more on his mind than love." She broke off, perceiving that Miss Chumley, a rather shy friend of Courtney's, was standing alone, and went off to bully young Mr. Kitteridge into dancing with her.

As Bronwyn applied such ruthless tactics successfully among the younger set, Lady Winslow was occupied in spreading her considerable charm among the older generation. Not by so much as a tremor in her confident hands did she betray any of the difficulties afflicting her. Her tongue continued to jabber a mile a minute, and the serenity of her countenance was untouched by anything except the genuine pleasure of a lady enjoying a comfortable evening with old friends.

"It must be the stage for her after this," her son murmured to Alexa in passing.

She smiled, glad to have the chance to chat with him. "You don't think anyone suspects?"

"Heavens, no!" He polished his quizzing glass. "Everything is just as it ought to be. I think even Auberville is having a good time. Luckily, Philpots is here as well." He saw the puzzlement in her eyes. "The two are horse mad and consider it poor sport if any event they are at doesn't provide them with the opportunity of boasting about their precious cattle."

Laughter sprang to her eyes. "And what about Archie? I've lost sight of him."

"Oh, he's somewhere about, never fear," the earl replied. "On his best behavior, too. One would never consider him a detective at all."

Alexa sighed. "You and he are behaving splendidly, and your mother is a paragon, but I shall undoubtedly collapse before the evening is at an end."

"Are you feeling ill?" the earl asked immediately.

The concern in his voice came as a shock to her. "Oh, no. It was merely a stupid jest." She had no further opportunity to enlarge on that, because Major Jayneway joined them with a benign expression on his face.

"Alexa, a first-rate party, my dear."

"Never mind that." She brushed aside his compliments impatiently. "Has anything useful turned up?"

Her eagerness won a smile from both men.

"It would be a stroke of pure luck if anything did develop here in the ballroom," the major pointed out. "I'm placing my hopes in the cards. You did have tables set up in the card room?"

She nodded. "Three, just as you ordered."

"Good." He rubbed his hands together in anticipation. "Between the countess, Sebby and myself we shall have all the whist players covered."

"While I am doomed to remain behind."

"They also serve who only stand and wait," the major advised.

"That sounds like something Mr. Hormfeld would say," Alexa said crossly, "and I do think, Archie, you would have more sense than to recite poetry to me at such a time."

He laughed and glanced about. "I had hoped to pay my respects to Mrs. Finch and her charming sister before I tackled the card room."

"They are in the corner." Alexa indicated the location with her fan, and he set off at once. "Archie seems rather taken with Courtney."

"With whom?" Winslow asked absentmindedly.

"Courtney, Bronwyn's sister," Alexa explained impatiently. "I wouldn't be surprised if they made a match of it."

She had his complete attention now. "Match? Do you mean marriage?"

"Well, certainly marriage!" She dealt him an incredulous look. "Major Jayneway is hardly the type of gentleman who would offer carte blanche to a girl just a step removed from a schoolroom."

"He's not the sort to offer carte blanche to any female period," Winslow said frankly. "But I don't fancy him married. Archie, a married man?" He pondered the image for a moment in his mind's eye. "No, I don't see it."

"And I don't suppose you see yourself as a Benedick either?" a voice asked tartly as Lady Hackett-Jones, resplendent in a lilac turban accentuated by two purple ostrich feathers, descended on them. "But that is always the case, my dear Winslow. The marriage trap sprung when least expected. Although you were not so much trapped as captivated, is that not so?''

''Far be it from me to argue with you, Lady Hackett-Jones,'' Winslow said suavely. ''I daresay you sprung many a trap in your salad days.''

She gave a bark of laughter, which caused the two feathers to dip alarmingly close to the earl's nostrils. ''In truth, it was your mama who had the sprigs of our day dangling after her until your papa arrived and took command. And that reminds me, your mother has put your betrothal party for the seventh, is that not so?''

''Yes, if nothing amiss should occur.''

She cast a baleful eye at him. ''Do you plan on something amiss happening?''

''No, but one never does know,'' he said lamely and then with a rueful shake of his head bestowed an enchanting smile on the older lady. ''My dear Lady Hackett-Jones, you perceive a bridegroom aflutter. I hope you shall take pity on me if I don't speak too sensibly.''

''Prettily said, Winslow,'' she complimented with another bark of laughter. ''Aflutter, indeed.''

''I also know of your great fondness for whist,'' he said, turning the topic. ''And I believe that is Lord Cavanaugh making his way toward the card room. I believe he is one of your prime pigeons, is he not?''

''So he is,'' she agreed, her attention instantly diverted. ''Never can tell a good hand from a bad one,'' she confided, and, excusing herself, she made haste to follow Cavanaugh toward the card room.

''Winslow, about that betrothal party,'' Alexa said, a tiny frown on her brow.

''It shan't come off, I promise you, Alexa,'' he assured her quickly.

She fixed her hazel eyes on his handsome face. ''I seem to recall you promising me that about this engagement of ours.''

His lips turned up in a smile. ''Unfair, Alexa! I gave you a chance to bow out earlier this week, as you know very well.''

"Yes, but that was nothing but fustian."

"Coming to cuffs again, Sebby?" Lady Winslow asked as she approached them with a tinkling laugh. "My dear boy, I would be remiss in my duties as a mother if I did not tell you that such is not at all the thing in a ballroom, and particularly with a lady who is your hostess."

"We were not coming to cuffs, ma'am," Alexa said sweetly. "Merely espousing a difference in opinion."

"Yes, of course you were," Lady Winslow said wisely. "But for now I must call a truce to this skirmish and take Sebby off to the card room to beard the counterfeiter in his den."

So saying, she marched off with her son, the two figures trailed by Alexa's envious eyes. How she wished she could follow them, but that would be shirking her duties as hostess.

For the next half hour, she fended off the entreaties to dance from some of the younger gentlemen. She had no intention of making herself an object of sport by dancing with men who were only a step out of the nursery! That was Penny's providence, and she was glad that her niece was enjoying herself in the midst of her young swains. Even young Miss Chumley had fought off a case of the dismals and as the evening progressed had made a notable conquest in young Mr. Lawry, who not only continued to dance with her but regarded her in the light of a goddess, a tidbit furnished by Bronwyn herself.

Alexa could not help laughing at her friend's attempt at matchmaking. "He seems a nice lad, although young."

"Heavens, Alexa! They are all young here except for us."

"Now, that is quite enough," Alexa said severely. "I have no intention of feeling like Methuselah or his sister, tonight of all nights. Just who is this Mr. Lawry?"

"Peter Lawry's son," Bronwyn explained obligingly. "There is a sister, I believe. Invalidish, they say, but a sweet chit nevertheless. And I can only count it a stroke of luck that Penny invited Miss Chumley to this ball, along with Mr. Lawry."

"Bronwyn, you're not thinking they might make a match of it already!" Alexa protested.

Her friend shrugged. "And why not? I'm sure her parents wouldn't object. Young Lawry is supposed to inherit a tidy fortune from his godfather. And I know his parents wouldn't object to such a shy, sweet thing. . . ."

"Perhaps not, but she is so young."

"She is just as old as Courtney," Bronwyn replied, a pensive note in her voice.

Alexa gazed at Courtney, who was surrounded by a bevy of admirers. "Courtney seems to have made many a conquest herself."

"Including Major Jayneway," Bronwyn said a trifle dourly.

The note of disapproval in her voice caught Alexa by surprise. "My word, Bronwyn, you sound as though you hold Archie in dislike."

"Don't be idiotish, Alexa," her friend retorted. "Archie is pleasant enough and also boasts a goodly income. He explained all about selling out his commission to me rather tediously one morning when he came calling and found Courtney absent. It was almost as though I were her mother instead of her sister!"

Alexa swallowed a laugh. "Since your mama rarely leaves Yorkshire, I suppose he thought you the one to acquaint with his plans," she said reasonably.

"Well, I wish he hadn't, for it made me feel as though I were in my dotage. And, anyway, I don't want Courtney marrying him."

Alexa's brows lifted. "Why on earth?"

"I wouldn't like my sister married to a loose screw or a gamester!"

"Oh, Bronwyn, Archie is no such thing!"

Bronwyn bestowed a pitying look on her. "I saw him at that dressmaker's shop, remember? And several of my other friends have spied him there before. If that doesn't speak of a weakness for the muslin company, what does?"

At this Alexa fell silent, realizing that Archie had no

doubt frequented such shops in pursuit of the bogus bank notes.

"And," Bronwyn continued, "you saw yourself how quickly he went off to the card room. As though he were shot from a cannon."

"Yes, I know it looks that way," Alexa said weakly, wishing that she could clear the major without implicating Lady Winslow. "I'm certain he has a reason for his behavior."

"You may be charitable enough to think that, but I do not," Bronwyn replied. "Anyhow, it is past speaking about Archie for Courtney. She has no tendre for him."

This revelation came as a mild disappointment to Alexa. "What a pity. Archie certainly dotes on her."

"Yes, I know. The devoted hound. But I asked her, and she said that she is not in the least bit in love with him, which I cannot really believe myself. . . ." She colored somewhat as these words slipped off her tongue, and Alexa dealt her a quizzing look. Before she could speak, however, Bronwyn excused herself, leaving Alexa to ponder just what Bronwyn really thought of Archie himself.

Seventeen

True to their agreement, *Winslow, Jayneway and the* countess waited for Alexa in the Crimson Saloon at the close of the ball. The minute she had dispatched the yawning Penny off to bed, Alexa stepped through the drawing room doors, barely able to suppress the excitement which had been building all evening.

"Well?" she demanded, glancing anxiously from face to face.

The trio seemed loath to speak, but Winslow finally broke the silence.

"Nothing," was his reply.

"Nothing?" Alexa sank into a chair, not quite believing her ears. "Surely you must have discerned something. The three of you were in that card room half the night, not even coming out for a morsel of food."

"I know that well enough," the major said mournfully, having suffered through exquisite pangs of hunger in the line of duty.

"Our effort was not without some discoveries," Winslow

spoke blandly. "Lady Hackett-Jones, for instance, has the cunning of a hawk when it comes to whist."

"And Mr. Fielding cheats," the major volunteered as he slumped in his chair. "When he thinks no one is looking," he amended. "And while that is a reprehensible trait in his character, it is not evidence that he is our counterfeiter. So I'm very much afraid that we are back to where we started from."

"You must not chide yourself, Archie." Lady Winslow spoke up from her corner where she had been sitting all but forgotten. The fatigue of the long evening was now visible on her face. "I shall behave with every discretion when you pack me off to gaol."

"Lady Winslow!" the major protested.

"Mama, don't even think such a thing!" Winslow commanded.

"My dear Sebby," the countess responded with dignity. "What else am I to think? There is not a jot of sense in being difficult about my situation. And, I assure you, I shan't blame Archie in the least for his suspicions. We all know I am the only link to the person putting out these bogus bills. And I shall try to act properly when the dungeon doors swing shut!"

The earl cast a mute appeal to the length of the room; and Archie picked up the cue at once. "I hardly think I shall be remanding you to the gaol, Lady Winslow," he said gently. "In fact I'm certain I shan't. But I do wish to heaven I were taking the culprit there. Are you certain that no one else among your circle of intimates was at Brighton, London and Bath?"

The countess looked helplessly at him. "No one's memory is faultless, and at this point I'm not certain of anything. I daresay I may have forgotten someone, but who it could be I have no idea. Unless they suspected the game was up. I'm sure you did your very best, Sebby, to look just as you ought, but you were watching everyone so avidly that it would confirm suspicion."

"Did I really?" Winslow asked. "I'm just not as adept as you, Mama. You were superb."

"Indeed you were," Alexa echoed.

For the first time since the ball ended, the countess smiled.

"We shall just have to try again," the major muttered.

The earl snorted. "I think even the slowest top in Bath shall realize something is in the wind if we continue to sponsor such games of whist. And Alexa might find herself accused of running a gaming hell."

"I shouldn't mind that if it would help your mother," Alexa said absentmindedly. "But I own people shall think it deuced out of character for me."

The clock on the mantel chimed just then, halting the discussion. "It's late," the major announced, stifling an enormous yawn with the back of his hand. "We'd best be getting home. Try not to worry, Lady Winslow. It's vexing, but it shall come to rights in the end."

"I certainly hope so, Archie," Lady Winslow said, giving him a gallant smile. "I had heard that dungeons are deplorably drafty, and I shouldn't like to endure more than a night there."

"Mama, do put off such thoughts. I beg of you," Winslow pleaded.

"Sebby is right," Alexa said, kissing the countess's powdered cheek. "Try not to worry, ma'am. We shall find the counterfeiter."

But just how they were to accomplish that was something none of them wished to speculate on.

The next day, Major Jayneway's customary optimism had returned, and he laid in front of the earl and the countess his latest plan for foiling the counterfeiter. The bulk of this scheme, he explained, had to do with the necessity of giving the lie to any rumor which might arise about the countess by accepting the many invitations for balls, routs and breakfasts that had been tendered to them. At the same time, they would be able to keep their eyes out for anything suspicious.

To this plan of his friend's Winslow uttered a brief and, as his mother put it later, abominably rude rejoinder. The scheme did win favor with the countess, who bestowed her wholehearted approval and demanded to know just how many of the invitations the major thought it best for them to accept.

"As many as possible without causing you to collapse, ma'am," he said promptly.

Much to the major's surprise, Lady Winslow, far from suffering a collapse from her hectic racketing about during the next week, seemed to thrive on each nightly revel. In high fettle, she flitted from one soirée to another on the arm of her handsome son, whom she dragooned into accompanying her, much to the delight of the Bath hostesses.

On occasion they were joined by the captivating Miss Alexa Eiseley, and by the end of a week's time it was the earl who was in need of assistance, not his beloved mama.

Not only was the countess indefatigable in dragging him from one rout to another—some nights as many as three—but she had the temerity to chatter continuously to one and all about his coming nuptials to Alexa.

"And that will make it even more awkward if we break it off," he complained to Alexa one morning.

"If?" Alexa's hazel eyes widened as she surveyed her caller. "If, Winslow? I would rather have said *when* we cried off."

"I meant when," came his reply testily, piqued by her evident desire to be rid of him. "But Mama still hasn't been cleared."

"She will in time," Alexa said with considerably more confidence in her voice than in her heart. "You must be patient."

"That's easy enough for you to say. Ain't your mother facing such trumped-up charges."

Alexa bristled immediately but managed to keep a civil tongue in her head. "You should know, Sebby," she said evenly, "that your mama is very dear to me."

The earl bit his lip. "Of course I know that. Do forgive me, Alexa. It is all this botheration. I did sound like a coxcomb just now, didn't I?"

"Like several coxcombs," she told him cordially. "But

I'll forgive you on account of your mama. How is she these days?''

In spite of his worry, Winslow smiled. "In high gig still. I'm convinced that she is having the time of her life dashing from one ball to another. Meanwhile, I shall undoubtedly succumb to an infection before this nightmare is complete."

"It can't have been so horrid for you," she teased. "Once or twice, I own I glimpsed some measure of pleasure on your face in the ballroom."

"That's only because you were there," he blurted out.

This unexpected comment appeared to astonish him as much as it did her, and he was beginning to wonder just what it was about Alexa that caused him to make such foolhardy remarks when, fortunately, a footman entered and announced Major Jayneway.

The major, had he been rather less absorbed in his own thoughts, might have been a trifle surprised at the cordiality he was greeted with by Alexa and Winslow, both relieved at the interruption.

"I'm glad you're here, Sebby," Archie said after greeting Alexa. "Your mama told me you were probably here."

"If you wish to see Winslow in private, I can leave, Archie," Alexa said.

"No, don't go," he said, halting her. "Actually, I wanted to see you both. This showed up last night at Lady Rendell's," he announced, holding out what appeared to be another fifty-pound note. Winslow snatched it out of his hand.

"In the card room?"

"Where else?"

"Not from Mama, I should hope," the earl said, passing the bank note on to Alexa for inspection.

"No, we may rest easy there. Lady Winslow was playing at another table."

"Thank God." The earl's relief was evident. "Then this clears her?"

"So it would appear," Jayneway murmured in a low tone with none of the expected glee.

Winslow exchanged a meaningful look with Alexa.

"Why so gloomy, Archie?" he demanded. "We've cleared Mama. Isn't that what you wanted? And you have the real culprit in your grasp."

The major took possession of the bogus bill again. "I'm not so certain of that, Sebby."

Alexa could not hold in her rising curiosity. "Archie, just who was it who passed you the bill?"

He stared at her. "Mrs. Finch."

"Mrs. Finch?" Winslow roared as Alexa simultaneously cried out: "Bronwyn? Impossible!"

The two men watched her pace agitatedly across the room. "It can't be Bronwyn. She hates whist."

"Which makes it highly improbable that she was in the card room to begin with," the major pointed out. "I don't wish to believe it of her either, and yet what else can I believe? She played a few hands of whist and lost. Not badly, mind. The fifty pounds accounted for most of it. She dropped the bill on the table and left. When I picked it up, I knew I had another counterfeit for my collection."

Alexa was shaken by this recital but still adamant in her friend's defense. "You must be mistaken, Archie," she repeated.

"Is Bronwyn purse pinched?" Winslow asked her.

Their eyes met. "Harry left her well off," she protested. "And there is no earthly way Bronwyn could be responsible for such a crime."

"I hope not," Jayneway murmured.

Alexa halted by the window. "I'm going over to see Bronwyn now."

"We'll go with you," Winslow said at once.

"To accuse her?" Alexa asked, lifting her chin.

"No," he replied gently. "Just as you wished to help me when my mama stood accused, so do I wish to help you and Bronwyn now."

"I feel the same way," the major put in.

Her cheeks flushed as she felt thoroughly ashamed of herself and her suspicions. "I'm sorry," she apologized. "I daresay I can use all the help I can get at this point." So saying, she led the way toward the entrance hall, stopping dead on seeing Bronwyn, garbed in an exquisite blue walking dress, just crossing the threshold.

"Alexa, my dear!" Bronwyn trilled gaily. "I thought I recognized Sebby's carriage on the flagway." She turned to Major Jayneway. "You are up very early, Major, for one who didn't leave Lady Rendell's ball until the wee hours of the morn."

"Bronwyn, you are the very person I wish to see," Alexa put in before either the earl or the major could speak. She turned to them. "Would you wait for me in the library, Winslow? And take Major Jayneway with you, please. I shall just be a few moments with Bronwyn."

This effort at privacy won Alexa a scold from her friend when they were alone.

"That seemed rather a crude way of fobbing off poor Sebby, don't you think, my dear?" she asked as Alexa bullied her into the Crimson Saloon. "And why on earth did you banish him to the book room of all places?"

"Never mind, Sebby! Bronwyn, what were you doing playing cards with Archie last night at Lady Rendell's?"

A mild flush overcame Bronwyn. "My dear, what are you prattling about?"

Alexa pulled her down onto the couch next to her. "The major told us you lost to him at whist last night. And I know you rarely play cards."

"Rarely, yes," Bronwyn acknowledged. "But I have indulged at times. I'm not Quakerish!"

"No, but by heaven I wish you were."

Bronwyn looked confused at this vehement remark. "What an idiotish thing to say! I wasn't deserting Courtney, if that's what you think. And I must say that if Archie came here only to boast about winning a paltry fifty pounds from me, it is the shabbiest thing. His luck must be running deplorably thin to boast about such a trifle to his friends!"

"He didn't come to boast. And I wish you hadn't played cards last night. And where did you get that fifty-pound note?"

"From my reticule, of course, silly goose!" Bronwyn

said, looking frustrated by all the questions. "And why are you so curious?"

Alexa saw no way around telling her friend the truth. "Bronwyn, that note you gave Archie was counterfeit."

"Counterfeit?" Bronwyn laughed. "Don't talk fustian!"

"I am not talking fustian!" Alexa corrected. "I wish to heaven I were. Listen to me." She grabbed her friend by the shoulders. "Archie has been investigating a counterfeiting scheme that has been operating in the kingdom for the past four months or so. Some of the bogus bills have been passed in London and Brighton, and now they've appeared in Bath. At one time he thought Lady Winslow might be the link in the chain. Winslow and I were trying to catch the culprit, but whom do we catch? You!"

"Is that why Archie has been frequenting the dressmakers and the card rooms?" Bronwyn asked.

"Yes," Alexa said, impatient with her continued interest in dressmakers. "Now, where did you get that fifty-pound note?"

"Well, I don't know," Bronwyn said, looking bewildered. "Who can remember such a thing? Do you remember where every bank note in your reticule came from?"

"I suppose not," Alexa acknowledged truthfully. "But what were you doing in the card room anyway? It can't have been because you had a sudden impulse for cards!"

Bronwyn colored ever so slightly. "If you must know I was trying to cast out a lure."

Cast out a lure? Alexa looked blank, then as the meaning of the words sank in, she looked up in amazement.

"Do you mean you were flirting?"

"It had not gone that far," Bronwyn objected. "And now I greatly fear it shan't be allowed to get anywhere at all."

"Bronwyn," Alexa said, excitely putting two and two together. "Don't tell me you were trying to cast out a lure to Archie!"

"Of course I was, you dolt! What else would I be doing in that stupid card room?"

Eighteen

"You have a tendre for Archie!" Alexa *cried out as she* clasped her friend to her bosom. "Oh, Bronwyn! I am in transports. I never thought I'd see the day again, not since poor Harry got killed!"

"Alexa, if you love me, you shall contrive to lower your voice," Bronwyn pleaded. "It would not be at all the thing for Archie to overhear you."

"Oh, he can't. The library is at least four doors away, and the walls are quite solid," Alexa averred, but she obligingly dropped her voice an octave. "Now tell me everything."

Bronwyn gave a shaky laugh. "There's nothing to tell."

"You were in the Rendell card room because he haunted the card rooms in Bath?"

"Yes, but mind you don't tell him so."

"But how else shall we convince him that you're not a criminal?"

"Counterfeiting, I suppose, is a serious offense?" Bronwyn asked.

"Most serious," Alexa emphasized, thinking again about

the counterfeit bills, which had slipped her mind in the excitement over her friend's tendre for Archie. Then she snapped her fingers and did a quick gig around the room.

Bronwyn watched her warily. "Alexa, I don't think I could bear it if you, of all people, lost your wits. Only think how *uncomfortable* it would be for you to live in Bedlam, and I should have to visit you. . . ."

"I haven't lost my wits," Alexa retorted. "I've just rediscovered them. You haven't been to Brighton or London this year, have you?"

"Of course not. You know perfectly well I make my home in Bath! Why?"

"Because the bogus bills were first discovered in London and Brighton. We had forgotten that you rarely set foot out of Bath. I must tell Sebby and Archie the news at once."

Before she could make good on this statement, Bronwyn held her back. "Alexa, promise me you shan't breathe a word to Archie about me."

An impish smile grew on Alexa's lips. "Why, Bronwyn, I've never known you to be so missish!"

"I am not being missish," her friend contradicted, stamping her foot in frustration. "I'm trying to behave with some particle of decorum. After last night's lapse into idiocy, I promise I shall never chase a gentleman into a card room again. But he must not suspect what I feel."

Alexa patted her soothingly on the back. "I'll dream up some tale to explain your presence in Lady Rendell's card room," she promised. "You stay here, and I'll bring Winslow and Archie back with me. They might want to ask you a few questions themselves about the bogus bill. So do try and think of how it fell into your hands."

Leaving her friend to ponder over that, Alexa made for the library, toying with several promising Banbury tales to lay in front of the major. The truth would have been simpler, but she felt a strange empathy for Bronwyn's feelings toward the major. It was much akin to her own feelings for Winslow, which, impossibly enough, seemed to grow deeper with each passing day, and admission that wild horses would not have been able to drag from her.

"Well?" a voice demanded.

She jumped, her heart in her throat as Winslow loomed in the doorway to the library.

"Bronwyn doesn't know a thing about the counterfeiting," she divulged when she had caught her breath. "And we are all hare-brained in thinking she might have been involved, for she stays in Bath year-round and hasn't been to London or Brighton in years, much less three months."

"That clears her, then," Winslow said, slapping his fist into the palm of the other hand. "Although she could have sent the bills out through friends."

"I'd call that rather farfetched," the major commented. "What a cake I've been. I don't know why I forgot such a simple thing as her living in Bath year-round."

"Did she say where she got the bill?" Winslow next inquired, turning to Alexa again.

"She can't remember."

Relief gave way to disappointment in the major's eyes. "Bad luck there," he said softly. "Of course, it would have been wishing on stars to have her remember." He lifted his head. "Did she say why she went to the card room last night?"

"As a matter of fact she did," Alexa drawled, feeling her way carefully. "Apparently, this is only the merest deduction on my part, she has developed a tendre for a gentleman who just happened to be frequenting the card room last evening."

At this revelation, Winslow broke out in a broad grin. "Is Bronwyn nursing a tendre then?" he asked, amused. "Well, well, first rate. I thought she might still be wearing the willow for poor Harry."

"Oh, she is well over that!" Alexa said, keeping a surreptitious eye on the major's countenance. "But she feels bashful about this tendre, Winslow, so please don't tease her about it."

The earl promised that he would behave with admirable discretion. "But I can't help wondering who the fellow in question might be."

"Probably Goodwin," Major Jayneway murmured, adding as the earl glanced up, puzzled, "Lionel Goodwin. You must know the fellow, Sebby. Tall chap, beak-nosed, said to be as rich as Croesus."

"What makes you think it's him?" Winslow asked, saving Alexa the trouble of voicing that very question herself.

"Because of the way she looked at him during whist last night. Each time I chanced to look up she was staring off in his direction. That's how she came to lose the fifty pounds to me. Sheer distraction."

Winslow clapped Archie on the shoulder. "Perhaps you ought to thank Goodwin, then. For if Bronwyn hadn't lost that fifty pounds to you, she wouldn't constitute your latest lead to the counterfeiter."

Despite this statement, it soon became apparent that Bronwyn's part in the counterfeiting scheme constituted the merest thread of a clue, since she, like Lady Winslow before her, had not the slightest idea of how the bogus bill might have come into her possession.

"I don't keep strict account of my financial affairs," she protested later in the Crimson Saloon. She looked more composed and demure than Alexa expected. Indeed, the agitated Mrs. Finch had vanished, leaving behind only a cool, elegant lady of fashion.

"Most of my finances are handled by my banker. For the daily activities I have a small account, which I dip into as needed. I use it and sometimes Courtney as well, but she is hardly a counterfeiter!"

"Still, there must be a link between you and Lady Winslow," Alexa mused aloud. "Perhaps some shared interest. A common bond. A mutual friend."

Bronwyn gave a tinkling laugh. "I should think we have many mutual friends, the countess and I. You forget that with Bath so thin of company everyone here knows everyone else. That might not be *de rigueur* in London, where the proprieties are stricter, but here such familiarity is the rule rather than the exception."

The major gazed at her intently. "Do you see any connection between yourself and Lady Winslow?" he asked, following Alexa's lead.

Bronwyn shrugged. "The countess is one of the leading lights in London, while I lead a rather sedate life here in Bath. The two of us do share an affection for Alexa and Sebby, but I doubt that they are your counterfeiters."

"It might be simpler all around if we were," Winslow barked. "Devil take it, there must be something else that has escaped us. Do try and think, Bronwyn. What do you do with yourself here?"

"I ride," she supplied helpfully.

He shook his head. The countess loathed riding.

"And," Bronwyn went on, "I hunt when the weather is warmer."

"No, Mama cannot abide a hunt. She feels an inordinate amount of sympathy for the fox."

Ten minutes of further questions elicited the information that Mrs. Finch was skilled in both French and Italian in addition to her native English; that she enjoyed music, plays and the theater in Bath; and that she was a strong supporter of Tory politics. While this last detail might have been of middling interest to Major Jayneway, who was himself a staunch Toryite, it did not lead him closer to solving the mystery of the counterfeiting ring.

"We don't have the faintest glimmer of light," Winslow complained plaintively.

"Actually, Sebby," Bronwyn said slowly, "I do have a common fate with your mama. We're both widows, after all."

"I scarcely see how the demise of my father and your poor Harry has anything to do with the counterfeiting of fifty-pound notes," Winslow protested.

Alexa, however, was less certain, and at Bronwyn's words, she sat up straighter in her chair.

"Bronwyn is right," she said, her eyes glinting in thought. "She and Lady Winslow are both beautiful widows. I'm convinced that Bronwyn might have married at least a dozen times since Harry's death! And the countess keeps a dozen suitors on her string."

She turned abruptly toward Major Jayneway, who appeared to be lost briefly in his own thoughts. "Don't you agree, Archie, that Bronwyn could quite easily attach some gentleman? Someone like Mr. Goodwin, for instance.''

The major appeared a trifle taken aback by the audacity of the question, but not nearly as much as Bronwyn herself, who shot a dagger look at Alexa, who appeared oblivious to it.

''I'm certain that Mrs. Finch could attract any number of gentlemen suitors,'' Major Jayneway said gallantly.

''As could my mama,'' Winslow added almost absent-mindedly, ''only she prefers her widowed state to that of re-marriage. General Cathcart keeps popping the question, or so he revealed in his cups one night, but Mama won't have him.'' He looked over at Bronwyn. ''Don't suppose he's on your list of admirers.''

''My list of admirers doesn't run to elderly military men, Sebby,'' Bronwyn answered tartly.

''What about young military men?'' Alexa put in and earned another thunderous look from her friend.

The earl resumed his pacing. ''Well, I for one think this is a muddle. Nothing connects Mama and Bronwyn.''

''There must be something,'' Alexa insisted, her chin propped in her hand. ''Only we are too stupid to see it. They are both widows. Let's start there. What to make of it?'' She appealed to the two men. ''Harry died at Salamanca, and your father, Sebby?''

''In a carriage accident,'' he supplied.

Even the most scrupulous investigation could not link these two disparate events.

''Now their widows. Both Lady Winslow and Bronwyn are highly courted, and you needn't blush, Bronwyn, for everyone in Bath knows that. Perchance could they have the same admirer?''

Confusion mounted on the earl's brow. ''I thought we had absolved General Cathcart of this affair,'' he complained.

''Sebby is right,'' Bronwyn agreed. ''While I might have a few admirers, and not the horde that you envision, I scarcely think any of them are paying homage to Lady Winslow as well as to me.''

"I can think of one who is," Alexa said slowly. "Mr. Hormfeld."

"Mr. Hormfeld?" Winslow looked stunned.

"Yes," she replied, the thoughtful expression on her face more pronounced than before. "Mr. Hormfeld."

Bronwyn fluttered nervously. "Heavens, Alexa. He isn't an admirer of mine. Far from it. And moreover, he's a poet!"

"Yes, and he has been running tame in your establishment, and I daresay making as great a nuisance of himself at Pulteney Street?" This latter question from Alexa was directed to Winslow.

"More than a nuisance," he replied, his eyes locking with hers. "But a poet?"

"They are notoriously poor, are they not?" she demanded and appealed again to Bronwyn. "Weren't you just telling me that he applied to you for a loan?"

"Well, yes," she admitted, "and while I didn't like it much, he already paid me back."

"How much money did you loan him?"

"Fifty pounds. And he handed me a fifty-pound note in payment . . ." Bronwyn stopped, realizing what she had just said. Her eyes widened in consternation. "Oh, Alexa, you don't mean that you actually believe . . ."

"Are you thinking what I'm thinking, Sebby?" Major Jayneway asked.

"Thanks to Alexa, I'm way ahead of you, Archie," the earl said grimly.

"But it can't be Mr. Hormfeld," Bronwyn protested weakly. "He cares nothing for worldly possessions except for those dismal volumes of his verse."

"That's what he says," the earl replied, the dangerous glint in his eyes very pronounced. "It makes an interesting scheme, don't you think? Mr. Hormfeld manages to ingratiate himself into your household, borrows money from you and repays you with bogus bills. You are too kindhearted. As is my mother, and I'm certain he used the very same ploy with her."

"How did your mama first take up with him?" the major asked.

"She was introduced in Brighton," came the reply. "I shall have to ask her just who did the honors."

On returning to Pulteney Street an hour later, he put the question to his mother, who stared at her only son with unveiled astonishment.

"Good God, Sebby, what peculiar questions you do ask. And why the sudden interest in Mr. Hormfeld unless"—the mirthful look came into her eyes—"you fear I shall suddenly elope with him."

"That fear is the furthest from my mind, Mama," he assured her with an indulgent laugh. "But do please try to remember who it was who introduced you to the poet. I know you told me it was in Brighton when you made his acquaintance."

"Oh, I didn't say that," she denied, laying aside the romance she had been reading. "I couldn't have, for I met him much earlier in London. But it was in Brighton that he became enamored of me."

Winslow sat, his hands on his knees. "About that tendre of his, Mama, just how did it come about?"

A look of pure devilment crossed the countess's face. "Sebby, that is hardly the sort of thing a mama would wish to confide in her son."

"Now, don't be missish, Mama," he said, unable to resist smiling back at her. "As though I don't realize you have half the gentlemen of the ton dangling after you."

"Yes, the half over sixty," she pointed out.

His lips twitched. "It is still an accomplishment. And now your tendre for Hormfeld."

A look of mild revulsion swept across the countess's face. "Good God, I don't have a tendre for him," she said at once. "Quite the reverse. He developed a passion for me the first moment he clapped eyes on me, or so he declared. And I'm rather inclined to doubt such a statement, since he is a poet and they are so prone to exaggeration. All the same"—she bestowed a pretty smile on her harassed son—"it is a very civil thing to say, and perhaps more gentlemen ought to say such pretty things to the women they love."

"Yes, but how did you meet Hormfeld, Mama?" Winslow asked with dwindling patience.

His mother surprised him by answering the question. "Through Lady Toppingham. He had been smitten with her and was writing verses to her beauty, which I confess must be a hum, since she is not a beauty now and never was, even in her salad days."

Winslow was not about to be waylaid into a discussion about Lady Toppingham's flaws. "About Hormfeld, Mama."

"Dearest, I am telling you. Even Lady Toppingham grew tired of his tedious verse, and when I happened to call on her one morning in Green Street he became smitten with me. And he followed me to Brighton, which I own was rather tiresome of him, and then on to Bath."

Winslow fought to control his excitement. "Mama, do you remember ever giving Mr. Hormfeld any money?"

The countess gaped. "Certainly not. What sort of hoydenish female do you take me for?"

"I beg pardon." He moved quickly to rectify this error in judgment. "I didn't mean to imply anything untoward in your conduct with Mr. Hormfeld, but I believe you once divulged that he had borrowed some sums from you."

"A mere pittance. And he paid me right back, Sebby. I'd given him the hundred pounds for his ridiculous verse, and he paid me back the money less the amount for his books."

"I don't suppose when he paid you it was with a fifty-pound note?"

"It may have been," Lady Winslow conceded, wrinkling up her nose. "Why all the questions?"

"We have been making some progress in capturing our counterfeiter, Mama," he informed her.

Her eyes flew wide, and she clapped her hands. "How? So far all you've done is prattle on and on about Mr. Hormfeld." She halted, staring at him quizzically. "Oh, Sebby, not Mr. Hormfeld."

"I fear so, Mama," he said quietly. "Last night at Lady

Rendell's ball Major Jayneway came upon another of the bogus bills. This one was given to him by Mrs. Finch.''

The countess appeared baffled by such an incident. ''Mrs. Finch? Impossible.''

''That's what we thought. And after a talk with Bronwyn we discovered that she had lent some money to Mr. Hormfeld and that he had finished repaying her to the tune of fifty pounds.''

''Oh, dear. Oh, dear.'' Lady Winslow wrung her hands. ''I never thought he would amount to much as a poet, mind, but I never thought he'd stoop so low. You have proof?''

''Unfortunately, no. But we do have strong suspicions. And I have a plan to get the proof we shall need.''

''What sort of plan?'' the countess asked, raising her curious eyes to his.

He smiled. ''I am planning to cultivate an interest in matters poetical, Mama, and you, my dear, must assist me!''

Nineteen

The next day Lady Winslow dispatched cream-colored invitations to her friends inviting them to partake of the pleasure of a poetry recital by Mr. Hormfeld that evening at her residence. Among the recipients of these strange invitations was Lady Hackett-Jones, who immediately informed her lord that Elizabeth must be getting dotty to foist such an evening of boredom on her friends and lost no time in sending her regrets.

Those with a more charitable view of Lady Winslow's invitation included Alexa, who would not have missed the performance for worlds and who overrode the protests of Penny, who could not fathom why they must spend an entire evening listening to verse.

"It is one of the things that people in London do for entertainment," Alexa pointed out as she slipped a gold bracelet onto her bare arm. "You must learn that not all of the Season shall be riveting. There may be times when you will be heartily bored. And you must know how to contrive."

Among those also accepting Lady Winslow's invitation

for the evening were Bronwyn, Courtney and Major Jayneway, who had previously eschewed all forms of literature as being horridly dull and who could not help wondering what his able mentor General Cathcart might say at having his residence put to such purposes.

Happily, General Cathcart was not at hand to witness the gathering under his roof that evening. But most of Bath's literati had assembled, buzzing amongst themselves in response to Lady Winslow's clarion call. As for Hormfeld, he was in his element as the pièce de résistance, waxing profuse in his thanks to the countess as he entered the drawing room and planting a kiss on her hand.

"Tonight, thanks to you, dear lady, I shall display my muse for all to see!"

"Yes, well, you needn't display *all* of it," Lady Winslow said hastily. "Just enough to give people a taste. Shouldn't wish to frighten them off. And you needn't read all the verses in your charming little book."

The poet frowned, looking, Winslow thought, more simianlike than usual.

"I had thought the evening was designed for just such a performance," Mr. Hormfeld protested.

"So it is," she fluttered. "But you know how people these days just don't appreciate too much of a good thing. You must keep them yearning for more. That is a saying they have in the theater, I believe. But you needn't worry. You shall have ample opportunity to sell your verse. You did bring extra copies with you?"

Mr. Hormfeld puffed his cheeks out and nodded. "Indeed, yes."

"Good." Lady Winslow nodded toward a tall, thin lady in the corner wearing a vivid violet gown augmented by an equally vivid turban. "Lady Farrington might be persuaded to buy a few. She is practically a bluestocking."

Mr. Hormfeld directed an interested face toward Lady Farrington. "Indeed," he murmured.

"And"—the countess added the clincher—"she is a widow."

Mr. Hormfeld's look of interest deepened. "Indeed," he repeated.

With a brisk clap of her hands, the countess quieted the buzz of anticipation in the room.

"Friends, friends, please, your attention. Our guest of honor is ready to begin." She indicated the simpering Mr. Hormfeld, at her elbow, who took his cue to stroll toward the center of the room and began to read a ponderous sonnet.

Alexa, Bronwyn and Lady Winslow had heard it before, but it was new to the ears of Winslow and Major Jayneway, and each gentleman heartily wished it had remained so.

"Winslow, do stop your fidgeting," Alexa whispered midway through the sonnet. "He will wonder what you are doing here."

"I'm beginning to wonder that myself," the earl muttered as the sonnet came to a merciful conclusion. A polite round of applause followed, which encouraged Mr. Hormfeld to launch into what Alexa recognized as the beginning of a rather ponderous ode.

"Can people really listen to such bibble babble?" the earl whispered.

Lady Farrington turned around in the chair in front of them and glared majestically at them both.

Alexa took pity on him. "Let's see if things are ready in the refreshment room," she suggested and led him away, an exit Major Jayneway envied.

"Whose idea was this, anyway?" Winslow asked when they were surveying the table of treats. Bath buns, lobster patties and eels were heaped on platters.

"Yours," she told him tartly, "and do at least try to appear interested in this recital."

"I'm more interested in a sherry, but I suppose I can wait. What do you make of Hormfeld, Alexa? A pretty cool fish, don't you think?"

She nodded. "But he doesn't suspect a thing," she pointed out as she gave in to the temptation to share one of the lobster patties with the earl.

"Do you really think he's the culprit, Sebby?" she asked, chewing thoughtfully.

"I might have had doubts before, but after listening to such verse there's no telling what a man who can write such vile stuff might do."

She chuckled, finished the lobster patty, refused a taste of the eels and bullied him back into the drawing room just in time for Mr. Hormfeld to read one of his prized sestinas, a form of verse that was a particular favorite of Lady Farrington.

Encouraged by her enthusiastic reception, Mr. Hormfeld opened his budget and read a work in progress, apologizing beforehand for its rough edges.

It was, Alexa later informed Penny, who had dozed off during the opening sonnet, a rather tedious account of a love affair between a gentleman known as Hernando and a lady known as Francesca. Since Mr. Hormfeld did not furnish any other clues, she could only deduce that the two were Italian.

The story of Hernando and Francesca bore unmistakable similarities to Mr. William Shakespeare's account of Romeo and Juliet, with one difference. Mr. Hormfeld had eschewed blank verse in favor of heroic couplets. Although the rhymes did strain at times, he acquitted himself admirably, at least in the opinion of Lady Farrington.

"Such originality, don't you agree, Lord Winslow?" she said, leading the applause and turning to the earl.

Winslow, whose eyelids were a trifle heavy, pulled himself up with a start. "I beg your pardon?"

"Mr. Hormfeld's verse. I vow I could listen to him forever," Lady Farrington confessed, occasioning a strangled sound from the earl.

Fortunately, Lady Winslow had already deduced from the glassy-eyed stares of her guests that she would do well to silence Mr. Hormfeld or be left friendless in Bath.

"Dear Mr. Hormfeld," she trilled now as he delved into his book again for another poem. "Such passion. Such wit. Such originality. We cannot thank you enough, can we, Sebby?"

The earl, hearing an appeal for help in his mother's voice, rose to the occasion.

"No, indeed, Mama. Obliged to you, Hormfeld," he said with what he earnestly hoped was just the right touch of ringing sincerity. "You have made this evening the *on-dit* of the week." He offered the poet his hand, thinking that the other man could not shake hands and recite verse at the same time.

"I have more to come," Mr. Hormfeld whispered agitatedly to Lady Winslow.

"No, you mustn't. Spoil us, I mean. Just enough to whet the appetite, as it were. There, I see Lady Farrington just bursting to speak with you."

Lady Farrington did indeed give the look of a matron about to burst. She surrounded Mr. Hormfeld at once and with the fervor of the true devotee demanded to know the origin of each and every poem he had recited that evening.

"Is it over?" Penny asked, opening her eyes and looking about.

"Yes, my dear child," Alexa replied, laughing at her. "It is over, and you have behaved admirably."

"More admirably than you and Sebby," Bronwyn quizzed, leaning over the back of her chair and yawning. "Bolting the room as soon as the performance was under way."

"We wished to make sure the refreshments were ready," Alexa said lamely.

At the mention of refreshments Penny, who had been settling back in her chair, looked up eagerly.

"Aunt Alexa, could Courtney and I—?"

"Yes, my dears," she said, dispatching them. "But not too many lobster patties. I won't have you awake all night with the stomachache."

While Lady Winslow's guests were moving amiably toward the refreshment room, Mr. Hormfeld was still receiving the full tide of Lady Farrington's appreciation.

"Might I possibly prevail upon you to sign one of your volumes of verse for me?" she asked with a simper.

"Nothing would be more pleasurable, dear lady," the poet said gallantly. "But I lack quill and ink."

"That can be found in the book room," Winslow said,

shamelessly eavesdropping. "I shall show you the way. Coming, Archie?"

Alerted by the imperious look in Winslow's eyes, the major lent his presence to the book room. Alexa watched the exodus with mounting curiosity and prevailed upon Bronwyn to forgo the lobster patties and follow the earl into the library.

"We can always eat lobster patties," she pointed out. "We can't always see how this affair shall end."

"Very well," Bronwyn said good-naturedly, "but I don't see why Sebby should be so very anxious for Mr. Hormfeld to autograph his wretched books. I would think those volumes have caused us all enough grief as it is."

As the two ladies entered the book room, Mr. Hormfeld was finishing autographing the first page of his volume.

"Such a strong, powerful, masculine hand, don't you agree?" Lady Farrington asked, displaying the page to all in the room.

The poet had the grace to blush.

"Now then, Mr. Hormfeld." Lady Farrington returned to her quarry. "Are you in the habit of giving recitations? I should very much like to sponsor you for an evening. I know several friends who would adore hearing you read."

The poet gave a wintry smile. "My dear lady, nothing would give me greater pleasure."

She beamed. "Good. Shall we say Tuesday next? Eight o'clock on the dot. I shan't forgive you if you're late." She wagged a playful finger at him.

The poet frowned.

"Is anything wrong with next Tuesday?" she asked.

"No, no. It's just that I have been overstaying my time here in Bath, and there are pressing matters that need my attention elsewhere."

Lady Farrington went rigid. "I am offering you the highest strata of Bath literati! Your efforts would be met with universal favor and encouragement." She dropped her voice an octave, unaware that Major Jayneway hovered nearby. "Lady Winslow is the kindest creature! But she has no real appreciation of the muse!"

"True," he murmured. "I have often observed that first-hand. And yet a poet's life is not without trials. There are difficulties at the moment."

"Are you in dun territory?" Lady Farrington asked bluntly.

The poet made a moue. "No, no, my dear lady. It is merely the inconvenience of being caught a trifle short. And pressing bills, but truly nothing to signify. As soon as an allowance from my uncle in London arrives, all will be well. But he enjoys keeping me waiting. He disapproves of my poetry."

Lady Farrington's cheeks flushed. "The ogre!" she sympathized quickly. "You must allow me to be of some assistance. I daresay you can pay me back when your allowance from your uncle comes in. Now, how much shall it be? Oh, why do we quibble? I have two hundred pounds in my reticule. It is yours."

"Lady Farrington, I cannot!" Mr. Hormfeld declared, the very image of outraged masculinity. "My pride."

"Your poetry must come before your pride, my dear sir. Art comes first."

"But two hundred pounds!"

Lady Farrington laughed. "Silly boy. It's the merest pin money to me."

"But I can't allow it," Mr. Hormfeld said, extracting his purse. "Lady Farrington, this is my last fifty pounds. If you insist on giving me the two hundred pounds, you must take it."

"Of course I insist, and you are being absurd. Keep your fifty pounds."

"But I insist," he said, pressing the note into her hand to accept. "Now I owe you one hundred and fifty pounds."

"You are being ridiculous, Mr. Hormfeld," Lady Farrington protested.

"Coming to cuffs so soon?" a voice inquired, and the two turned to find Winslow and the major an attentive audience to their exchange.

Lady Farrington smiled. "Mr. Hormfeld is just being absurdly male."

"How is this, ma'am?" the earl inquired.

"He won't hear of accepting a loan of two hundred pounds from me and insists on giving me his last remaining fifty pounds. Now, gentlemen, have you ever heard of anything so absurd?"

The poet bridled. "My honor is at stake."

"Is that his fifty-pound note, Lady Farrington?" the major asked and, at her affirmative nod, plucked it out of her hand before she might wonder what the major wished to do with a paltry fifty-pound note. Just one touch of the bill soon convinced him that their long search was over.

"Mr. Hormfeld." His voice was quiet but firm. "I must ask you to come with me."

"Come with you?" Lady Farrington ejaculated. "My dear Major Jayneway, Mr. Hormfeld is promised to me for the rest of the evening. We are planning to eat a few of Lady Winslow's lobster patties and discuss that thrilling closing line in one of his sonnets."

"I'm afraid the only place you shall have to discuss Mr. Hormfeld's sonnets with him shall be in gaol."

"G-gaol?" the poet stammered.

"Now, look here . . ." Lady Farrington began to bluster.

"Your hoax is over, Hormfeld," Jayneway said, ignoring the furious matron next to him. "Bogus fifty-pound notes, indeed. And using ladies to pass them for you!"

"I have no notion what you mean, and just who are you?" the poet demanded angrily as a burly gentleman who had been loitering in the hall came forward at a hand signal from the major.

"This is Constable Fenwick," the major replied. "He's the one who shall be arresting you. We'll need this as evidence." The major handed the bogus bill to the constable.

"Now, see here," Mr. Hormfeld gurgled, easing the collar from his neck with a finger. "I am a gentleman, and I protest such treatment."

"You are a counterfeiter," the earl put in, enjoying the spectacle of the poet wriggling on the hook.

Hormfeld paled and turned sickly white. "No, never that. Perhaps I took some of the bills, but I wasn't the only one."

"I'm sure you weren't," Jayneway said cuttingly. "Your scheme cut a wide swath through the kingdom. And you can give the full particulars to the constable. I'm sure he'll be an avid listener."

The constable smiled. "Oh, yes, indeed, sir. Nothing I like more than a good Banbury tale."

"Where are they taking him?" Lady Farrington asked.

"To gaol, ma'am," the major replied. "But you needn't worry about him. I daresay he is only one link in the chain. But he shall lead us to the one responsible for these bogus bills."

"Then you were serious about the charge."

"Yes, but pray don't concern yourself unduly. With the gaol as an inspiration, Mr. Hormfeld may pen yet another epic poem to hold you in raptures."

"Now, that was quite naughty of you, Archie," Alexa said, repressing a gurgle of laughter as Lady Farrington stalked away.

"You did not have to sit through that odious ode," Major Jayneway put in.

"I had heard it before," she said dampeningly.

"I think we should tell Mama how the scheme turned out, don't you?" Winslow asked and led the way toward the refreshment room, where Lady Winslow was doing her best to defend herself from the onslaught of guests demanding to know why she had taken leave of her senses and sponsored, of all absurdities, a poetry recital.

"Because she was endeavoring to catch a criminal," Major Jayneway replied. "And she succeeded admirably."

"Did I really, Archie?" Lady Winslow inquired.

He nodded.

"How famous."

"Criminal?" Lady Cleeves, who considered herself one of Lady Winslow's oldest friends, looked totally bewildered. "Elizabeth, just what is going on here?"

While Lady Winslow supplied her friends with the true story behind the poetry recital, earning accolades for originality, courage and superior acting, her son was beset with more mundane emotions. His relief that his mother was finally cleared of any duplicity in the counterfeiting scheme was considerable. But now he had no further cause to keep the pretense of his engagement to Alexa. And he was oddly reluctant to have to end it.

The plain truth of the matter was that the earl, who long had been one of the prizes of the London marriage mart and had spurned over the years the lures of the most beautiful ladies of the ton, was now top over tail in love with Alexa. And he had not a smidgeon of an idea of what he should do about it.

To make matters worse, he had no idea of what, if anything, she felt for him. Oh, she liked him well enough, but he could not help thinking that it was the affection she would feel for an older brother. He watched now as she bit into a Bath bun and returned a sparkling laugh Penny's way. Not once had Alexa shown him any sign of partiality or of accepting his attentions as anything other than the sham they were enacting. In fact—memory made him grimace sharply—she had very nearly sought to match him with Bronwyn.

How had he come to fall in love with such an absurd, delightful, demanding creature? he wondered as he circulated about the refreshment room, returning the greetings of his guests with a profound air of distraction. Cupid's revenge, he told himself, was total. He had been struck not so much with an arrow as with a full quiver!

Winslow was not the only gentleman present that evening to have felt the dubious sting of Cupid's arrow. Several doors away from the refreshment room Major Jayneway sat, gloomily staring into the fire. Constable Fenwick had taken Hormfeld off, and his own duty to his uncle was accomplished. He should have been savoring the results. Instead, he felt curiously out of sorts. And he laid the fault for that on the pretty shoulders of Bronwyn Finch.

Why was it, he wondered, that she reduced him to jelly and his speech withered on his tongue whenever in her presence? Scowling, he turned at the sound of the library door opening and rose to his feet at the sight of Bronwyn crossing the threshold.

"Oh, Archie!" She came to a confused halt. "I didn't know anyone else was here. I tore my hem, and Lady Winslow was good enough to supply some thread and needle. But if you are using the room . . ."

"Don't scurry away," Jayneway said hastily, leading her toward the sofa. "A torn hem, did you say?"

"Yes, someone trod on it in the refreshment room," she revealed. "But it is not as bad as I feared, and I daresay that Amelia at home can keep the garment from ruin."

"Thank heaven for that. It is very pretty. It becomes you greatly."

"Why, thank you, Archie," she said, rather surprised at such praise from him.

The major stared at her for a moment, well aware that he should depart, but he rarely had the chance to speak to her in private. Usually, she was surrounded with people or, at the very least, Courtney.

"Is your sister here tonight?" he asked, realizing as soon as the words were out of his mouth that it was a stupid question to ask.

"Courtney? Oh, yes." She chuckled. "She and Penny are set on devouring all of the lobster patties. I only hope Courtney doesn't give herself indigestion!"

A silence fell.

"Now that Mr. Hormfeld is dispatched, will you be leaving Bath soon?" she asked.

"I suppose so. In perfect truth I hadn't thought that far ahead. Are you so eager to see me go?"

"Not at all," she denied quickly, so quickly that he looked at her curiously. "I mean"—she stammered a little—"we shall be sad to see *any* friend go."

"We?"

"Why, yes, all of us here in Bath. Winslow, Alexa and Courtney."

"Ah, yes, Courtney," the major said in his rather abstracted way.

To Bronwyn, he appeared lost in thought, but he suddenly shot his head up.

"Bronwyn, there is something I must speak to you

about." He clasped his hands around one knee. "The thing is I've had it in mind to marry for considerable time. I never found the right lady before, but now I believe I have." He felt suddenly very shy and decided to take his fences in a rush. "Mrs. Finch—Bronwyn—do you think there is any hope for a fellow like me?"

"I'm afraid not, Archie," Bronwyn said as quietly as possible, for it was obvious that he was offering for Courtney, who was oblivious to the major's charms and not disposed to thinking of Archie as a husband at all. "In fact, Archie, I'm all but certain your suit would be hopeless."

A weaker man would have staggered under such a blow, but the major absorbed it with some difficulty.

"I had hoped that it might be different. You shall let Mr. Goodwin know that I consider him the luckiest man alive."

Bronwyn looked up, puzzled. *"Mr. Goodwin?* Pray, what does Mr. Goodwin have to do with Courtney?"

"Well, I don't know," Archie began, then stopped abruptly. "And what the devil do you mean Courtney?"

Her puzzlement grew into exasperation. "Haven't you just finished making me an offer of marriage for my sister?"

"An offer of marriage for Courtney?" he expostulated. "Do you think I'm queer in the attic? She's a mere school-room miss. A nursery brat. Not that she ain't a taking little thing and will score a huge triumph during next year's season, but for my wife! Really, Bronwyn, don't think me such a nodcock!"

She paled. "But if you weren't trying to fix an interest in Courtney, why all this talk about marriage and your hopes? You cannot have been offering for *me*, Archie," she said, stunned.

"And why not?" he demanded with some passion. "I suppose your tendre for Mr. Goodwin makes it impossible that any other man might wish to marry you?"

Bronwyn stared at him open-mouthed. "My tendre for whom?" She gave her head a shake as though to clear it. "Archie, I fear all this counterfeiting business has unhinged you. How did you come to such a besotted notion that I nursed a tendre for Mr. Goodwin?"

"Well, I don't know," the major said, rather confused by this reversal. "You were gazing at him so intently during Lady Rendell's ball when you were in the card room."

"I was staring at him, you silly gudgeon, because I was terrified that you might see I was interested in you!"

It was his turn to stop and stare. "Interested in me? Bronwyn, do you mean you aren't smitten with Goodwin?"

"The only one I am smitten with is you," she said with a smile. "And you hardly paid me a moment's notice."

"Not true!" he denied emphatically. "I noticed you—more than noticed, if you want me to be frank. And I've thought of you for days and weeks. I even came close to offering for you last week, but you did persist in talking of Courtney."

He broke off, alerted to the fact that Bronwyn's lovely face was only inches away from his and that anything else he wished to say could be delayed while they exchanged a kiss, which proved so successful that no further words were necessary between them on the topic of love, marriage or each other!

Twenty

Fifteen minutes later Alexa, chancing to pass the library, witnessed the emergence of Major Jayneway with one arm about Bronwyn's waist. One look at their glowing faces and she deduced immediately what had come to pass.

"I do wish you happy," she said, hugging them one at a time.

"And we return that wish, Alexa," Bronwyn said, for now that her own romantic affairs were settled she desired nothing more than to set Alexa's straight.

Her friend, however, did not rise to the bait. "That is naught but an air dream of yours," she declared. "My engagement to Winslow is just a hum. Nothing that has happened changes that. And now that his mother is clear of any taint of wrongdoing, I can cry off with a clear conscience."

"Alexa, you must be the most aggravating female I know! Can you really be so idiotish as to cry off?"

"Yes," came the reply as Alexa avoided her friend's skeptical gaze and the major's quizzing one.

"Well, I think you're shamming it," Bronwyn went on. "You're as much in love with Sebby as he is with you."

"You are no doubt right," Alexa said cordially. "For Winslow and I are both agreed that we are nothing more than good friends."

"Well, if such is the case, I would tell your prospective mother-in-law. For she is all atwitter about your betrothal party this coming Friday. You can't have forgotten that, I hope?" She quizzed as Alexa bit her lip. "And if you do cry off later, it shall make her appear rather foolish, don't you think?"

Put in mind of the betrothal party, Alexa made several attempts that evening to detach Lady Winslow for a moment of private discourse but to no avail. As she later rode back to Milsom Street with Penny, she resolved to set out the next morning to nip Lady Winslow's plans for a betrothal party in the bud.

This admirable plan suffered an immediate setback when Alexa descended the Adam stairs after a leisurely breakfast in bed and beheld Mr. and Mrs. George Eiseley stepping over the threshold of the establishment, accompanied by a portmanteau, Baby and his nurse.

"George? What in the name of heaven are you doing in Bath?" asked that gentleman's sister as she pecked Maria on the cheek.

George, who had suffered through a bone-shattering ride to Bath, turned a peevish face toward his sister.

"What kind of bacon-brained question is that, Alexa?" he demanded. "As though I enjoy being jolted all over the kingdom. This is all your doing."

"Mine?"

"Actually, George is only partly right, Alexa." Maria intervened in this familiar family skirmish. "And I suppose my notion as well, for I couldn't bear not being at hand for your betrothal party. So exciting! Lady Winslow wrote to invite us, you see. And nothing could keep me away."

"Lady Winslow invited you?"

Maria's blond curls bobbed up and down. "Yes, of course. Quite a most civil invitation, too, I might add. But why are you looking so agitated, my dear? I hope Penny has been behaving yourself and hasn't run you to death.''

"No, Penny is fine," Alexa said quickly. "At the moment she is in bed. We had a rather late evening of it. And far from racketing me about, she's been a splendid companion. Everyone in Bath who has met her dotes on her.''

Although Maria was delighted to hear about Penny's triumph, she was not dissuaded from her original plan, which was to learn all the details about the impending betrothal party. After Baby and Nurse had been dispatched upstairs and she and George were comfortably seated in the drawing room, she turned an expectant face toward Alexa.

"Now, about this betrothal party, Alexa . . .''

"Actually, I'm not so certain there will be one," Alexa said weakly.

"What do you mean?" George spluttered half his sherry back into his glass. "Winslow's family invited us.''

"Yes, I know that. But really, George, nothing is definite. And I'm not sure the thing will come off the way everyone seems to imagine.''

"Not come off?" Mr. Eiseley turned several shades of red before reaching his favorite purple. "My dear Alexa, if you think you have gotten me here on a fool's errand, not to mention Baby being carriage sick right in front of me . . .'' The laughter which greeted this last remark brought the color higher in his cheeks. "I see nothing humorous about Baby being carriage sick," he said frigidly.

"No," Alexa acknowledged, struggling in vain to contain her mirth. "You are quite right. A horrid affliction for him, and quite horrid for you to witness as well. But you needn't pinch and scold me, George, because I have nothing to do with the plans for the betrothal party. All that is left to the countess. And now you must excuse me, for I meant to call on her today. She and I have certain things we must thrash out." And without giving her brother time to mutter another word about what a ramshackle creature she was, she quitted the room.

With George and Maria in Bath it became even more imperative that Lady Winslow learn the truth, Alexa decided, and she summoned her carriage and her courage to do the deed.

A half an hour later, dressed in a new lemon muslin frock, she entered the countess's sitting room and found Lady Winslow up to her eyebrows in all the details of the betrothal party.

"It is all these tedious decisions," the countess said, looking up with relief to greet her caller. "It makes one want to sink."

"It must be tedious for you," Alexa agreed.

Lady Winslow gave a little sigh. "But I do so wish it all to be perfect for you. Now, tell me. Do you prefer red roses or yellow ones? I own that yellow is rather pretty, and I have always been partial to the color myself, but traditionalists prefer red. What do you think?"

"It really makes no difference to me," Alexa said, trying not to be deterred from her task. "Lady Winslow, before we discuss the roses or the music or the menu for the party, there is something quite urgent I must tell you. It's something Winslow himself should have told you weeks ago, but he fought shy of doing so."

"Then it must be something unpleasant," Lady Winslow said acutely, putting aside her papers. "Poor Sebby turns positively *craven* at doing anything remotely disagreeable. And if it is so disagreeable as to put him into a quake, perhaps you had better not tell me."

"But I must," Alexa insisted. "I beg your pardon, but it is essential that someone do so, for I have put it off much too long as is. And now you are so preoccupied with the plans for the party that I see no alternative but the truth."

"Alexa, you needn't trifle yourself . . ."

"Ma'am, you have been kindness itself to me, and my relationship to your son is not what it seems," she said in desperation.

Lady Winslow's expression turned thoughtful. "In what way, my dear?" she asked calmly.

"Heavens, in every way!" Alexa exclaimed, making a clean breast of things. "And it is all Winslow's fault that we allowed it to get this far. I wanted to tell you long ago that

our engagement was naught but a sham, but he wouldn't allow me. It was never, ever, intended that Winslow should
marry me, nor I him.''

"Oh, I know that," the countess said, reaching over to
touch Alexa's cheek. "But do you think, my dear, after
being engaged to him these few weeks that you might not
have changed your mind and might wish to marry him after
all? He is the kindest creature as a rule, even though I as his
mother say so!''

Alexa gasped, hardly believing her ears. "My dear Lady
Winslow, have you heard what I just said? My engagement
to your son is nothing but a hoax concocted between us.''

The countess chuckled. "Yes, my dear. I am well aware
of that.''

"You are?" Alexa asked, stunned by this blithe remark.
"Did Winslow tell you finally?''

"Oh, no! I daresay Sebby would not even know how to
divulge such a thing. Fortunately, I received a letter from
Leigh some weeks ago, and he revealed the charade that had
arisen after you came so conveniently to his rescue. And,
my dear, I haven't begun to thank you properly for that! I
should have hated for him to succumb to an infection, what
with the cold and the wet of the storm. And he is my eldest
grandson, you know. But there is not the least danger of
that, for he certainly seemed hale and hearty in his letter.
And I do believe he is well over his infatuation for Miss
Fornhurst!''

Alexa felt in no frame of mind to discuss young Leigh's
infatuations. "If you knew the truth, ma'am," she said doggedly, "why didn't you say something to me or Sebby? If
you only knew how we have been worrying about your reaction to our bogus betrothal!''

Lady Winslow raised a playful brow. "But is it really so
bogus, Alexa?''

"Y-yes, of course it is.''

The countess cocked her head at her young guest. "My
dear Alexa, I might have known that your betrothal to Sebby
was just temporary, but I also knew in my heart that Sebby
could not have chosen a better bride than you. And I hoped

that given enough time you might feel some inclination to accept him. I know a mother shouldn't boast, but he is alleged to be the leading prize on the marriage mart!''

A strangled laugh escaped Alexa. ''I am well acquainted with Winslow's reputation, ma'am.''

''Oh, are you?'' A worried look creased the countess's brow. ''I assure you he has never been very deep in the petticoat line.''

''Lady Winslow! I could not marry Winslow just to suit you!''

''No, of course not,'' the countess agreed. ''That would be freakish but obliging of you. But can you actually sit there and tell me you would not like to marry him?''

Alexa felt unable to meet the countess's eyes. ''It doesn't matter,'' she answered stoutly. ''For Sebby has no wish to marry me.''

''Then you do wish it!'' The countess pounced on this hopeful clue with relish. ''I knew you could not be so immune to his charms. And I am so glad you have fallen in love, for nothing is more dreary than marriage without affection!''

''Lady Winslow,'' Alexa protested, making another attempt to stem the tide of felicitations. ''I am not in love—''

The countess looked at her closely. ''That seems such a pity, Alexa, for I vow I would have wagered anything that you were in love with him and he with you. In fact, when Mrs. Finch came by to see me earlier this morning she assured me that the two of you would see the light very soon.''

''Oh, she did, did she?'' Alexa said, looking grim.

''But I was of much the same opinion myself,'' the countess said quickly. ''Only think for a moment how excellently suited you are in temperament and position. And best of all you are in love! Why do you fight it?''

''Because Winslow . . . Because I . . . Oh, heavens,'' Alexa blurted out. ''This is not the way it should be.''

''No,'' Lady Winslow agreed. ''Sebby should be here making this offer to you properly. But that dratted boy is never about when one has need of him. Ah.'' She smiled suddenly. ''I think I hear his step.''

"Oh, merciful heaven," Alexa exclaimed as she jumped to her feet. "I must be off." But before she could make good her escape, Winslow crossed the threshold.

"Mama, there is something I wish to speak to you about," he said but came to a rigid halt when he noticed Alexa in the room with his mother.

"I beg pardon, Mama. I didn't know you were busy."

"Come in, Sebby." Lady Winslow waved him in with a happy smile. "You are the very one we wish to see. It appears only you can put an end to a ridiculous argument between Miss Eiseley and myself. She has just finished telling me that she doesn't wish to marry you and that you share those feelings!"

"I merely told your mother the truth about our engagement, Winslow," Alexa put in quickly. "It was time one of us did."

"I see," the earl said slowly, an odd expression in his blue eyes. "Well, then, Mama, I hardly know what else to add. Alexa is correct."

"Then it's true that you had no intention whatever of marrying her when you proposed this engagement to her?" the countess asked.

"I know the gentlemen of your generation probably did it differently," Winslow said hastily, "but it seemed an urgent business at the time." He looked at Alexa. "Did you tell her about Leigh?"

"I didn't need to," she said darkly. "Leigh wrote her himself."

The earl's head swiveled toward his mother. "Indeed, Mama? Why wasn't I told?"

"I had my reasons," the countess said defensively. "For I am certain if I had told you you would have made a bigger mull of this business than you have so far."

He smiled. "I have no doubt you think it a ramshackle affair."

Alexa cut short his explanation. "Lady Winslow," she said as she rose, "there is no further need to delve into the matter. Winslow himself has told you the facts as I stated them earlier. Now I must take my leave. My brother,

George, and his wife have descended on me this morning—"

She got no further. Lady Winslow clamped an iron grip on Alexa's wrist and pulled her back down to the sofa.

"Nonsense, child. You shall stay here. We are having this out once and for all. I could never believe that I gave birth to a dolt. And if you, Sebby, mean to sit there and tell me that even with all your charm, grace and fortune that you could possibly find a better bride in Christendom than Alexa, you must be a skittlebrain."

"I'm sure I'm no such thing, Mama," Winslow said mildly.

"Hmmph!" the countess snorted. "And no doubt you mean to tell me that you don't wish to marry her?"

"By no means," Winslow said blandly. "There is nothing I wish more in the world."

"Winslow, there is no need for such flummery," Alexa exclaimed as she became aware of a pounding in her chest. "We needn't humor your mother any further about our marriage."

"I fear you mistake my devotion to my mother, Alexa," Winslow replied. "However much I adore her, and I do, I would not allow myself to be leg-shackled to some female merely to placate her."

"Quite right," Lady Winslow interjected, rising from the sofa and directing a long, appraising look at her son. "I'm relieved that you finally came to your senses, Sebby. I only ask that you make your offer to Alexa in a civilized way, for you have made too much of a mull of things as it is. Or"—she paused—"do you wish me to stay and lend you my support?"

"I think I can carry on now that you have started me on the path, Mama," Winslow said manfully.

"Sebby, there is no need to play the gallant with me," Alexa said the instant his mother had left the room. "We both know that this is nothing but a hoax."

"I know it started that way," Winslow said, still smiling at her in a way that caused her heart to beat alarmingly in her chest, "and while I might not have been wholeheartedly in love with you back then, I certainly feel some part of me must have already loved you, for how else could I have toppled so completely in love with you in so short a span?'' He picked up her hand. ''And I do beg you to accept my proposal, Alexa, for I really could not see myself explaining to Mama the mortification of a rejection. She would be bound to think I had made a mull of things yet again.''

''But this is idiocy, Winslow,'' Alexa murmured, trying to snatch her hand back and finding it impossible. ''You must be all about in your head.''

''Of course,'' he agreed with aplomb. ''Every man in love is! And perhaps I should have persuaded Mama to remain, for I must say that while I don't know how the gentlemen of my father's generation offered for their ladies, I'm sure they could not have met with such cavalier treatment as this. To be accused of idiocy in the middle of a proposal!''

''I suppose that was uncivil of me,'' Alexa murmured, feeling a trifle giddy as his eyes continued to linger on her face.

''Horridly so,'' he said now with a smile. ''I am not a lunatic!''

''Oh, no. I'm sure I didn't mean that, and I do apologize if—''

She was destined to get no further for the earl, deeming that the time for talking was over, cut her apology short by taking her into his arms and covering her lips with his. For a long, electric moment the world spun giddily about in Alexa's head.

''I love you,'' he whispered against her hair, each syllable of that declaration sending a thrill of pleasure up and down her spine.

''Are you sure you aren't offering for me merely to please your mama?'' Alexa teased some minutes later as she sat back, making a feeble effort to compose her slightly disheveled head now resting on the shoulder of the earl's coat of Bath blue superfine.

''Of course I'm not marrying you to please Mama,'' he retorted. ''Actually, I'm doing it to save you from one of George's thunderous scolds.''

She lifted her head a fraction, the better to stare at him. "Do you mean my brother George?"

"Unless you have another relation by that same name hidden away," the earl replied, blenching at such a prospect. "Old George, bless his heart, thinks rather highly of me as a brother-in-law. And if you let me slip through your fingers, he'll hound you for life!"

Sighing, Alexa burrowed her head deeper into his embrace. She felt warm and contented.

"My brother and your mother, Sebby. Do you think we ever stood a chance against them?"

"Not a chance in the world, my love," he said soothingly and bent his head to kiss her soundly once again.

ABOUT THE AUTHOR

Also the author of SAMANTHA, Clarice Peters is presently at work on her third novel. She lives in Hawaii.